The
VINEYARD
VICTIMS

ALSO BY ELLEN CROSBY

THE WINE COUNTRY MYSTERIES

The Merlot Murders

The Chardonnay Charade

The Bordeaux Betrayal

The Riesling Retribution

The Viognier Vendetta

The Sauvignon Secret

The Champagne Conspiracy

THE SOPHIE MEDINA MYSTERIES

Multiple Exposure

Ghost Image

Moscow Nights

The
VINEYARD
VICTIMS

ELLEN CROSBY

Minotaur Books
New York

THE VINEYARD VICTIMS. Copyright © 2017 by Ellen Crosby. All rights reserved. Printed in the United States of America. For information, address St. Martin's Press, 175 Fifth Avenue, New York, N.Y. 10010.

www.minotaurbooks.com

Library of Congress Cataloging-in-Publication Data

Names: Crosby, Ellen, 1953– author.
Title: The vineyard victims / by Ellen Crosby.
Description: First edition. | New York : Minotaur Books, 2017.
Identifiers: LCCN 2017024855 | ISBN 978-1-250-07662-5 (hardcover) | ISBN 978-1-4668-8810-4 (ebook)
Subjects: LCSH: Montgomery, Lucie (Fictitious character)—Fiction. | Vinters—Fiction. | Vineyards—Virginia—Fiction. | Murder—Investigation—Fiction. | GSAFD: Mystery fiction.
Classification: LCC PS3603.R668 V54 2017 | DDC 813/.6—dc23
LC record available at https://lccn.loc.gov/2017024855

Our books may be purchased in bulk for promotional, educational, or business use. Please contact your local bookseller or the Macmillan Corporate and Premium Sales Department at 1-800-221-7945, extension 5442, or by email at MacmillanSpecialMarkets@macmillan.com.

First Edition: November 2017

10 9 8 7 6 5 4 3 2 1

For Dr. Sondra Melzer,
my extraordinary eleventh-grade English teacher,
with grateful thanks for teaching me how to write

He that dies pays all debts.
—*The Tempest*, ACT III, SCENE 2

For most of its nine-thousand-year history,
winemaking was only a small step above witchcraft.
—GEORGE M. TABER, *To Cork or Not to Cork*

Prologue

M y mother warned me to stay away from bad boys even before I started dating, but she'd married one herself—my father—and, as they say, apples don't fall too far from the tree. So I already knew I was going to get my heart flung to the ground and the life stomped out of it, but here's the other thing every girl who falls for the wrong guy knows: You want him anyway.

A few years later my mother was dead, killed in a freak accident when her horse stumbled jumping a low stone wall on our 225-year-old farm in Atoka, Virginia, and the sudden brutal void she left channeled my anger and grief into taking the kind of foolish risks anyone with a lick of sense knows will get you in trouble. That's when Gregory Knight walked into my life. We met at a party the summer I turned nineteen, and it was like taking a lighted match to a can of gasoline. Already there was too much free-flowing booze, no one old enough to legally drink, and no responsible adults around to stop us. As soon as I laid eyes on Greg I knew he was the kind of guy my mother had been talking about, but after a couple of mojitos he was also exactly what I was looking for. Dark haired, lifeguard-bronze skin, hot, hungry eyes, cool, dangerous smile. Someone you know you can't tame—just like my father, Leland.

He drove a bloodred Corvette convertible like he owned the road, too fast and with the music up and the top down. Most days I liked it, the wind whipping my hair, the smug feeling of invulnerable immortality that belongs exclusively to the young and reckless, but today he was angry, which made it different. We were fighting, the worst argument we'd ever had in a relationship that had barely survived one tumultuous year. I'd caught him in a lie—I knew he'd been with someone else when he told me he hadn't—and now he wouldn't look at me, just kept his foot pressed on the gas pedal until he was pushing sixty on a winding country lane where the legal limit was twenty-five.

It was dusk at the end of a washed-out day of rain, so he'd put the top up. Late spring only a few days after I'd come home from college, still tired and hollow eyed from the last push of exams. The roads were wet and slick, with plenty of low spots where streams had overrun their banks, not only flooding the shoulders but creating treacherous small ponds that covered the asphalt as well.

"Greg," I said. "Look at me."

A muscle twitched in his jaw as he took a corner too fast, knocking me into the passenger door. The car fishtailed and spun onto the muddy shoulder, tires squealing. He regained control and we bumped back onto the road. I grabbed the door handle and hung on. By now the car windows had fogged up from our body heat and our anger. The closed-up air felt suffocating.

"Dammit," I said. "Slow down, will you? You're going to get us killed."

He ignored me, fiddling instead with the temperature controls until cold air blasted the windshield and the fog disappeared like a stage curtain rising before a performance.

"Who told you?" he said. "How'd you find out?"

He sounded mad.

I almost said, *You've got some nerve.*

There's cheating and there's cheating. The worst kind is when you know her, because you've been doubly betrayed. Your best friend. A sister or a cousin. And then there's when he cheats and it's your brother's fiancée.

"What difference does it make?" I wasn't backing down. Not this time.

Usually he laughed it off when I asked who she was, telling me I was imagining things, believing stories made up by jealous rivals. I'd accepted the excuses because I didn't want to believe he'd lie to me. Or cheat. But he hadn't denied this one. And I knew I couldn't forgive him if he'd really done it, either. If he'd really slept with my brother Eli's fiancée, Brandi, what was left of our falling-apart relationship wouldn't make it past today.

"Does Eli know?" he asked, finally flicking a glance my way.

I gave him an icy look. "I'm not my brother's keeper. Ask him yourself if you want to know."

"Lucie," he said, cajoling, "come on, baby. Don't take it so hard. It didn't mean anything."

"Then why did you do it?" I hated myself for asking, for sounding like a nagging girlfriend.

He shrugged. "I don't know."

"That's a stupid answer."

Another tiny tightening of that muscle in his jaw, a burst of speed from the Corvette, and no response from him.

"What you did was cruel," I said. "To me, to Eli, and even to Brandi, though she's just as much to blame as you are. If it didn't mean anything, then you just used her to hurt me and Eli."

"Oh, come on. I did you all a favor. Eli's better off knowing who he's marrying before the wedding instead of after she's got the ring on her finger, don't you think?"

"I don't know and I don't care," I told him in a cold voice. "Stop the car. I'm getting out and walking the rest of the way home. You're driving like a maniac. I'm done, Greg. I don't care what you do and who you see anymore."

His right arm came across my chest like a vise, pinning me to my seat. "You're not going anywhere," he said. "I'm taking you home. The roads are flooded and we're nearly at your place, anyway."

"Let me out." I grabbed the car door handle but he hit the door-lock button and swerved on purpose so I fell against him.

He leaned over and said in my ear, "Stay away from your door and stop acting like a little kid. I told you I'll take you home."

The windows had steamed up again. I swiped my side of the windshield with my fist so I could see where we were. "Then you'd better turn right this second or you're going to pass Sycamore Lane. Pay attention to the road, why don't you?"

He wrenched the steering wheel, and the tires squealed again as he made a hard turn onto the dirt-and-gravel road that

led to my house. This time I braced myself against the dash-
board, and when I looked up, we were barreling straight toward
one of the stone pillars and the high wall that marked the entrance to the vineyard as though he'd lost control of the car.

"The pillar . . . Jesus, Greg. Turn the wheel or we're going
to crash into it."

They say your life flashes before you when you think you're
about to die. Mine compressed into a few terrifying seconds.
He was doing this on purpose to scare me. I knew he was hot-
headed and stubborn enough to play chicken, threatening not
to turn away unless I took back what I'd said.

"Tell me we're okay," he said in a lazy drawl, "and I'll
do it."

"You're crazy," I shouted. "You're going to kill us both."

His gaze snapped back to the looming wall as he jammed
on the brakes too late, locking the wheels. The car skidded on
the muddy gravel and spun sideways so the passenger door—
my side of the car—was going to take the direct impact of the
crash. I remember throwing my arms up in front of my face to
shield myself, and I think I yelled something. Or maybe he did.

We slammed into the pillar, the awful sound of metal con-
necting with stone, followed by an agonizing pain in my legs.
And blood. On my hands, my legs, my face. The impact sent Greg
careening onto me like a football player tackling the other
team's quarterback. He groaned, and after what seemed like
an eternity, he slowly pulled himself off me.

"Lucie?" His voice sounded faint. "Are you okay?"

It took all my effort to answer. "No. My legs."

He managed to open his door and I watched him fall onto
the ground and start crawling away from the Corvette.

"Don't . . . leave . . . me . . . please." I tried to shout, but the words came out in a whisper.

He turned his head toward me and stared as if he were trying to figure out what he should do next.

"Help me," I said, but he just kept right on staring.

Then I passed out.

One

TODO

TODAY

could see the car speeding toward me on Atoka Road, a small dark speck that was maybe a mile away but definitely traveling well above the limit on the two-lane country road that ribboned out in front of me. The car disappeared into the trough of a hill and then popped up again, accelerating as it grew closer. A cold, hard rain that had fallen for most of this early spring day had finally abated, leaving large puddles in the usual low spots and wet, slippery asphalt that could be treacherous if you took a turn too fast.

The driver was motoring like he had stolen something, fast and careless, weaving back and forth across the road into my lane. By now the car was close enough that I recognized the gold SUV that belonged to Jamie Vaughn, who six months ago had been a candidate for the office of president of the United States. It looked like Jamie was behind the wheel, alone in the car. Even though it was just past noon, I wondered if he'd been drinking. Like me, Jamie owned a family vineyard, and after a devastating loss in November, I'd heard rumors about how he was coping—or more like not coping—though I'd never actually seen him drunk.

He hadn't shifted back into his own lane, so I leaned on my horn and waited for him to correct himself, then wondered why he didn't. Maybe he was unwell—a heart attack, a stroke . . . something. By now we were both approaching the turn to Sycamore Lane and the entrance to my vineyard, heading directly toward each other like a pair of jousters preparing to do battle. I'd have to cut across the road in front of him to make it into the turnoff before he reached it since I assumed he'd keep barreling right past me—or through me if I didn't get out of the way in time.

One more look at his car and the speed at which he was traveling and I knew I wouldn't make it without being broadsided. I swerved hard onto the opposite shoulder and my Jeep bounced into a deep, rutted puddle, jolting me so hard my teeth rattled in my head. I swore under my breath and fought to hold tight to the steering wheel to avoid crashing through my neighbor's split-rail fence. Jamie was driving like a lunatic.

I heard the screech of his tires before I could turn around to see what happened, followed by what sounded like a car engine accelerating. Then the crash—metal smashing into unyielding stone, so eerily reminiscent of my own accident ten years ago. I cut the engine to the Jeep and looked in my rearview mirror.

He'd hit the same pillar Greg had plowed into, and part of it had collapsed onto the hood of his car. I grabbed my phone from the console and my cane from the backseat, scrambling out of the Jeep. By the time I reached Jamie, I'd called 911. The air smelled of gasoline along with the acrid odor of deployed air bags. The impact and the toppled stone pillar had crushed the frame of the car so Jamie's door was jammed shut, but luckily his window was open. A fine coating of air bag dust had settled over the car interior and on Jamie's navy blazer and khakis. His dark brown hair looked like it had been coated with powdered sugar. Either he'd already unhooked his seat belt or he hadn't been wearing one. I guessed it was the latter. Everyone around here knew he drove without buckling up. He'd even got called out on it during the presidential campaign.

There was blood on his face from a gash in his head, and he was wheezing as if he couldn't catch his breath. His internal injuries were probably worse, maybe a gut punch from the air bag or he'd hit the steering column without the restraining protection of the seat belt.

I reached in and shook him gently. "Jamie, it's Lucie. Lucie Montgomery. Can you move? We need to get you out of here. I smell gasoline and I think your engine is about to catch fire."

He gave me a confused, glassy-eyed look. "No."

I yanked on his door, which budged a little. "Help me," I said, urgency creeping into my voice. "We haven't got much time. Push against the door, will you? I'll keep pulling."

It was the same spot where I'd been trapped inside Greg's Corvette. The *exact* same spot. That time the fire department needed the Jaws of Life to extract me, but at least the car hadn't caught fire. I felt like I was going to throw up.

Jamie reached through the open window and clutched the sleeve of my jacket. His hand was red and raw, probably from air bag burns.

"I'm sorry," he said, with surprising force. His eyes, now trying to focus on mine, were feverishly bright, and I wondered if he was a bit high, what he'd taken. "Tell him I'm sorry."

I leaned closer and smelled alcohol on his breath. Maybe he'd mixed booze with pills. "What are you talking about? Jamie . . . we have to hurry."

Something slipped through his fingers and fell to the ground, landing at my feet. A MedicAlert bracelet. It must have snapped and fallen off his wrist with the impact of the air bag. I picked it up and shoved it in my jacket pocket. When the ambulance arrived, they would need the information on it.

"Tell Rick," he said and coughed up blood. "Do you hear me? Tell Rick I need him to forgive me." He tried to wipe away the blood with the back of his hand. "I'm sorry. So very sorry."

"Sure," I said. Anything to placate him. "I'll tell him. Now come on, you have to help me."

"No," he said again, his voice thick with blood. "S'okay. You promise, right?"

"Jamie—"

"Lemme alone, Lucie. It's too late." He coughed, spitting a spume of blood like a projectile. It sprayed over me, stinging my face and leaving a trail across my jacket, my shirt, and my jeans, as shocking as a hard slap. For an instant I froze, then my brain kicked in again.

Get him out of there. He's choking on his own blood.

"It's not too late. Dammit, Jamie." I was losing him. The heat from the fire that had started under the hood was as hot as if I were standing at the open door to a furnace. I tugged on the car door. "Come on."

I didn't hear the other vehicle until the brakes screeched as someone pulled up behind me. When I turned around, Mick Dunne, my next-door neighbor, was scrambling out of his Land Rover, hollering as he sprinted toward me.

"Lucie, get away from the car. The engine's caught fire."

I glanced at Jamie, who was now unconscious, eyes closed, blood still trickling from one side of his mouth. Black smoke poured from the front of the car and flames appeared through the front driver wheel well and around the edges of the smashed-in hood. The heat burned my skin. My clothes felt like they were becoming congealed to my body.

"I know," I said. "Mick! Hurry!"

"Get out of there," he yelled. "Now!"

"Jamie Vaughn is trapped inside. I can't open the door. Help me!"

Mick reached me and easily scooped me into his arms. He smelled of horses and hay and sweat. "The engine's going to blow up any second. Come on."

"No!" I pummeled his shoulders with my fists. "We can't leave him to die like this. He's still alive. Mick, he's your friend."

Two pops sounded like gunshots and we both flinched. "That's the tires exploding," Mick said in a tense voice. "Lucie, dammit, we can't save him."

The thick smoke, which had morphed into a black funnel cloud, now engulfed us. My eyes stung and my lungs felt like they would explode. Over the roar of the blaze I heard Jamie's agonized scream as the flames spread to the interior of the car, burning it like a funeral pyre.

Mick pulled my head down, jamming my face against his shoulder. "Don't look," he said as we moved away from the fire. "Just don't."

"Put me down. Get away from me." My voice was muffled against the scratchy denim of his jacket. I punched his shoulder with my fist, but this time I knew it was too late. "Let me go."

He obeyed, setting me down as soon as we were out of range of the fire and the vicious smoke. I stumbled away from him and dropped to my knees, gasping as I tried to catch my breath. My cane was somewhere near Jamie's car. I'd dropped it when Mick picked me up.

"Lucie—" Mick was on the ground, too, coughing convulsively. "Lucie—"

"We let him die."

Sirens wailed in the distance. I turned away so Mick wouldn't see my tears. The smoke was now an enormous column that plumed into the sky like a dark, ominous genie. Below it, the fire blazed, turning the car into a charred metal skeleton like the picked-clean bones of an animal devoured by a predator.

Jamie was dead, gone, consumed by the fire.

Mick came over to me, grabbing my arm. "Don't you ever say that again." His mouth was next to my ear and his anger cut through me like a whip. "If we'd stayed to help him, we'd have been immolated just like he was. Do you hear me? I saved your damn life."

He shook my arm hard and dropped it, walking away as the first fire truck roared up Sycamore Lane.

Immolated. Killed or sacrificed by fire.

What a bizarre word choice. Except I was the only person who'd actually witnessed Jamie's car as it crashed into the wall. Or seen most of it. Not only had it seemed deliberate—he'd aimed directly for the stone pillar and hadn't slowed down—but he also didn't help me open the door and free him before the car caught fire.

Everyone knew how devastated he'd been by losing the election in spite of a gracious, upbeat concession speech. His loss had floored everyone—the media, the pollsters, his party . . . the country. What made it worse was that he'd won the popular vote but lost massively in the electoral college. Jamie's opponent—now the president—had scooped up the big-prize states, claiming an overwhelming mandate, and even turned a few states the other way for the first time in decades. It had been Jamie's first time in national politics, galvanized by the belief that he could do something to change the ugly polarization and deadlocked status quo that had mired Washington for decades. His charisma, boyish good looks, and personal charm had soon elevated him above the other candidates in his party so that he'd wrapped up the primaries early in the season, swept through the national convention as his party's shining star: an appealing new candidate who was smart and telegenic, and possessed the savvy political instincts of a pro. A successful self-made businessman with a multimillion-dollar empire in international real estate, well known for his generous philanthropy, beloved in our community—one of our own—and a devoted family man. Jamison Vaughn had it all.

What had just happened?

And who was Rick, someone so obviously on Jamie's mind—or his conscience? I realized now his dying request was for me to find him and tell him Jamie was sorry. *So sorry,* he'd said. *Forgive me.*

For what?

Something so awful that it had driven him to commit suicide? Surely there had to be another explanation for why he drove into my wall. Not suicide, but a tragic accident. Maybe a lethal combination of drugs and booze.

Jamie's death would be national—no, international—news. As the only witness, there was no way I wanted to tell anyone I suspected it had been suicide and destroy the reputation of a man who had done so much good in his lifetime.

But in my heart of hearts that's exactly what I thought had happened: Jamie Vaughn had deliberately taken his own life in a gruesome and violent way.

And I was the only one who had witnessed what he'd done.

Two

The first fire truck from the Middleburg Fire and Rescue Station roared into Sycamore Lane, lights flashing and sirens blaring, followed by a blur of emergency rescue vehicles, an ambulance, and a brown-and-gold Loudoun County Sheriff's Department cruiser. A moment later the battalion chief's car pulled up. A man suited up in firefighting gear got out of the SUV.

"I'll handle this," Mick said.

Before I could protest, he sprinted over to the battalion chief, pointing to the flames shooting out of Jamie's car and to me. Then he shook his head. I knew why. He was saying we'd arrived on the scene too late to save Jamie.

I wrapped my arms around my waist and watched two fire-fighters train a hose on the SUV. It didn't take long for the flames to subside and the sooty black smoke to dissolve into a grayish-white mushroom cloud enveloping what remained of the chassis and drifting over nearby rows of my dark brown grapevines on the verge of bud break.

Mick and the battalion chief split up and he joined me again. "You obviously told the nine-one-one dispatcher it was Jamie's car, which is why a battalion chief showed up right away," he said. "I told him what happened."

"Yes, I'm sure you did." I kept my eyes locked on the firefighters who were still dousing the SUV with water.

"Are you okay?" he asked.

"No." I gave him a you've-got-to-be-kidding-me look. "I'm not. You shouldn't be, either, after what just happened."

He blew out a short, angry breath. "Bloody hell, Lucie, we couldn't have saved him." His voice had an edge that I didn't like. "You're not going to say anything different, are you?"

Part of me knew he was right, that we probably couldn't have gotten Jamie out of the car before the fire reached him. What bothered me—actually, haunted me—was that Jamie hadn't wanted to escape and Mick hadn't tried to yank open the car door. He and Jamie had known each other for decades; they'd met their freshman year of college at the University of Virginia, and Mick, who was from London, had practically been adopted by Jamie's family, spending every holiday and school break at the Vaughns' home in Richmond when he didn't return to England. Everyone knew they were as close as brothers. Did Mick know Jamie had some kind of death wish?

Or why?

"I'm not going to lie," I said to Mick, my voice stiff with anger, "if that's what you mean."

There is also some history between Mick Dunne and me:

We've slept together. Sex changes the dynamics of everything, especially if it's in the past and the relationship didn't end well. Forever afterward you know each other with an intimacy that leaves you vulnerable and more emotional when you're together, plus there's a hidden subtext in every remark or casual comment you make. At least we'd managed to stay friends—we were, after all, neighbors who owned adjacent vineyards—but the backstory of our tumultuous affair still tripped us up. Like it was doing now.

"Lucie." He reached for my shoulder, but I jerked away and kept my arms folded across my chest.

A female EMT with close-cropped gray hair and wearing a navy jumpsuit walked across Sycamore Lane, striding toward Mick and me. Her medical bag was in one hand and she was looking intently at us like she was on a mission. When she came closer, I realized that her face was young and the gray was probably premature. She pointed to my blood-spattered face and clothes.

"Are you injured?" she asked. "What happened?"

"It's not my blood," I said. "It's Jamie Vaughn's. I got to him before he lost consciousness. He started spitting up blood before he passed out."

"Would you like me to clean your face?"

"Yes, please."

She knelt and opened her kit, pulling on a pair of purple exam gloves. Then she took a couple of gauze pads from a box and sprayed them from a bottle marked "Saline Wound Wash."

Her touch was gentle and I closed my eyes as she wiped the blood off my face. "He probably sustained some pretty severe internal injuries, which caused the vomiting," she said.

"More than likely a couple of crushed or broken ribs. There . . . all done."

"Thank you." I opened my eyes. "He wasn't wearing a seat belt."

She groaned. "Seat belts save lives. He might still be alive if he'd used his. Did you see the crash?"

"Not exactly," I said. "I had to pull off onto the opposite shoulder to avoid him. He was speeding down Atoka Road, probably doing at least sixty. I heard the impact, then I turned around and saw his car smashed into the pillar."

"Can you stick around?" she asked. "I'll let the deputy from the sheriff's department know you were there when it happened."

"I live here," I said. "I'm not going anywhere. Thank you for . . . what you did."

"You're welcome. I'm just sorry we were too late for Jamie Vaughn."

She left and Mick picked up where we'd left off. "It's going to utterly gut Elena and the boys if this goes down as a suicide, Lucie."

I flinched at the word "suicide." "If it wasn't deliberate, then what happened?"

"I don't know. He was taking medication to deal with . . . losing the election and that brutal campaign. He'd also been drinking more than he ought to. He could have mixed alcohol and pills and then made an unwise decision to get behind the wheel of a car." He shrugged and gave me a look I didn't understand. "To tell you the truth, it wouldn't surprise me."

"You're right about the alcohol," I said. "I smelled it on his breath. And I think he'd taken something, too. He seemed kind of . . . I don't know . . . out of it."

"Which would mean he was driving while impaired. That doesn't make it suicide, Lucie. Just a horrible accident."

Maybe Mick was right. But something had weighed on Jamie's mind before he died, and now I wondered if it had upset him enough to prompt him to mix that deadly combination of alcohol and pills. "Who's Rick?" I asked. "Do you have any idea?"

"Pardon?" He frowned. "Rick?"

"Before you got here, Jamie asked me to tell someone named Rick he was sorry," I said. "I wondered if you knew who he meant."

Mick gave me a long, steady look. When he spoke, his voice was cool. "I have absolutely no idea what you're talking about. Jamie was unconscious when I reached him. If he said anything a moment before he passed out, you can hardly expect it made sense."

"It didn't make sense, but it's what he said."

"You also just told me he'd been drinking and possibly mixed it with drugs. Look, Lucie, Jamie's had a hell of a comedown since November. It hit him hard. He's been trying to deal with it as best he could. Forget what you think he said to you and don't stir up trouble or hurt anybody with speculation you can't justify. Think of Elena and Jamie's sons. And the millions of people who voted for Jamie, believed in him."

I stared at him, open-mouthed. Mick had been the one who walked—no, ran—away from that car without trying to help open Jamie's door. And I was supposed to feel guilty if I told

Jamie's wife what I'd seen and heard? Wouldn't she want to know?

"You can't be serious, Mick."

"Let it go, Lucie. I mean it."

I stared at him in frustration and disbelief. Then I turned my back on him.

Two more sheriff's department cruisers pulled up on the shoulder of Atoka Road in front of where Mick and I were standing, forming a barrier between us and a gathering crowd of neighbors and curious passersby who had stopped their cars to watch the unfolding tragedy. With the front entrance to the vineyard blocked, someone—probably Quinn Santori, my winemaker and, as of a few weeks ago, my fiancé—had opened our south service gate farther down the road. I guessed that a lot of the cars driving past us came from the vineyard itself, people who'd stopped in to taste or buy our wine. One of the deputies began directing traffic, which had backed up along the road as cars slowed down to see what had happened. The other deputy took over crowd control, herding everyone who was standing around like spectators riveted to a sports event where something has gone horribly wrong, until they moved across the street and out of the way. Two people I didn't recognize were filming the scene with their cell phone cameras. My stomach churned. We'd probably be watching someone's homemade video of Jamie's burned-out car on the evening news.

I pulled out my own phone to call Quinn. There were half a dozen missed calls, three from him and a couple of text messages. He answered even before I heard the phone ring. "There's an accident at the main gate," he said. "A car hit the wall and caught fire. Antonio put up barricades at the turnoff on our side of Sycamore Lane and we're having folks leave through the service entrance." He paused. "I hope whoever was driving managed to get out before the fire started."

"It was Jamie Vaughn," I said, "and he didn't. I saw the crash."

"Jamie Vaughn? Oh, my God . . . Jamie." He sounded stunned. "Lucie, are you okay? Are you hurt?"

"No . . . no, I'm not hurt. I'm fine."

"What happened? He lost control of his car? Was anyone with him?"

"No, just Jamie." There would be time later to explain to him that I wasn't sure it was an accident. "I'll tell you about it when I see you."

"Where are you now?"

"By the entrance, with Mick Dunne."

"Mick," he said, not sounding happy. The relationship between my fiancé and my ex-lover wasn't always smooth. "What's he doing there?"

"I'll tell you about that when I see you, too."

"Give me five minutes," he said. "And you can tell me everything."

BY THE TIME QUINN'S pickup truck pulled up behind the two police cruisers, a misty drizzle had turned the landscape into a washed-out watercolor. The deputy who'd been the first to arrive, a young guy with a buzz cut and the demeanor of an ex-marine, had taken me aside—away from Mick—to question me about the accident. I told him the truth, about Jamie's speeding down the wrong side of the road before turning into Sycamore Lane and crashing into the pillar. And that I'd smelled alcohol on his breath.

Over his shoulder, I could see Quinn talking to Mick. If body language was anything to go by, it didn't look like the conversation was going well.

"Are you saying you think he was drunk?"

"I'm saying he didn't seem like himself."

"Well, it's a single-vehicle crash and there aren't any skid marks, which is consistent with someone not trying to stop," the deputy said. "Did you see him swerve to avoid something, an animal, maybe? Any indication he was distracted? On his phone? Texting?"

I shifted my gaze away from Mick and Quinn and focused on him. "I don't know. I couldn't say one way or the other. I was too busy trying to avoid him and then keep control of my own car so I wouldn't crash through my neighbor's fence."

"Then you didn't actually *see* Mr. Vaughn make that last turn?"

"No, but his car didn't levitate off the ground and make a sharp right on its own."

He gave me a don't-be-a-wiseass-to-a-cop look. "There's no such thing as an earwitness, Ms. Montgomery. You just said you didn't know if Jamie Vaughn was avoiding something or otherwise distracted and lost control of the car because you didn't see that crash happen."

Black or white. Yes or no. All or nothing.

"That's correct," I said. "But there's something else."

He paused from making notes in a reporter's notebook and looked up. "Yes?"

"He was conscious when I got to him, and he said something. He asked me to tell someone named Rick that he was sorry."

The deputy tapped the end of his pen on his pad. "Do you know who he was talking about?"

"No, I don't. He also didn't want me to help him get out of the car."

More pen tapping while he considered that. "What do you mean?"

I shrugged. "Just what I said. He wouldn't help me try to get his door open. He told me to move away from the car, to leave him."

"Was he trapped in the car?"

"Yes."

"Could the two of you have opened the door?"

"It would have been very difficult . . . I don't know. Probably not."

"Do you think Mr. Vaughn realized that it was futile to try to rescue him and that the car was about to catch on fire?"

"I suppose so."

"In other words he might have been trying to save your life. Make it easier for you to walk away."

"I . . . maybe. I mean, yes." Mick had said practically the same thing.

The officer wrote something in his notebook, then closed it and clicked his pen. Even to my own ears it sounded like I wasn't sure about anything anymore. Unreliable witness. Maybe that's what he'd just written down.

"Thank you for your help, Ms. Montgomery."

"You're welcome. What happens now?"

"We'll inform his next of kin and the ME will perform an autopsy. As to whether it was an accident or something else, our investigation will track with what the medical examiner's office determines is the cause of death." He rested a hand on my shoulder. "Take it easy, okay? You've just witnessed an awful crash, someone you know perishing in a fire. It's going to affect you. There's no way it won't."

I nodded because I was afraid my voice would crack if I spoke. Afraid I would crack. He walked back to his cruiser. Quinn broke away from Mick as soon as I was by myself and ran over to me. In the past few minutes the rain had turned into a cold, steady drizzle. The drops of blood on my clothes started to run like pink Rorschach inkblots.

"Mick gave me this. He said you dropped it." Quinn handed me my metal cane, a puzzled look on his face that turned to shock as his eyes took in my blood-spattered clothes. "What happened? Are you hurt?"

Obviously Mick hadn't explained the circumstances that led me to drop the cane, that he'd been carrying me kicking and screaming away from where Jamie still remained trapped inside a burning car.

"I'm okay," I said. "Don't worry."

Quinn pulled me into his arms. "You've got blood on your clothes."

"It's Jamie's."

He hugged me tight, his chin resting on the top of my head. "Come on, let's get you out of here," he said in my ear. "It's going to start pouring any minute. I just saw a television crew arrive. One look at you and they'll be all over you for a story."

"I wonder if anyone called Elena," I said as we walked back

to the truck. "Or the kids. It would be awful if they found out on television or through some social networking site."

"Mick's on his way to Elena's," Quinn said. "He phoned her while you were talking to that deputy. I didn't realize those two were so friendly with each other."

"What do you mean?"

He shrugged. "Nothing. Just some vibe I thought I picked up."

"They've known each other for decades. Of course they're good friends. Mick is godfather to one of the twins. Owen, I think."

"Yeah, maybe." He opened the passenger door to the truck and held it for me. "You look like you could use a drink. And a shower."

"Yes to both." I said. "Wait a minute. My car is still where I left it after Jamie ran me off the road. I ought to get it before anyone else puts two and two together that I was here when Jamie crashed. I'll meet you at the house."

"Leave that to Antonio or one of the other guys," he said. "You'll be mobbed by people asking questions before you get anywhere near your car. This is going to be enough of a three-ring media circus as it is, once word gets out that Jamie Vaughn died in a fiery crash practically at our front door—if it isn't already out by now." He held out a hand. "Here, give me your keys."

I climbed into my seat and gave them to him. "You're probably right."

"I know I'm right." He climbed into his seat, put the truck in reverse, and did a neat three-point turn.

I glanced in my side mirror. A petite woman in a bright

blue windbreaker with a D.C. Channel 3 news station logo stitched on it ran toward us. Her hood shielded her hair and face from the rain so I couldn't get a look at her. Before Quinn could pull out onto Atoka Road, the deputy who had been directing traffic pointed at us and held up his hand, indicating for Quinn to wait until one of the fire trucks maneuvered onto the road on its way back to the station.

"Damn," I said as the reporter came around and rapped on my window, an engaging smile on her face as she tried to make eye contact. Her cameraman was right behind her.

Quinn frowned. "Ignore them."

I groaned. "That's what's-her-name from Channel 3. She's a pit bull."

I stared at my hands in my lap and pretended not to see either the reporter or her cameraman as Quinn drove away. Thank God that EMT had cleaned Jamie's blood off my face. I checked the mirror again and saw the cameraman filming the truck, and the reporter, no longer smiling as she stabbed her finger in our direction.

This would not turn out well.

"I don't want to talk to anybody," I said to Quinn. "Or answer questions about what happened. I mean it."

"You don't have to do anything you don't want to do." He sounded like a parent soothing a child who just insisted monsters were hiding under the bed. He shot me a perplexed look. "What's wrong, Lucie? You look almost like you're about to pass out."

Here it was. I took a deep breath. "I don't think that crash was an accident. I think Jamie deliberately drove his car into our wall."

"Jesus, are you serious? You think it was suicide?"

I nodded, and his eyes held mine as he took in the implication of what that meant.

"How sure are you?" he asked.

"I heard him accelerate right before he hit the wall. Unfortunately—or fortunately—I didn't see the actual crash because Jamie ran me off the road and I ended up in that puddle on the shoulder where you saw the Jeep. So according to the deputy who interviewed me, I'm not technically an eyewitness. And there was alcohol on Jamie's breath."

Quinn had taken the long way back to the house, through the vineyard with its neat rows of dark brown vines and down an allée of pink flowering Yoshino cherry trees my mother planted years ago. Though the blossoms had reached their peak a few days ago, the trees were still lovely and ethereal, jarringly beautiful after the fire-charred wreckage we'd just left behind. Today's rain and wind had scattered hundreds of petals so they carpeted the road like pink snow. It was one of the places where I always felt most at peace, and I guessed that was why Quinn had brought me here.

He stopped the truck under the sheltering protection of the trees in a spot where their lacy branches crisscrossed above us. A few flowers drifted down and landed on the windshield. "Here's what I think we should do," he said in a gentle voice. "I think we need to call Frankie. Warn her that the vineyard is probably going to be swarmed by reporters nosing around for a story in the next day or so. If that woman back there knew you were a witness, it won't be long before the rest of the pack gets wind of it, and you're going to be hounded."

"What are we going to tell her?" I asked. My brain felt like it had frozen.

"That if anybody asks, all she should say is that Montgomery Estate Vineyard has no comment except that our hearts go out to the Vaughn family. The less said the better."

Francesca Merchant—Frankie—ran our tasting room and the day-to-day retail operation of the vineyard with military efficiency. She'd be more than up to coping with anyone who came around or called asking questions about the crash or trying to pry into my knowledge of what had happened.

"I'll call her," I said. "I'm the one who was there." I pulled my phone out of my pocket as he reached for his. "Who are you going to call?"

He gave me a long look. "Persia. It might be a good idea to get Hope out of the house before you get home, don't you think? Maybe she can stay at Persia's place until you get cleaned up."

Last fall I hired Persia Fleming, a middle-aged Jamaican woman who'd recently become a widow, as my housekeeper when it finally got to be too much to keep up Highland House, my family's 225-year-old home, along with my increasing responsibilities at the vineyard. A few months later my brother Eli and his three-and-a-half-year-old daughter, Hope, moved in after Eli's marriage fell apart. It hadn't taken long for him to poach Persia as Hopie's daytime caregiver when she wasn't at preschool, but Persia adored Hope as if she were her own and the house had never run so smoothly.

"That's a good idea," I said. "What are you going to tell her?"

"As little as possible for now. She'll just fret, otherwise."

My thoughts moved in a straight line from Persia to Hope to Eli. "Oh, God, Quinn, what about Eli? He needs to know. I think he had client meetings all day so he's spending the day driving all over Loudoun County. If he's in his car, he'll have satellite radio tuned to some music station."

"First call Frankie," Quinn said. "Then call your brother. Though if Elena knows, he might have found out by now as well."

Over the winter my older brother, Eli, had begun going out with Sasha Vaughn, Jamie's daughter from a brief marriage to a college girlfriend who inconveniently got pregnant. Eli and Sasha met at Hope's preschool where his daughter and her four-year-old son were in the same class. Before long I knew Eli was timing his school pickups and drop-offs so he could "accidentally" bump into Sasha. It was a rebound relationship for both of them—Eli's first since his acrimonious split up with Brandi and, for Sasha, the first time she'd dated since her marine husband filed for a divorce and went back to Iraq to marry his girlfriend. In recent weeks it seemed to me things between them had become even more serious.

"Elena's going to call her own sons and make sure Owen and Oliver are okay before she tells Sasha," I said. "They don't have the easiest stepmother-stepdaughter relationship. Eli still might not know."

Frankie answered her phone over the blare of a television. It sounded like people were shouting.

"Lucie." Her voice was breathless and agitated. "Are you okay? I'm watching CNN. They're saying that an eyewitness said two cars were involved in the crash that killed Jamie Vaughn at our front entrance. The story is all over the place."

"I'm fine," I told her. "I wasn't anywhere near his car when it hit the wall. And there wasn't anyone else around when it happened. So if there's another eyewitness, it's news to me."

"Thank God you're okay. Look, I closed the tasting room for the rest of the day and sent all the staff home. Do you want to come by for a drink? You probably could use one."

"Thanks. I think I'm just going to head home with Quinn and get cleaned up."

"Cleaned up?"

"I'm . . . uh . . . all muddy."

She let that go and we discussed what she should say if anyone called the vineyard, specifically anyone from the media.

I hung up with Frankie as Quinn clicked his phone off after talking to Persia. "Persia is going to take Hope over to her apartment and give her dinner there," he said. "She'll bring her back later in time for bed."

"Good," I said. "I guess I'd better call Eli."

Quinn laid a hand on my arm. "He knows. He's on his way home, too. First he wants to see you. Then he's going over to Sasha's place. She canceled all her patients for the rest of the day and went to pick up Zach from preschool."

"That poor little boy," I said. "I hope Sasha can keep him from seeing or hearing any stories on the news so he doesn't have to know how his grandfather died. It's going to be hard enough explaining death to him as it is."

Quinn started the truck. The rain was coming down hard,

drumming on the roof in a metallic staccato that jangled my nerves. "Persia and Hope are probably gone by now," he said. "You look wiped out. Let's go home."

I FOUND QUINN AND Eli on the sofa in the parlor drinking beer out of the bottle when I came downstairs after showering and changing. I had scrubbed for a long time under a stream of hot water as if Jamie's blood had somehow penetrated my clothes clear through to my skin.

The television was on mute and a commercial flashed on the screen, a couple cavorting in a field on a sunny day with a dog. You never know what they're selling anymore. Based on the rest of the images it could have been a sexual performance—enhancing drug or a cell phone plan.

My brother got up and gave me a look as if he hadn't been sure what to expect when he saw me. Like Leland, our father, Eli wasn't good with weepy, emotional women. For that matter, neither was Quinn. I am neither weepy nor emotional, but I was pretty wrung out.

"Relax," I said, forcing lightness into my voice. "I'm okay."

He gave me a one-arm hug. "You sure?" His smile was half-hearted.

"Absolutely."

"What can I get you to drink, sweetheart?" Quinn asked.

"Scotch, please. Neat. The shower helped. I threw out my jeans and my shirt. I can't wear them . . . again."

Eli's eyelids flickered, so I knew Quinn must have told him about the blood.

"Jamie's death is going to be the lead story on the local

news at six," Quinn said. "They've been talking about it non-stop. We don't have to watch if you'd rather not."

He left the room, his hand caressing the back of my neck on his way out. Eli and I sat down on the sofa. "When Quinn and I left the accident scene about an hour and a half ago, a reporter from Channel 3 and a cameraman were already there," I told him.

"One?" he said. "Just one? I saw half a dozen as I drove by a few minutes ago. If this keeps up, we're going to end up with more satellite trucks and reporters doing their stand-ups outside the vineyard entrance than the O.J. trial."

Quinn returned with my Scotch and caught the tail end of what Eli said. "Was Jamie's car still there?" he asked.

Eli nodded. "They were moving what was left of it onto a flatbed truck. It was too wrecked to tow. Fortunately, there were a couple of officers from the sheriff's department handling crowd control, keeping people away from the actual crash site. What's still standing of the pillar looks pretty unstable. We're going to have to rebuild it eventually. Along with that whole section of the wall."

I was glad he didn't say "again" or mention that it was the same one Greg's car had crashed into. Last year when Eli and Hope moved in with me, we made a deal that in return for free rent, my brother—an architect who had converted the lower level of our old carriage house into his studio—would supervise all construction work at the vineyard pro bono. I knew he'd take care of fixing the wall as well. I also knew that when it was finished there would be no trace of today's destruction, no seam between the old stonework and the new repair. Nothing visible to remind me—or anyone else—of what had happened there. He would make sure of it.

"How's Sasha?" I asked him.

"In shock."

"How'd she find out? From Elena?"

He drank his beer and made a face. "No. Garrett called her. He and Owen and Oliver were at the house with Elena."

Garrett Bateman was Jamie's shadow, his indispensable right-hand man. He'd been the director of communications and a senior adviser for the presidential campaign. Before that Jamie jokingly called him the vice president of everything, since Garrett played an integral role in every aspect of Jamie's international real estate empire. Like Mick, Garrett met Jamie at UVA, so they went back a long way. No doubt Jamie's death was as hard for Garrett to deal with as it was for Elena and Jamie's children.

I wondered whether he would know if something had been troubling Jamie before he died. Maybe he even knew who Rick was. If anyone understood Jamie Vaughn and could get inside his head, it was Garrett Bateman.

"The six o'clock news," I said. "It's starting."

Quinn picked up the remote. "Sure you want to watch?"

"Yes. Channel 3, please."

He switched channels and clicked on the sound as the theme music for *News Channel 3* came on and an authoritative Voice of God introduced the male and female anchors. The lead story was, as promised, Jamie Vaughn's tragic death. The words BREAKING NEWS kept flashing across the screen and the anchors went straight to Pippa O'Hara, their investigative reporter on the scene, who had an "exclusive interview" that would be a "bombshell revelation." The camera cut to a petite redhead in a blue windbreaker.

I groaned. "Pippa O'Hara. She's the woman we drove away from, Quinn. She hypes everything. I wonder what her bombshell is."

"Shh," Eli said. "Listen."

". . . right here," Pippa was saying as she strolled down Sycamore Lane and pointed to the yellow police tape that had been strung up around the vineyard entrance, "where former presidential candidate and international real estate mogul Jamison Vaughn died tragically in a fiery car crash earlier this afternoon. His SUV, reportedly traveling at high speed, crashed into a stone wall at the entrance to Montgomery Estate Vineyard in Atoka and caught fire."

She went on about what a sleepy little village we were in the middle of Virginia's affluent horse-and-hunt country and what a close-knit community Atoka was. By now she was standing next to the sign for the vineyard.

"*News Channel 3* has obtained exclusive information"—she paused for maximum dramatic impact—"that there was a witness to this accident. Lucie Montgomery, owner of Montgomery Estate Vineyard, was on the scene when Jamie Vaughn's car crashed into the stone wall at the entrance to her vineyard."

"How in the hell did she find out—"

"Shhh," Eli said again as the camera cut from Pippa to the earlier footage of Quinn's truck speeding away this afternoon, along with a close-up of my Jeep tilting at a crazy angle in the mud puddle where I'd left it.

"Unfortunately, Ms. Montgomery, whose vehicle you see here, refused our request for an interview," she said.

"I did not—"

"However, we spoke to a neighbor off-camera who told us there is a history of tragedy on this very spot. Ten years ago, Ms. Montgomery herself was involved in a high-speed car crash when a vehicle driven by a former boyfriend ran into this same wall, destroying part of it and seriously injuring Lucie Montgomery. That man, Gregory Knight, is now serving time in jail for murder."

I caught my breath. How had she found out? Who told her about my accident, remembered those precise details from ten years ago? I thought the only one who carried around a cinematographic memory of what happened to me was me. And maybe Greg.

The camera panned the accident scene again, lingering on the heat-scorched stone wall, the charred earth where the car had burned, and the rubble where the pillar had been demolished. Then it refocused on Pippa. Her smile was grave, but there was a satisfied gleam in her eye as if she'd hauled in the biggest fish of the day while everyone else still had bait on their lines. "Keep it on *News Channel 3* for the latest updates on this developing story. I'll have more for you at eleven, but now back to you in the studio."

Quinn hit Mute on the television remote as the picture returned to the two anchors, and the three of us sat in silence. I caught Quinn and Eli exchanging uneasy glances, but inside I was raging.

There was no reason to tie my accident to what had happened to Jamie, to drag up the past as though it had some connection or link to the present. I told Quinn I didn't want to talk to a single soul about Jamie's death because if I did and I told the truth, the only conclusion anyone could reach would be that Jamie had deliberately taken his own life. The shock waves from that news would reverberate far and wide. Now Pippa O'Hara had just dragged me into the middle of the maelstrom in a very public way.

I wondered what would happen next, because I had no doubt there would be more.

Much more.

Three

Eli left for Sasha's place after we turned off the news, promising to be back in time to kiss Hope good night, if I wouldn't mind putting her to bed once she came home from Persia's. I told him I wouldn't mind at all. Quinn found a plate of Persia's southern fried chicken left over from yesterday's dinner, along with a head of Boston lettuce and some arugula in the refrigerator.

"I'll make us a salad," he said. "The heirloom tomatoes you bought the other day ought to be ripe."

"What can I do?" I asked.

"Choose the dinner wine."

Since he moved in with me in February, Quinn had gone to work taking an inventory of what was left of Leland's old wine cellar in the basement and restocking it with new wines. As any winemaker knows, drink too much of your own stuff and you get what's called a cellar palate. Eventually you start over-looking deficits in your own wine, your palate is no longer honed to notice the nuances in other varietals, and you become numb to the differences you would have noticed if you drank more widely. So by choice we almost never drank our own wines for dinner unless we were having friends over or hosting a party. And even then we still made a point to choose a variety of wines from around the world.

I found a German Kabinett-style Riesling that had a bit of sweetness in it in the wine refrigerator Quinn had installed. The day could do with some sweetness to counter everything bitter and ugly that had happened. Quinn nodded approval when he saw my choice and handed me the corkscrew as my cell phone rang. I looked at the display: Kit Noland.

Anyone can be a friend when times are good, but a true friend sticks around through the heartache and bad times, and still loves you even if you've just made a fool of yourself or done something you're both going to regret. Kit Noland was that kind of friend. We met when we were five years old, and though we'd gone down different paths as we'd grown older, we'd never grown apart. She was still my best friend in the world.

Five years ago Kit moved back to Atoka to care for her mother, who had suffered a debilitating stroke, which meant leaving a job as assistant foreign editor for the *Washington Tribune* and an offer—a promotion, actually—to go to Russia as the *Trib*'s Moscow bureau chief. She swore she had no regrets about the arrow she'd shot into the upward trajectory of her career, and she meant it. Kit had that kind of tenacity and grit, even when she took over as bureau chief for the *Tribune*'s Loudoun County office, which was about as far from Russia as you could get geographically and psychologically. She also married the boy back home, Bobby Noland, a detective with the Loudoun County Sheriff's Department.

It didn't take a genius to know why she was calling now: Jamie Vaughn.

"It's Kit," I said to Quinn.

Maybe she had new information about Jamie that she'd picked up from Bobby, though it was just as likely she didn't. "I sleep with the guy and he still makes me work my ass off for anything I get," she always complained. "Actually, I probably work harder than anyone else so he can make sure it doesn't look like he showed me any favoritism."

"Take it," he said. "It's not like dinner's going to get cold."

I flashed him a grateful smile and answered her call.

"Hey," she said. "Are you okay?"

"Not really," I said. "Who's covering the story from the *Trib*?"

"National affairs and the guy who followed Jamie on the campaign trail are all over it. We, uh, sent a photographer out to the vineyard. The crash site looks pretty horrific." She cleared her throat. "The Loudoun bureau is covering the local story, obviously, since he lived here . . . and died here."

Her unasked question hung in the air between us. "And you want to interview me."

"I thought maybe we could talk about that." She sounded uncomfortable, which surprised me. Kit was fearless when it came to getting the story. "Are you by yourself?"

I looked over at Quinn, who was whisking olive oil and lemon juice for our salad.

"No."

"Could you be?"

"Give me a minute." I signaled to Quinn, pointing to the phone and the door to the veranda. I held up five fingers to let him know I wouldn't be gone long.

He nodded. I stepped outside, pulling the kitchen door shut and immediately regretting not grabbing a sweater. The sky was still overcast so there was no spectacular sunset behind the Blue Ridge Mountains to the west, just the leaden sky turning the even dirtier color of ashes. In the waning daylight the temperature had dropped, so it was sharply cooler.

"Okay," I said. "It's just me."

She took a deep breath and said, "I saw him yesterday."

"Saw who? Jamie? What do you mean, 'saw him'?"

It was too early in the season to put out the cushions for the patio furniture, so there was no comfortable place to sit down. I paced the veranda and listened to Kit. The gardens had morphed into insubstantial shadows and the Blue Ridge Mountains were slowly fading into the sky, which was now the color of an old bruise.

"I mean I met him," she said. "It was at my request. At our favorite off-the-grid drinking place." She paused. "It didn't go well."

Our favorite off-the-grid drinking place was the old Goose Creek Bridge just outside Middleburg, the next town over from Atoka. It was built in 1802 during Thomas Jefferson's presidency, and at two hundred feet long, it was the longest arched stone bridge in Virginia. It was the site of the Battle of Upperville, involving Colonel J.E.B. Stuart's soldiers, who hid out in ravines and behind old stone walls—and the bridge—hoping to delay Union troops who were desperate to find Lee's army.

Ten days later, they finally met. At Gettysburg. Five years ago, it landed on the National Register of Historic Places.

I stopped pacing. "Why did you meet Jamie Vaughn at the Goose Creek Bridge?"

"Because it's private, hardly anybody goes there, and he figured it would be the last place anyone would see him talking to me."

I wasn't expecting that answer. "Oh."

"I just left Mom's apartment a few minutes ago. I had to run by to drop off some medicine and I'm still in her parking lot. Bobby's working late tonight because of everything that happened today." She sounded tentative, still not at all normal Kit. "I really need to talk to someone about all this."

She was fifteen minutes away. All what? I had no idea what she meant.

"Quinn and I are about to have dinner. There's enough for three. Leftovers, but it's Persia's fried chicken. Come on by."

"I won't turn down Persia's fried chicken, but this conversation has to be between you and me."

"Okay. We'll talk after dinner, just the two of us," I said. "See you soon."

I disconnected and went inside. "Kit's coming for dinner," I said. "Then she wants to stick around to have girl talk, okay? Bobby's working late tonight."

"Sure." He pulled me to him and ruffled my hair. "I'll get lost. My feelings aren't hurt."

I rested my hands against his chest. "You can smoke one of your cigars on the veranda with a cognac and feel guilt-free since I'll be occupied."

I had one hard-and-fast rule: No cigars smelling up the house. He nodded. "I might just do that. You want to get an extra wineglass?"

I took one out of the cabinet and set a third place at the table. Kit had said her meeting with Jamie at the Goose Creek Bridge hadn't gone well. The next day he was dead.

Earlier I had wondered if someone close to Jamie—perhaps Elena, one of the twins, or Garrett Bateman—knew who the mysterious Rick was. Now it occurred to me that maybe someone he didn't know so well might have an answer to that.

Maybe Kit knew.

DINNER WAS SMALL TALK, anything but the subject that was really on everyone's mind. Quinn was the one who finally brought up Jamie, though in a roundabout way.

"I wonder what's going to happen to the Jefferson Dinner now," he said.

"They'll probably cancel it, don't you think?" Kit asked.

The Jefferson Dinner was a ten-thousand-dollar-a-plate dinner that was officially an opportunity to taste several rare vintages from the celebrated eight-thousand-bottle wine cellar of Jamie Vaughn at a meal served on china and silverware that dated from the era of Thomas Jefferson. Unofficially it was a fund-raiser organized by Jamie's friends to help pay off some of his staggering campaign debts.

The highlight of the evening would be a tasting of what, in our business, is known as a "unicorn wine"—a wine so rare and sought after that it is priceless. Jamie's unicorn wine was an 1876 Norton's Virginia that had been salvaged from a shipwreck off the coast of North Carolina a few years ago, made from a little-known native American grape discovered in Virginia in the early 1800s by Dr. Daniel Norton of Richmond. Twenty-five people who had paid another ten thousand dollars would get a taste of that wine at the dinner.

"Jamie's campaign still has debts," I said. "If they cancel they'll have to return the money they took in. Although I'm sure that's probably the last thing Elena and everyone else is thinking about now."

"Maybe, but the dinner is Saturday and they made a big fuss about it being held on Thomas Jefferson's birthday," Kit said, covering the top of her wineglass with her hand and shaking her head as Quinn picked up the bottle of Riesling to refill it. "Are you two going?"

The dinner was being held at the Goose Creek Inn, a local restaurant owned by my cousin Dominique Gosselin. The Inn consistently won regional and national dining awards and regularly made the list of "most romantic places to dine" in the D.C. Metro area. If anyone could pull off a pricey fund-raiser involving a dinner replicating Thomas Jefferson's favorite foods, plus handle the national buzz of attention the Norton wine tasting was getting, my cousin could.

"If we had forty thousand dollars to spare—or even twenty thousand—it would go for a new destemmer," I said. "The price of the tickets was too steep for us."

"Still, I'd give my right arm to try that 1876 Norton." Quinn got up and started clearing away our plates. "I think I'll go out on the veranda and smoke my after-dinner cigar," he said, "if you two don't mind."

"We'll miss you," I said.

He grinned and dropped a kiss on the top of my head before he left the kitchen.

"Come on," Kit said. "I'll help you do the dishes. We can talk then."

"There's really nothing to do. I'll clean up later. How about I make us some tea and we can sit and talk in the library?"

Kit still insisted on cleaning up while I made a pot of lavender, lemon, and sage tea, which she carried into the library. The room had once been Leland's office, stamped with his larger-than-life personality, a place of gloomy shadows and dark corners that seldom saw daylight, something he said was necessary to protect his collection of rare first editions that used to line the floor-to-ceiling bookcases. Light, he'd told me, not only destroys wine, it also destroys books.

A few weeks after he died, a fire burned much of the first floor of Highland House, especially the library. The exception had been my father's hand-carved gun cabinet, which wasn't even scorched. Eli had handled the renovation, staying true to the original architecture and rebuilding the bookshelves, but I'd painted the library walls a soft mint green and had the new furniture upholstered in soothing earth colors. The dark-green-and-cream-striped curtains were now drawn only in the evening.

Kit and I sat on opposite ends of a caramel-colored crushed velvet sofa with our feet propped up and mugs of tea, so we faced each other.

"Okay," I said, "what's going on?"

She tucked a bottle-green throw pillow behind her head and blew on her tea. I knew she was stalling.

"A couple of weeks ago the senior national editor asked me

to put together a story about Jamie's political campaign for the Sunday news magazine," she said finally. "Ten thousand words, something in-depth. How he bypassed more experienced politicians to win primaries and the nomination, put together his organization starting from next to nothing, the whole megillah."

"And?"

She gave a noisy, unhappy sigh. "You know the saying, 'When you want to dig up dirt, go find a worm'?"

"Sure."

"A worm found me. I have no idea who it is." She looked uneasy. "I got an anonymous package from someone who claimed to have worked for the Vaughn campaign. According to this person, some of the donation money was used to pay Jamie's personal expenses. Or, more accurately, expenses for his family and his business. Whoever it is included photocopies of checks made out to Elena Vaughn. I'm talking thousands of dollars, too. Not little stuff. There were other checks made out to his vineyard, supposedly expenses for campaign fundraisers. It's freaking me out."

"I thought Jamie funded his campaign with his own money."

She sipped her tea and shrugged. "According to my source, the Vaughn Real Estate Group is not in as good financial shape as he made it out to be. He's got a couple of huge projects here and overseas that are completely stalled because the investment funding dried up. He's having a hard time raising any more cash. I don't know how much of his campaign financing really came from his own bank account."

"Who knows about this?" I asked.

"Well, me. The national editor. Our managing editor, who

told me the story had better be airtight before we run it. And now, you. The worm. And, as of yesterday morning, Jamie."

"What did Jamie say?"

"He denied it and told me if the *Trib* printed a word of it, he'd sue my ass off. And take the *Trib* to court as well."

"Did you believe him?"

"That he'd do it? You bet. As to whether I believe him that it's not true, I don't know anymore." She set her mug on the coffee table and folded her arms across her chest. "You saw the crash, didn't you? Bobby said there were no skid marks. Jamie obviously didn't try to stop."

The light from a hammered copper lamp on an end table behind Kit cast her face in shadow. I knew her as well as I knew myself. As a reporter she would do anything to get a story, but as a friend she would never betray a confidence, including what I was about to tell her.

"You can't use this," I said, "but I think he did it on purpose. He must have been going sixty on Atoka Road before he turned onto Sycamore Lane. I had to swerve to avoid him and ended up on the opposite shoulder. I almost took out the split-rail fence across the road. Before I could turn around, I heard him accelerating and then the crash."

"You didn't actually see it, but you still think it's deliberate?"

"That's right."

"Why?"

"Because I talked to him before he passed out and before Mick Dunne showed up. He didn't want me to help him get out of the car."

"I heard he was pinned inside," she said. "That he couldn't have gotten out if he'd wanted to."

"Maybe, but it still remains that he didn't want to."

"You're sure?"

Through the closed library door I heard the sound of the front door being unlocked and a moment later the door opening and Persia's singsong-accented English, as she spoke to Hope.

"Let's go find Aunt Lucie, pet."

"We're in here," I called. "The library."

I swung my legs off the sofa as Hope opened the door and bounced into the room, her dark hair done up in two high pigtails tied with pink ribbons. She wore jean overalls and a pink turtleneck with lace on the cuffs. I held out my arms and she ran into them.

"How are you, sweet pea? I've missed you today." I rested my chin on top of her head and mouthed "Thank you" to Persia, who stood in the doorway, leaning against the jamb and watching us.

Hope gave me a kiss on the cheek and said, "I missed you, too."

"Hey," Kit demanded. "What am I? Chopped liver? Don't I get a kiss?"

Hope obliged and Kit fiddled with the ribbons of her pigtails. "You look adorable, princess."

"I know."

Persia and I said, automatically, "Thank you, Aunt Kit."

Hope grinned and stuck her finger in her mouth. "Thank you, Aunt Kit."

"Lucie, would you like me to put Miss Adorable to bed? It looks like you two are in the middle of something," Persia gave me a concerned look over the top of Hope's head, so I knew she'd figured out that we were talking about Jamie.

"Would that be okay, Hopie?" I asked. "Just for tonight? Daddy will be home soon and he'll stop in and give you a good night kiss. I'll kiss you when I come upstairs, too."

Hope nodded and the pigtails bounced. "Persia, will you read me a story?"

"Of course, I will." Persia held out her hand and Hope ran to her.

"Thanks, Persia," I said. "And thanks for taking care of her this afternoon."

"Hope, love, go ahead and start up the stairs. Persia will be along in a minute," she said as Hope skipped out of the room. As soon as she was out of earshot, Persia said in her lilting accent, "I saw pictures of the accident on the evening news. That poor man, it must have been a terrible crash."

I set my empty mug on the coffee table and nodded. "Hope didn't see it, did she?"

Persia looked horrified. "Of course not. I would never let her see something so dreadful. She'd have nightmares for weeks."

"I know." I had nightmares for weeks after my accident, and I was already dreading that they might return for an encore tonight.

"Are you all right, Lucie?" she asked.

I heard Kit suck in her breath. Neither Kit, nor Eli, nor Quinn had referred to my accident so far, but Pippa O'Hara had made a point to tie what happened to me to Jamie's accident today. Persia hadn't been around ten years ago; she hadn't even been in the country. She couldn't know how hard it was to have my own history dragged up again, like scraping a scab off a wound that refused to heal.

"Don't worry about me. I'm fine."

She gave me a clear-eyed look that said we both knew I'd lied. "I'm glad to hear that. Excuse me. I'd better go take care of Hope."

After she pulled the door shut, I said to Kit, "If I ever meet Pippa O'Hara, I'll strangle her."

"Get in line." Kit sat back down on the sofa, cross-legged with her hands folded in her lap. "What were you about to say before your sweet niece interrupted us?"

"I don't remember."

"Like hell, you don't. You were about to tell me why Jamie Vaughn didn't want to get out of his car." She fixed her gaze on me. "Do you think it has something to do with what I told him yesterday?"

"You mean is it your fault?"

Her eyes were anguished. "Okay, yes. Was our conversation the last straw, the thing that pushed him over the edge?"

"Are you crazy? You were just doing your job. You can't blame yourself for what he did."

"What makes you so sure? I hit the tip of the iceberg with what I found out about his money problems. Jamie was trying to raise cash any way he could. I think his business empire had started caving in around him and he was desperate to stop it before anyone found out. What do you think the Jefferson Dinner is all about?"

I hadn't seen Kit upset like this in years.

"Hold it," I said. "Just wait a minute. There's something you still don't know."

"What?"

"Before he died, Jamie told me that I had to find someone

named Rick and tell him that he was sorry for something he'd done. He hoped Rick would forgive him."

"Forgive him for what?" Her eyes grew wide. "And who's Rick?"

"You don't know?"

"Why would I?"

"You're the one who has been poking around in his life. Any Ricks you've come across who work for one of his hotels or a building he owns? A staff person on his campaign? Maybe even your source?"

"No one sticks out, but that doesn't mean I haven't missed someone," she said, looking thoughtful. "I'll go through my files and notes and take another look."

"Thanks. Let me know, okay?"

She nodded. "What do you think Jamie did that it's so important to him that he needs to be forgiven? It almost sounds like a deathbed confession."

"I don't know," I said, "but I guess I'm going to have to find out."

Four

Quinn wasn't on the veranda when I went to find him after Kit left, nor did I detect the scent of his Swisher Sweets cigar lingering in the chilly April air. On other nights I'd know where to find him if he wasn't out here smoking: the summerhouse at the back of the garden where he would have taken out his telescope to study the night sky. Astronomy and anything to do with space exploration fascinated Quinn—the idea of an infinite universe beyond all imagining where billions and billions of galaxies existed that we would never know about, that perhaps a mysterious dark energy was out there expanding it even farther. That the light we saw from a distant star twinkling in the sky was billions of years old, and the air we breathed had been breathed by everyone else who had ever walked this earth.

Tonight, though, I was sure he wouldn't be out stargazing; the cloud cover was so dense and low it looked like you could reach up and punch a hole through it with your fist. I walked through the garden around to the front of the house. His truck wasn't where he'd left it in the circular driveway. Either he was over at the barrel room checking on something or, more likely, he had gone back to the vineyard entrance to see whether there were still any camera crews and reporters filming their news stories or gawkers who wanted to get a firsthand look at the crash site.

He answered right away when I called his mobile. "Where are you?"

"On my way home," he said, sounding too cheerful. "There was something I needed to take care of in the barrel room."

"Really? What was it?"

"I wasn't sure if I remembered to lock up the bonded cellar."

"Must have been tough to do since your keys are on the telephone table in the foyer," I said. "Including the cellar key."

He groaned and I heard a vehicle coming up Sycamore Lane. A moment later he pulled in to the driveway. When he got out of the truck I said, "You went to check on the crash site, didn't you?"

"I did." He put his arm around me and we went inside the house. A light on the phone blinked that there were messages and the answering machine beeped quietly. The display showed twelve missed calls. "The entrance was lit up like a carnival, there were so many television crews. Plus people stopping by to leave things, like a memorial or a shrine."

I pushed the button on the answering machine and a mechanical voice said, "You have nine new messages." I scrolled through the call log—the callers were friends, neighbors, and three news organizations.

"Are you going to listen to those?" Quinn asked.

"Not tonight. I'm sure everyone wants to know about the crash, and I don't want to talk to anyone from the press after what Pippa O'Hara did to me this evening. I've got six more messages on my cell phone and texts from ten different people."

"I'm wiped out. I can't talk to anyone about it anymore."

"How about an after-dinner drink?"

I threw him a grateful look. "What kinds of things are people leaving? Flowers? Cards?"

He walked into the dining room and got an open bottle of brandy and two glasses. When he came back into the foyer, he said, "A lot of flowers and cards and letters. Also two Fever baseball caps, someone's Fever basketball jersey, a makeshift cross with a yellow tie draped on it, American flags, Vaughn and Tanner bumper stickers and buttons, photographs, anything you can think of." He blinked. "Jesus, it's like an ocean of grief out there."

I would bet money some of those mementos were left by strangers as well as friends. Folks who felt they knew Jamie because they'd voted for him or shook his hand at a campaign stop or saw him at a Virginia Fever basketball game. Someone who had to be a witness to his death because it seemed personal to them. He had that kind of charisma. I thought about what Mick told me today about keeping silent and not destroying the faith and trust so many people had in Jamie. It still made me squirm.

Jamie had been part owner of the Virginia Fever, the newest NBA team based just over the river from D.C. in Alexandria, and he'd attended every home game and as many away games as he could. He'd also been known for the sunshine yellow tie he wore on the campaign trail, which he later claimed was his lucky tie because every time he wore it on primary day in some state, he won.

I suppose it should have occurred to me that the crash site would become a shrine to Jamie, to honor him and his big-hearted philanthropy, but people push boundaries in ways you'd never expect, even when they're expressing their grief and sympathy. In the past we'd had families show up prepared to have a picnic—along with bottles of someone else's wine—on our land, figuring it would be okay even though we were closed. Another time we found a bride and groom and their entire wedding party drinking champagne and posing for pictures at the Ruins, the burned-out Civil War tenant house that Eli had renovated as a place for outdoor concerts and plays. The couple chose it because it was so picturesque with the vineyard and the mountains as a backdrop and never thought they needed to ask permission. Then there were those who thought it was okay to pick our grapes—just to try them. What always floored me was how surprised everyone was when we asked if they'd leave, even when we explained that we could lose our license allowing an after-hours illegal party on our property. And the grapes were ours.

"I wonder if we should have someone keeping an eye out there tonight," I said as we walked into the parlor and sat down on the sofa. Quinn poured our brandies and handed me my glass.

"I called the sheriff's department when I was driving back here and asked them to send a cruiser," he said. "Someone went inside the yellow police tape and put lighted votive candles all along the top of the wall and lined up others like stair steps on the broken pillar. It looks like a church altar for high holy Mass."

I shuddered. "That's creepy. Besides, that pillar is unstable. Nobody should be climbing on it. What do they think the yellow tape is for? Decoration?"

"We'll have to use the south service entrance for anybody coming and going from the winery until Eli can get a stonemason to rebuild the wall."

"I know." I drank some brandy and leaned back into the crook of his arm. "I think I ought to pay a visit to Elena tomorrow and offer my condolences. Especially since I was the last person to see Jamie before he died."

Quinn tilted his brandy snifter so the amber-colored liquor gleamed in the reflected lamplight. "Are you going to tell her you think her husband deliberately crashed into our wall?"

I looked into my own glass as though I might find some kind of wisdom or guidance in it. The officer from the Loudoun County Sheriff's Department who questioned me said they'd follow the lead of whatever the medical examiner's office determined was the cause of death. Maybe I should just keep my mouth shut until they did that. It's what Mick had asked—no, practically ordered—me to do.

I traced a finger around the rim of my glass and made my decision. "If she asks, I'm not going to lie. And I'm definitely going to ask her if she knows someone named Rick."

"Want me to come with you?" He rubbed my shoulder, working out the kinks of my knotted muscles. I tilted my face and kissed his cheek.

"I do, but it might be easier if it's just Elena and me, especially if I end up telling her I don't think it was an accident," I said. "You don't mind, do you?"

Plus I had promised Kit I wouldn't say a word about what she'd discovered concerning Jamie using campaign money to pay Elena and reimburse his vineyard for expenses the campaign incurred. Maybe Rick was someone Jamie had betrayed financially. I didn't like keeping secrets from Quinn, but Kit's information wasn't my secret to share—especially since her boss had said he wouldn't run the story until she had airtight proof. Otherwise the *Washington Tribune* would probably be staring down the barrel of a nasty lawsuit.

He grinned, looking sheepish and relieved. "Honestly, no. I'm not very good at those things anyway. You know that."

"I'm not sure how good I'm going to be at it myself." I finished my brandy and set the empty glass on the coffee table.

"How about an early night? It's been a hell of a day," Quinn said.

"Eli's not back yet."

"You can talk to him in the morning, sweetheart. You ought to get some sleep."

"I'd like to watch the eleven o'clock news. We ought to see if they're saying anything new about the crash."

"And let that woman get you all torqued up just before you go to bed? Don't give her the satisfaction." He leaned back against the sofa and stared at me. "What's going on, Lucie?"

Quinn and I had never really talked about my accident, about the girl I used to be before it happened—someone he never knew—how the months in the hospital where I was told I might never walk again had dyed me darker and changed me forever. It had taken a long time to get over the nightmares where I relived that crash again and again, learned to adjust to what had happened to me—that I was now disabled—and not look back and say "what if?" What if I hadn't gotten into that car? That day? What if we hadn't been arguing or it hadn't been raining or . . . a million other variables. But it had been like crawling out of a long dark tunnel on my hands and knees.

Greg Knight had been in a prison in southern Virginia for the last five years, serving a life sentence for the murder of my godfather, Fitzhugh Pico. I tried to think of him as little as possible because any thoughts I had were still filled with anger, along with plenty of self-recrimination about why I'd ever gotten involved with him when I knew he was trouble. On days like today it all bubbled to the surface again like a poisonous stew, and that scared me.

Among the many reasons was this immutable truth: I was kidding myself. I was far from being over what had happened to me, and later, Fitz's death—really over it, at peace—so that I was finally able to move on, forgive and forget. I hated the corrosive power those memories held over me, the self-blame that I had allowed this serpent to slither into the garden of my thoughts and now it wouldn't leave.

Tonight when I went to bed, what I feared most was that I would not only relive Jamie's accident, I would relive my own. But I didn't want to tell Quinn any of this, drag it all up again, go through all that tortured angst.

Instead I said, "You're right, darling, it has been an exhausting day. I promised Hope I'd kiss her good night after Persia put her to bed. Maybe we should go upstairs."

He stood up and held out his hand, pulling me with him.

"I'll clean up and put the brandy away. You go on ahead and kiss Hope. I'll meet you in the bedroom in a minute."

Hope didn't stir when I bent to kiss her soft baby cheek and whisper sweet dreams in her ear. She looked like a sleeping angel with her dark hair fanned out over her pillow, one hand thrown over her head, the other hugging her favorite pink rabbit. More than anything I wished I could wrap her in my arms and protect her from the wicked ways of the world. But she'd lived through her parents' toxic divorce, and every so often she'd say something that hammered home how aware she was that Mommy and Daddy didn't love each other anymore. And that Mommy was gone and didn't come back to see her, either.

You can't protect someone you love forever. Maybe not even for very long. No matter how hard you try.

Quinn showed up in our bedroom holding a glass of water and a pill in his hand when I was already undressed and in my nightgown. "Take this," he said. "You'll sleep."

I had worked hard, so very hard, to wean myself from pain medications after the accident, fighting to not become addicted to or dependent on anything, which so often happens. Ever since then I took almost no medication at all.

I held out my hand without a word and let him drop the pill into it. Then I threw it into my mouth, downed it with the water, and slept the dark, semicomatose sleep of the dead as if I were inside a tomb.

When I woke up the next morning, my mouth felt like someone had stuffed it with cotton balls and my head throbbed with the kind of headache that I knew meant I was completely dehydrated. The clock on my side of the bed read 5:10 A.M. The alarm wouldn't go off until six, but usually one of us woke up in time to turn it off so the buzzer never actually sounded.

Quinn didn't stir when I slid out of bed and walked into the bathroom to get a glass of water, nor did he move when I pulled on the clothes I'd changed into yesterday after the accident, which were still heaped on a chair where I'd tossed them last night. Before anybody else showed up for the day, I wanted to see the makeshift memorial for Jamie Vaughn for myself. Surely at this hour no one would be there.

Eli's bedroom door was closed and so was Hope's. I hadn't heard my brother come in last night, which would have made the alarm sensor on the front door beep quietly, but according to the display panel in the upstairs hall he hadn't set the alarm either, so I wouldn't need to turn it off and wake up anyone as it squawked that it had been disarmed.

I went down the back staircase that led to the kitchen and pushed open the door. The room was warm and homey with the lingering scent of Persia's baking. The sun wouldn't be up for another hour, and the thermometer attached to one of the kitchen windows showed forty-four degrees.

My jacket hung on a hook in the mudroom just off the kitchen. I reached for it before I remembered I had worn it yesterday and that it was blood spattered. There was no way I could put it on, not now and probably not ever again. I bunched it up to throw it in the trash when something clattered on the old quarry tile floor. The MedicAlert bracelet that had fallen out of Jamie's hand yesterday when he reached for my arm. I'd kept it, thinking I would give it to the EMTs who would need the information on it. I picked it up. Apparently Jamie was allergic to Coumadin, a drug I knew only too well. It was a blood thinner that helped prevent the formation of blood clots. My doctors had prescribed a similar drug for me after the accident—heparin—because I'd spent so much time immobile in bed. I hadn't realized Jamie had a problem with thrombosis and, to be honest, I didn't ever remember seeing him wearing this bracelet, which looked old and scratched up. Something cheap that you'd buy on a drugstore carousel, the way you bought generic reading glasses, for a couple of bucks.

I slipped it into the pocket of my jeans to return to Elena when I saw her. Quinn's oversized jacket hung on the hook next to mine. It came down to my knees, but when I pulled the collar around me I smelled the vague tangy scent of the barrel room mingled with the bath soap he used, his Swisher Sweets cigars, and the cologne he occasionally wore.

My Jeep was in front of the house where someone, probably Antonio, our vineyard manager, had left it last night. The keys were under the floor mat. I drove through the vineyard as the sky turned rose colored in the east, and when I got to the service gate, I had to get out of the car to unlock it. The gate swung open with a rusty creak and I drove outside.

There was no one at the vineyard entrance. Today, unlike yesterday, the sky was sharp and clear with only a few long wispy clouds like streamers, holding out the promise of a gorgeous spring day. The air was cool and sweet, but as I came nearer to the rubble of the crash site, the heavy smoky smell of burned vegetation and wet ashes hit me.

As selfish as it sounded, I didn't want the entrance to the vineyard, to my home, to become a place of sadness and grief. A place where people stopped in their cars and said, "He died right here."

Quinn was right. Piled up against the stone wall were bouquets of flowers, some still in the clear plastic wrapper from whatever grocery store bin they'd come from, flags, campaign buttons, Virginia Fever paraphernalia, letters slipped into plastic page protectors, photographs of Jamie that he'd autographed for a fan. The large bouquet of red roses—from a florist, not Safeway—stood out among all the other mementos. I knelt and read the card attached to it.

What's done in darkness always comes to light.

Handwritten, no signature. What did *that* mean? Maybe someone knew about Jamie's financial troubles, that he'd used campaign money to pay for personal expenses, and this was a sly, oblique reference to them. Who would leave flowers at the place where he died with such a taunting, "gotcha" note? Maybe the elusive Rick had been here.

By the end of the day I was determined to find out who he was, meet him, and fulfill my promise to Jamie.

Then maybe my life could get back to normal. Though somehow I doubted that was going to happen.

Five

I t is because of a war that my Scottish ancestors acquired Highland Farm in the late 1700s. Hamish Montgomery, who fought with the 77th Highlander Regiment—also known as Montgomery's Highlanders—was given five hundred acres of land in the British colony of Virginia in recognition for distinguished service during the French and Indian War, and it was on this land that he built his new home. The Montgomery clan has always been a martial clan, a clan of warriors. We fight for what we believe in. Our motto *Garde bien*—watch well, watch out for us—is carved into the stone lintel above the front door of my home.

Though every Montgomery as far back as Hamish is buried on our land in a hilltop cemetery that commands a spectacular view of the Blue Ridge Mountains, there are a number of cairns—man-made piles or stacks of stones—that my father told me Hamish probably built as trail markers, although true Scottish cairns served as burial monuments after a battle.

The building of cairns to honor the dead is a Highland tradition, but they date back to prehistoric times, as far back as the Bronze Age. According to Highland legend, every man who was going into battle brought with him a stone that he stacked in a pile. When the battle was over, each survivor removed one stone from that pile. What was left represented the number of men who had been killed. Eventually, the unclaimed stones were built into a cairn as a war memorial, a perfect monument to honor each and every man who died.

I drove home thinking about Jamie's makeshift memorial and the pile of stones—what was left of the pillar—that now looked like rubble. Before long the flowers would start to rot. The pictures, Virginia Fever paraphernalia, campaign bumper stickers, and all the other tributes would not survive the next spring downpour. Perhaps later we could build a small cairn, as Hamish had done, for Jamie.

I was halfway down Sycamore Lane when I got Quinn's text. No punctuation, just *where are you*. I wrote back: *home in 60 seconds*.

He was seated at the kitchen table drinking coffee with Eli when I walked in 120 seconds later. Quinn's eyebrows went up when he realized I was wearing his jacket and then I think he remembered the blood on mine because he gave me a grim nod as I bent to kiss him.

"You went to see the crash site," he said. Not a question.

I shrugged out of his jacket, dumped it on a chair, and poured myself a cup of coffee. It was a rerun of last night's conversation, except in reverse.

"So many people have left things. It's so strange to see all of it."

"Was anyone there?" Eli asked.

I shook my head. "Not at six A.M."

My brother's dark hair stuck up in wild little tufts. He was wearing a faded Virginia Tech sweatshirt and baggy gray sweatpants. His eyes were puffy, with the hungover look of someone who hadn't gotten much sleep. I wanted to go over and give him a hug, he looked so beat down after a night of grief and sadness. But I knew that was precisely the wrong thing to do when he was trying to hold himself together, so I stayed where I was.

"What time did you get in?" I asked him.

He gave me a weary smile. "Two o'clock."

"How's Sasha?"

A regretful shake of his head and more regret in his eyes. "She's taking it hard. Unfortunately, she thinks Elena's treating her like a guest who overstayed her welcome now that Jamie's not around." He stood up to get more coffee.

I hadn't told Eli I thought Jamie deliberately crashed into our wall, so he wouldn't have told Sasha, either. Nor had I told him about Jamie's dying wish to find Rick somebody-or-other and ask for forgiveness.

"Sit. I'll get your coffee." I walked over to the table with the pot and filled his mug. "That must be tough. Especially right now."

"Families." He shrugged. "You know how it goes. Elena and Sasha's mother never got along anyway. Sasha said her mother hasn't decided whether she's going to the funeral or not. She's not sure she wants to deal with the drama."

"Have they made any arrangements yet?" Quinn asked.

Eli nodded. "The wake is Thursday afternoon and evening

at Hunt Funeral Home. The service is Friday morning at Trinity Episcopal. Ten o'clock."

"That was fast," I said. "Today is Tuesday."

"Well . . ." He looked uncomfortable.

"Well, what?" I asked.

"Elena thinks the Jefferson Dinner should go on as scheduled and that's on Saturday evening," he said. "And Saturday afternoon is the Goose Creek Hunt's Point-to-Point. With so many of their friends going to the races and attending the dinner, she figured it would be easier to have the funeral earlier."

"Elena always was practical," Quinn said in a laconic voice. "I think she's got one or two horses running in the Point-to-Point if I remember right."

"Quinn!" I gave him an admonishing look, though I had been thinking something along the same lines. "That's callous. Everybody grieves differently."

"He's right, she docs," Eli said. "Two horses."

"So how's she coping?" I asked.

"Better than Sasha, if you ask me. Elena's tough and she's got a lot of support. Owen and Oliver are with her," he said. "Garrett is taking care of all the press calls. He wrote the obituary that was sent to all the media outlets. Mick Dunne has been a big help, too."

Quinn flashed me an I-told-you-so look when Eli mentioned Mick's name, which I pretended not to see. "I thought I'd call her later and stop by, if she's up for it," I said.

"She, uh, knows you were the last person to be with Jamie," Eli said. "I'm sure she'd appreciate it."

Unless you lived on Mars, everyone and his grandmother now knew I was the last person to see him alive. A vehicle pulled in to the driveway—we could hear the whine of an engine—before I could answer him, and the three of us looked at one another.

"Do you think that's Antonio?" I said. "Although it doesn't sound like his truck."

Eli's phone rang and he pulled it out of the pocket of his sweatpants. "It's Persia," he said and punched a button. "Hi, Persia. How are . . . what?"

His eyes traveled to me and then to the bank of kitchen windows facing the front of the house. A high boxwood privacy hedge enclosed a garden my mother had planted, separating it from the driveway. At the moment, the garden was rioting with blooming tulips in vivid colors and daffodils in every shade of yellow, orange, and white.

"Right," Eli said. "Don't worry. Thanks. We'll take care of it . . . no, you sit tight. Sure. Right. Bye."

He hung up. "Persia says it's a television truck from Channel 3. She can see it from her kitchen window."

Persia lived in the upper floor of the carriage house above Eli's studio. She had a perfect view of the driveway. My heart lurched.

"How did they get in?" I asked, and then my voice died. The gate. I hadn't closed it on my way back from checking out Jamie's memorial. "Never mind. They drove in."

"They're still trespassing," Quinn said. "I'll call Antonio and we'll take care of this." He gave Eli a meaningful look, and I suddenly thought of Leland's gun cabinet in the library, stocked with enough weapons and ammunition to outfit a small militia.

And Quinn sounding like he was ready to pick a fight to defend me.

"You're not going to do anything crazy," I said. "Look, if it's Pippa O'Hara, she wants to talk to me. I'll go outside, get this over with, tell her what we agreed to say last night—that we extend our deepest sympathy to Jamie's family—and that's it."

There was more commotion outside, the sound of more vehicles pulling up.

"Wait here," Eli said in a tense voice, as he got up and left the kitchen. He was back a moment later with a report. "Two more trucks pulled up and there are about half a dozen people out there. They're camped outside the front door."

"I'll talk to them. I'm going to tell them all to get lost," Quinn said.

Quinn is all about action, physicality, getting the job done, not wasting time. If you want his opinion, you get it, unvarnished and with no filter. He has a clear-eyed view of what he believes is right and wrong and doesn't feel he needs to be diplomatic, especially if someone is flagrantly on the wrong side of an issue. The people outside our door didn't belong here and needed to be gotten rid of.

This is one of the big differences between us. I like to think things through, take my time, weigh my options. Sometimes you have to negotiate to get what you really want, meet the other person halfway, and you get more with honey than you do with vinegar. When all was said and done, they were journalists trying to do their job. Which included getting my side of the story about Jamie, whether I liked it or not.

"No." I held up my hand. "It will only make things worse.

They'll just stake out the winery when it's open later this morning. What are we going to do? Close for business? Hide out? I'm not going to be able to avoid the press forever. I might as well get it over with."

"You're sure you can handle this?" Eli asked.

"I talked to that reporter from the local ABC television station last year," I said. "And that went well."

"That," Quinn said, "was about the problem we were having with waterlogged vines that were splitting after they froze."

I gave him a defiant look. "I still talked to them."

"You want company, Luce?" Eli asked. "You shouldn't face them alone."

"You're in your pajamas, Eli. They're television reporters with cameras. But thank you anyway."

"I'll go with her," Quinn said.

I took a deep breath. "All right, then. Let's do this."

IT WAS HARDER THAN I expected to handle the barrage of questions that were hurled at me when Quinn and I stepped outside a few minutes later. For one thing, everyone was shouting at once, their microphones thrust in my face, waved around like brandished weapons. For another, I should have written down the few words I was prepared to say so all I had to do was read a statement. Third, and probably worst of all, a strong beam of morning sunlight happened to fall directly on the front door, blinding us like a spotlight for most of the time we were outside. Quinn and I had to squint and shield our eyes with our hands so we could see who was talking, which made me feel like a suspect in a police lineup.

"Can you tell us what happened yesterday?"

"Did you see Jamie Vaughn's car crash into your wall?"

"Was he speeding? Were you speeding?"

"Were two cars involved, yours and his? Did Jamie swerve to avoid your car, which was seen in a ditch by the side of the road?"

"Did you call nine-one-one?"

"Were you able to talk to him?"

"Did you try to save him?"

"Where were you when he crashed into the wall?"

"Lucie, can you describe your emotions as you watched Jamie Vaughn's car go up in flames? Take us through it, please."

Finally, Quinn held up his hand as though he were negotiating a truce. "That's enough. Please, stop. You're all talking over each other," he repeated in a loud voice until everyone quieted down. "Lucie has a statement and that's all she's prepared to say."

I found Pippa O'Hara in the crowd, which wasn't hard given her blazing red hair and electric-blue windbreaker, and tried to keep my face expressionless. "All of us at Montgomery Estate Vineyard extend our deepest condolences to Jamie Vaughn's family after the tragic accident yesterday that took his life. I have nothing more to say, other than like so many people, I am grieving the loss of a friend and a good man. Everything else you might want to know should be directed to the Loudoun County Sheriff's Department and the Middleburg Fire and Rescue Department. Thank you."

I turned to go inside when a voice drawled, "Lucie, Pippa O'Hara, News Channel 3. Why are you covering up what really happened to Jamie Vaughn?"

I spun around. "I beg your pardon?"

"Don't," Quinn murmured in my ear. "Let it go."

She had edged her way through the small crowd so she stood alone in front of everyone else. Now she planted herself directly in front of me, feet apart, a combative pose, staring me down. "Was this a single-vehicle crash or was your car involved as well and Jamie Vaughn swerved to avoid you? Maybe he lost control of his car?"

It is a slippery slope when you start trying to explain your way out of a situation with the intention of not saying anything about it at all. I was already angry with her for dragging my own accident into her story last night as though it were somehow related to what happened to Jamie. Pippa's questions were legitimate, but there was also a bit of schoolyard taunt in her voice.

"My car wasn't involved in the crash," I told her in a firm voice. "I'm not covering up anything. Feel free to ask the sheriff's department."

"If that's true, then when, exactly, did you arrive on the scene? Based on where your Jeep was found, it appeared you and Jamie Vaughn were traveling along the same road. Did you see the crash?"

She was picking at a tightly wrapped ball of string and finding loose ends to pull on.

"No comment," I said.

"There were witnesses to what happened yesterday who reported seeing you with your clothes covered in blood. How did that happen?"

"No comment."

"Was it Jamie Vaughn's blood? Did you get to him before he died in that fire? Was he conscious? Did he say anything to you?"

"No comment."

Quinn stuck out his hand and covered the lens of the Channel 3 camera, shoving it away from us. "We're done here, folks. That's enough. Leave her alone."

He reached behind us and opened the front door, a neat trick of apparent double-jointedness, stepping inside and pulling me in with him, a fast, ungraceful exit offstage. Then he slammed the door. There was a surge of voices outside and someone banged on the door.

I stared at him, breathing hard. "Make. Them. Go. Away."

"Go on upstairs," he said. "Take a shower. I'm calling Bobby Noland and getting someone over here from the sheriff's department. You'll be okay, sweetheart. You don't have to talk to her again. You did just fine."

"How can you say that? I did anything but fine." I tried to keep my screeching voice down so my outrage and anger wouldn't travel through the door to the listening world outside. "I did appallingly. She made it look like I'm covering something up. Like I had some responsibility for Jamie's accident."

Our eyes met and his locked on mine so it was impossible to look away. I knew what he was going to say next. "You are covering something up, Lucie. Just not what she thinks you are. You're trying to protect Jamie's reputation and in the process you had to take a hit for him."

"You were right. I shouldn't have said anything."

"Go take a shower. Calm down. What's done is done." His lips brushed mine. "I'll call Bobby."

I was halfway up the winding staircase when I heard Hope's singsong voice calling Eli's name, followed by uncontrollable giggling. Good. Eli was with her, meaning she hadn't accidentally witnessed what just happened, caught sight of it through a window.

I took a shower, as Quinn advised, but I didn't calm down. Yesterday I'd practically scrubbed myself raw because it felt like I couldn't get the stain of Jamie's blood off me. Today there was nothing visible to rub at, but I still felt unclean. Pippa O'Hara had thrown a lot of mud at me this morning.

And mud sticks.

BOBBY NOLAND TOLD QUINN that the sheriff's department would send a cruiser over to the vineyard to keep away reporters if we were prepared to state that they were trespassing and harassing us. I called Frankie at home and told her what had happened this morning with the press scrum outside my front door and that she should expect a brown-and-gold cruiser at the temporary vineyard entrance.

"Oh, don't worry. I'm ready for anything. Have you read the *Tribune* yet today?" she asked.

"No," I said, realizing Eli must have hidden it somewhere, because he usually brought it into the kitchen when we had breakfast. "What does it say about Jamie?"

"The headlines are huge. Under 'Tragic Death of an American Golden Boy,' which is a huge banner across the front page, it also says, 'More Questions than Answers in Fatal Crash Involving Jamie Vaughn.'"

"The sheriff's department is going to go along with whatever the medical examiner's office says as far as cause of death," I said. "That ought to put a stop to a lot of speculation."

"Do you know what really happened, Lucie? You do, don't you?"

"I didn't see the crash. I . . . swerved to avoid him and ended up on the other side of the road on the shoulder."

The line between truth and lying had just become as thin as a silk thread. If I stretched it any tighter it would snap in two. The officer who questioned me yesterday told me that I couldn't be an eyewitness because my attention had been diverted while I tried to keep my Jeep from plowing into a neighbor's fence. Now I clung to that technicality like it was a commandment written in stone.

But Frankie was right. I did know what happened to Jamie Vaughn.

He'd deliberately driven into that wall and committed suicide.

What I didn't know yet was why.

Six

Whenever I have something I need to get off my mind or some problem to think through, I seek out the wisdom and counsel of my mother. That she has been dead for more than a dozen years doesn't make those sessions any less real or meaningful for me. A visit to her grave in the family cemetery where I sit and talk to her, leaning against her sun-warmed headstone with its serene view of the layered, low-slung Blue Ridge Mountains, and it's as if she is still there for me. I needed to visit her now.

So when Quinn asked if I wanted to go out with him and check the vines in the south vineyard, I begged off. A week ago the daytime temperatures had warmed up enough for the sap to start running in the vines, which meant that it wouldn't be long before bud break—the first sign of green in the vineyard after a winter of dormancy—would begin. For one or two days the sun-warmed sap runs up through the trunks to the ends of the canes, where it oozes through cuts made by pruning and looks like thousands of sparkling crystal droplets falling to the ground like rain. We say that the vines are weeping. Quinn, the Californian, jokes that our Virginia grapevines weep in happiness because they survived another cold, snowy winter.

Unfortunately for us, in the past week nighttime temperatures had been flirting with numbers that were dangerously close to freezing, and a frost this late in the year would wreak havoc with all or part of a season's crop. If leaves appeared too early on the vines and temperatures plunged to thirty-two degrees or below at night, it would kill the tiny shoots and leaves, destroying the chance for any fruit for the year. Chardonnay, which is an early-budding grape, is notorious for this. At least once every eight years we lost the entire crop. Even more heartbreaking was the fact that even though we wouldn't have a harvest that year, we still had to care for the vines with the same attention and diligence as if we did. Nobody said life had to be fair.

"Do you want to stick around the house for a while?" Quinn asked me now. "I can take care of checking the south vineyard."

"I can't stay at home or I'll go nuts. I thought I'd stop by the cemetery and clean up the flowers I left at Easter. They'll be all wilted and brown by now. I'll join you after I'm done."

Quinn smiled and kissed my forehead. "Go talk to your mom. Tell her I said hi."

"I will," I said, grateful that this man, who was clear-eyed and pragmatic right down to his socks, never acted as if I were a bit loony, off to a session of mystic communing with the spirits or a séance where my mother was summoned back from the Great Beyond. "I won't be long."

I CUT A BUNCH of yellow and white daffodils from the flower garden my mother had planted outside the kitchen window and put them in a small delft blue-and-white floral vase to take with me. Before she died, my French mother had faithfully tended the Montgomery family cemetery, leaving flowers on special occasions or planting small American flags by the graves of those who fought for America on Veterans Day, the Fourth of July, and Memorial Day, sweeping gravestones, clearing away fallen branches. After she died, I took over the task since no one else in the family wanted to do it—including Leland. That's when I began talking to her. Ever since, I'd felt she listened.

Though the distant tree line of the Blue Ridge Mountains still looked winter-brown as I drove over to the cemetery, the flowering trees—cherry, Bradford pear, dogwood, and redbud—had bloomed within the past week. A few late forsythia bushes were bright splotches of yellow in an otherwise pastel landscape. From one day to the next, the skyline would be crosshatched with dark bare-branched trees, and then suddenly overnight a lacy filigree of yellowish-green would appear on the deciduous trees and the maples would turn a coppery reddish-brown. That's what I loved about spring. It never failed to surprise me.

I parked the Jeep and hiked up the hill to a low brick wall that surrounded thirty-seven headstones, urns, and small statues—generations of Montgomerys who had lived and died at Highland Farm. The wrought-iron gate creaked on its hinges as it always did when I opened it. The first thing I did was clean up the wilted Easter flowers I'd left two weeks ago and dumped them in a compost pile on the other side of the wall. Then I went to sit with my mother.

Both my parents had died violent deaths on our land, just like Jamie's death yesterday. My mother's death had been a tragic accident; my father's had been made to look like a hunting accident, but it wasn't. What about Jamie? Had his death been an accident, or had he deliberately driven into that stone wall and taken his own life?

We are all masters of our own destiny, my mother used to tell me. Even though we can't always choose what happens to us, we can choose how we respond. In the end, she said, the way we handle the tough things life throws at us—adversity, loss, hardship, rejection—is what defines each of us as a human being. Whether we face them with courage and grace and honesty or choose to feel sorry for ourselves, blame someone else, lash out at life's injustices with anger and cruelty—that's what makes us who we are.

It was not for me to write the final words of the last chapter of Jamie Vaughn's life: That was his responsibility. Eventually the truth would come out about what really happened yesterday.

I had promised him I would find Rick and tell him Jamie was sorry and had asked his forgiveness, and I intended to keep that promise. But I didn't owe Pippa O'Hara anything just because she asked or because she wanted to share that information with her television audience. The only question that remained was whether I would tell Elena, Jamie's twin sons, Oliver and Owen, and Sasha the truth about what I saw, or would I lie to be kind, to spare them knowing that I was fairly certain Jamie had wanted to die.

I sat and watched a few cotton ball clouds that floated across the lacquered blue sky imprint their shadows on the mountains and fields below. A cardinal chirped somewhere above my head and a flash of scarlet streaked by and disappeared into a grove of pines and hollies.

Would I want to know, if it were me?

I would. I would take knowing the truth over being deceived, even out of kindness or compassion. My mother's voice came into my head.

They won't be surprised. Neither would you.

Mick Dunne had said Jamie was having a tough time dealing with the loss of the presidential race and had been trying to cope with it privately. So perhaps his family already knew that something was wrong and that he was distraught and unhappy.

I stood up and brushed my hand across the top of my mother's gravestone. Halfway to the gate, I turned around. "I almost forgot," I said. "Quinn says hi."

QUINN PICKED ME UP in the Gator just outside the block of Norton grapes, one of the varietals we planted a few years ago when we went through a major expansion of the vineyard. Norton is America's oldest native grape—discovered right here in Virginia—and probably its least known. Like so much of the early history of winemaking and grape growing in Colonial America, the story of the Norton grape and the Richmond medical doctor who discovered it is a tale of heartbreak, betrayal, and loss.

When Dr. Daniel Norton lost his wife and newborn child in 1821, he became nearly suicidal with grief. What saved him was the solace of his garden where, as an amateur horticulturalist, he threw himself into experimenting with crossbreeding plants. Though he planted a variety of flowers, fruits, and vegetables, his real ambition was to produce a wine grape hardy enough to survive in American soil without succumbing to disease the way all European grapes had done so far. He also wanted this grape to produce not only a drinkable wine but also a wine that could hold its own with fine European wines, not something that tasted like a wet dog, which had been the case with much of the wine made in America.

By the 1830s, Daniel Norton was able to make the hearty red wine grape he had crossbred—known as Norton's Seedling— commercially available for purchase. It quickly found a home in Missouri, which had become the wine capital of America in the 1800s, with Norton as its signature grape. But after Dr. Norton's premature death in 1842, a new story spread about the true discoverer of the Norton grape, discrediting Daniel Norton.

A man named W. F. Lemosy claimed in an article published in *Horticulture* magazine that his father had come across the grape growing wild on a small island in the middle of the James River years before Daniel Norton knew of it. It was the senior Lemosy who recommended the grape to Norton for his experiments with wine-producing grapes. As the popularity of the Norton grape spread throughout the country in the mid-nineteenth century, the Lemosy story gained credence and Norton's name faded into obscurity. This, in spite of the fact that in 1830, five years before Lemosy claimed to have introduced the grape to Daniel Norton, it was described by and credited to D. N. Norton in a two-volume publication called *A Treatise on the Vine,* the first book on viticulture published in America.

After that, a one-two punch practically destroyed Virginia's fledgling wine industry: the physical damage and destruction caused by the Civil War, followed by Prohibition in the early twentieth century. The lone exception was a small revival after the Civil War ended in the area around Charlottesville, which experienced a wine boom with Norton's Seedling. By 1870 the region was known as "the Wine Belt of Virginia," though it was a short-lived accolade as California began its ascendency to become America's premier wine-producing region.

The grape fell farther out of favor thanks to Prohibition, which gave Americans a taste for hard liquor and the European *Vitis vinifera* wines they had grown used to drinking on the sly. So as America rebuilt its vineyards in the post-Prohibition era, winemakers planted the noble grapes of Europe and the Norton grape faded into obscurity.

It was a Virginian—Dennis Horton, the owner of a vineyard bearing his name—who revived Norton as Virginia's grape in the late 1980s and early '90s; later, Jenni McCloud, who owned Chrysalis Vineyard down the road from us in Middleburg, became one of its staunchest champions. Now Montgomery Estate Vineyard grew it, too.

Quinn liked it because it required so little care compared to other grapes. Our clients, especially the younger ones, liked it so much that it had quickly become our third-best-selling wine. I liked it because it was a Virginia grape, plus I had a personal connection since Daniel Norton's second wife, Lucy, was my great-grandfather's cousin on Leland's side of the family.

Quinn and I drove down the rows of neatly aligned grapevines without talking. He hadn't asked about my cemetery visit and I figured he was going to wait until I was ready to talk about it, even though he almost certainly knew that I'd gone there because I was still upset about Jamie's death.

Finally, he stopped the Gator in the middle of the Norton block. "I wonder what Jamie's bottles of old Norton taste like," he said. "I've never drunk wine that old, not Norton, not anything."

"It probably doesn't matter much what it tastes like," I said. "No one's drunk a Norton that old because Jamie's got the only bottles that anyone knows of. Even luckier for us is that the wine happens to be from a Virginia vineyard."

What had further catapulted Norton's Seedling back into national prominence was a marine salvage company's discovery of three perfectly preserved bottles of Norton in a metal trunk found in the hold of the *Virginia Belle,* an iron-hulled side-wheel steamship that had sunk off the coast of North Carolina in 1878. According to documents discovered after the *Belle* had been salvaged, the ship had been headed to Le Havre and from there the wine, renamed Virginia Claret, was supposed to be delivered to the International Paris Exhibition of 1878. A few years earlier, when the exhibition had been held in Vienna, a bottle of Norton from a vineyard near St. Louis, Missouri, had won first prize as "the best red wine of all nations." In 1878 a wine produced by the Monticello Wine Company near Charlottesville during that brief post–Civil War wine boom was hoping to duplicate that win in Paris.

The story of the sinking of the *Virginia Belle* had all the mystique and allure of a blockbuster movie: a true ghost ship that was rumored to be haunted by the captain who had mysteriously abandoned it. Originally a British ship named the *Titania,* the ship was found adrift off the coast of West Africa in 1876 with no trace of the crew or passengers on board. Like a more famous ghost ship, the *Mary Celeste,* the cargo and provisions for several days were still intact, as were the personal belongings of everyone on board. The lifeboats, however, were gone. Rumors about what had happened flew everywhere—paranormal intervention, piracy, insurance fraud, giant jellyfish—but no one ever discovered what had become of the crew and passengers who vanished as though the sea had swallowed them up. The following year the ship was registered in America and renamed the *Virginia Belle.*

Dogged by bad luck and reports of sightings of the ghost of the previous captain, in 1878 the *Belle* was attacked by pirates, who boarded the ship and took her over, only to sink during a fierce storm the following day. According to the ship's manifest, the legendary Star of Burma, a ruby as large as a pigeon's egg that supposedly carried with it a curse of a violent death to its owner, had been in the possession of one of the passengers. The Star had never been found—perhaps spirited off by the attacking pirates—but the bottles of Norton, as dark and bloodred as the ruby was reputed to be, still lay in the ship's hold and were a surprise when they were discovered. Experts said that the layer of silt covering the container probably helped preserve the wine.

Jamie Vaughn had paid an exorbitant price for the Norton bottles at an auction several years ago and had kept them locked away in his extensive wine cellar on the grounds of Vaughn Vineyards, where they were displayed to special visitors from time to time under extremely low light. The mystery surrounding the former ghost ship, the ruby, the pirate attack, and the wine on its way to compete at an international world's fair—obviously an excellent vintage if the owner was hoping to win a prize—had only enhanced the reputation of Virginia's native grape. When Jamie decided to offer a tasting of one of the bottles and sell the others at an auction as a fund-raiser to pay off his campaign debts, there had been a huge national interest in the dinner, which was to be held on Thomas Jefferson's birthday. A menu of dishes Jefferson would have known and enjoyed at Monticello, served on china and using silverware and wineglasses from the early 1800s, only added to the allure. The ten-thousand-dollar tickets for the dinner sold out in two days, but the twenty-thousand-dollar tickets, which included a small taste of the shipwrecked Norton, were gone in a matter of hours. Eventually, there had been a decision to allow bidding to off-site participants for the Norton bottles in addition to the dinner guests, so no one knew how big this was going to be.

"Not to sound crass, but Elena is going to rake in big bucks for Jamie's wine this weekend," Quinn said, as if he'd read my mind. "Since she's planning on going ahead with the dinner and the auction."

"I ought to call Dominique," I said. "If anybody knows what's happening with that event, she does, since she's closing the Inn for the evening to host it."

"Why don't you drop by and visit her?" Quinn said. "I still think you should take the day off."

He started the Gator again and turned onto the dirt road that led back to the winery.

"Thanks, but what I really need to do to take my mind off everything is work. It will do me good, a distraction." In spite of my protest, part of me believed that even a month of total peace and tranquillty in a remote mountain cabin or on a deserted tropical beach wouldn't be enough to scrub yesterday's images of Jamie's fiery death from my brain.

"I know," he said, "but if you show your face around here today, you're going to be hounded by folks who want to know what happened to Jamie. That includes reporters. I'm just thinking it might be a good idea for you to lie low, that's all."

He was right, of course, but I made one last feeble stand. "I can't hide out forever."

"Just until this whole thing blows over," he said. "Go get lost somewhere today . . . and maybe even tomorrow."

"All right, I will. Anyway, there's something I need to do," I said. "I need to find Rick."

He gave me a worried look. "That wasn't exactly what I had in mind. You could end up jumping out of the frying pan into the fire."

"That was a horrible choice of words."

"Oh, God. Sorry. You know what I meant."

I leaned over and kissed him. "I do."

"How are you going to find this guy?"

"Ask the people who knew Jamie best. Elena. Oliver and Owen. Garrett Bateman. Maybe talk to Mick Dunne again. I had a feeling he was holding something back yesterday."

Quinn raised a skeptical eyebrow when I mentioned Mick. "Something wasn't right when I was talking to him while that officer questioned you. He seemed . . . I don't know . . . anxious, maybe. I know he just watched one of his closest friends die in a horrible way. But there was something else."

"Do you think it was guilt?" The question came out before I could stop it.

Quinn looked surprised. "Do you mean because he couldn't rescue Jamie in time? Are you talking about something like survivor guilt?"

"I'm . . . I'm not sure." I stumbled over my reply. Was that what I felt, too? "What do you think? Was it survivor guilt?"

He considered the question and then shook his head. "No, not Mick. If you're right and the crash was deliberate rather than an accident, I think Mick might have had some idea what might have pushed Jamie over the edge. I think maybe he was trying to deal with that."

I had sensed something yesterday, too, when Mick scooped me up in his arms and carried me away from Jamie's car just before it burst into flames.

Before I visited Dominique or Elena Vaughn, I was going to pay Mick a visit. Even though he'd denied it when I'd asked him, I had a feeling he knew something about the identity of the mysterious Rick.

In fact, I was sure he did.

Seven

Usually Mick Dunne's housekeeper, an attractive young Hispanic woman with a sunny smile, opened the front door, but today Mick opened it himself even before I rang the Westminster chime doorbell. A wreath of dried pale blue hydrangeas hung on the door and I remembered with a small shock that Historic Garden Week had only been last week and that Mick's house had been one of the houses on the tour.

Virginia's Historic Garden Week is the oldest home and garden tour in the country. It goes on for eight days and is advertised as "America's Largest Open House" because it features more than 250 homes, gardens, and historic landmarks throughout the Old Dominion. Organized by the Garden Club of Virginia along with fifty local garden clubs, the money raised goes to restore our many historic sites, including the gardens of numerous presidents and founding fathers—Washington, Jefferson, Madison, George Mason, Woodrow

Wilson, to name a few. We are spoiled for beauty and history here in the Commonwealth of Virginia.

Because Historic Garden Week was always held early in April when only the first spring flowers had bloomed, it was actually more of a home tour featuring indoor arrangements—spectacular, creative displays of flowers and greenery—from the gardens of club members as well as the host's home. The Garden Club of Atoka had decorated Wicklow, Mick's nineteenth-century Georgian estate, and Elena Vaughn, who was a master gardener, was its president. I'd heard she had not only persuaded Mick to take on the considerable expense of opening his home to hundreds, if not more than a thousand, visitors, she had also staked her claim to provide the flowers as part of the deal. Although I'd bought tickets since it was a charity we always supported and the winery had been one of the venues where folks could pick up copies of the free program guide, it had been an exceptionally busy week for us with so many visitors in town that I never managed to get by to see any of the houses in our area.

Mick opened the door wider. "Come in," he said. "I've been expecting you."

He was unshaven and disheveled, looking as if he'd been up all night with a bottle of something keeping him company. I shouldn't have come by without calling first. He pulled me into his arms and crushed me to him like a drowning man clinging to a lifeline.

I'd never seen Mick fall apart, and if that's what was about to happen, I wasn't prepared to deal with it. Not Mick, the kind of macho guy who could be a prototype for an action character in a computer game—a military commander in an epic battle, an assassin with a mission to take out a dictator or drug lord, or an outlier in a dystopian universe playing hide-and-seek with the evil enemy. Someone who was always stronger, faster, smarter, and tough as nails. And always in control of his emotions.

He tilted his head and his lips were so close to mine I had a dizzy feeling he was about to kiss me. He was in no shape for this—definitely hungover—and neither was I. I needed to stop things before he went any further. The familiar scent of his cologne and the laundry soap he used were triggering too many memories.

"Mick." I wiggled out of his embrace. "Are you okay?"

Behind him an enormous silver urn filled with lilacs, viburnum, hydrangeas, and spirea sat on a mahogany oval table in the middle of his marble-tiled foyer. The arrangement was stunning. That would definitely be Elena's work. I went over and stood next to it, putting some physical distance between us.

"These are gorgeous."

The distraction worked. He stared at me as though he were coming out of a fog and then he half smiled. "Yeah. Elena and her gang did amazing work, didn't they? And I apologize for practically mauling you when you walked in. I'm still trying to deal with . . . Jamie. It's still such a bloody shock that he's gone."

"I know. And no apology necessary."

"So what brings you here?" he said. "You don't usually drop by like this anymore."

My cheeks turned red. "Like this" meant when we were still together, a couple. "I was hoping to talk to you about something."

He gave me a sharp-eyed look, but I met his eyes and hoped mine revealed nothing but innocent concern. When he spoke, his voice was cordial.

"Why don't we go into the library then? Would you care for a coffee?"

"Coffee would be lovely. You look like you could do with a cup as well. Or maybe even a whole pot. How much sleep did you get last night?"

He gave me another rueful smile. "I don't know . . . not much. I was over at Elena's until after midnight. When I got home I was absolutely shattered, but I just couldn't fall asleep. How about you?"

He put a brotherly arm around my shoulder and we walked down his long hall lined with oil paintings of bucolic English country scenes that I always thought looked as if he'd plucked them from the Constable and Turner rooms in the National Gallery of Art.

"We'll have coffee in the library, please, Maria," he said to the maid who reappeared. "And some of those scones."

Maria left for the kitchen.

"Quinn gave me a sleeping pill," I said, answering Mick's question. "I passed out."

"I saw you on the telly this morning," he said. All these years in America and he still slipped easily into Britishisms. "That Pippa what's-her-name was looking for raw meat to throw to her audience and she obviously zeroed in on you."

"She thinks I'm covering up what really happened to Jamie," I said as we walked into the library.

A few years ago when Mick bought Wicklow, he'd hired a mutual friend to redecorate the place and gave her carte blanche. His only requirement was that she had to remain true to the bones and history of the house, which left him free to focus on his passion: his Thoroughbreds and polo ponies and the expansive stables and training pavilion which his staff kept in immaculate condition. The vineyard had been an afterthought—the pride of having his name on a bottle of wine served at his own dinner parties, grapes grown on his soil. Finally, he realized it was too much like farming, rather than a romantic hobby, and turned it over to a professional winemaker and property manager to run.

The house itself had been redesigned in the early twentieth century by Nathan Wyeth, the architect of the Oval Office and the White House West Wing, and reminded me more of a museum than a home. Mick had spared no expense for historically correct details and furnished the rooms with fine American and English antiques. The library, its bookshelves lined with his collection of first editions and leather-covered books with worn gilt titles that gleamed in the lamplight, was my favorite, and that room, too, was filled with flowers. On either end of the broad fireplace mantel two celadon temple jars spilled over with freesia, lisianthus, delphinium, and roses. Though there was no fire in the stone fireplace, the room smelled faintly of woodsmoke overlaid with the strong sweet peppery perfume of freesia.

We sat on a green leather sofa and faced each other. "Lucie," Mick said. "Elena and I don't want you dealing with any more journalists or media inquiries. I just got off the phone with her. We want you to turn them over to Garrett. He's a pro. He'll handle it so you don't get broadsided the way you did this morning."

Garrett Bateman, Jamie's vice president of everything. Fixer of all problems. Garrett, who was fiercely protective of Jamie, took no prisoners, and would be more than a match for Pippa O'Hara.

It sounded like an order, not a request. Still he was polite, making it seem as if it were for my own good. I shook my head. "I appreciate that, Mick, but it only makes it look worse, like I've really got something to hide. Garrett wasn't even there yesterday."

"He's the family's spokesman. We don't want to muddle the message with conflicting stories."

Or perhaps the truth. And Mick kept saying "we." Not "Elena and Owen and Oliver." Or just "Elena."

"And what is the message?"

There was a knock on one of the French doors, and Maria entered carrying a silver tray with our coffee and a basket of scones, along with jam, butter, and a small pitcher of what I knew would be clotted cream. You can take the boy out of England . . . Mick got up and took the tray from her. After she left, he fixed our coffees and passed me a scone on a blue-and-white Wedgwood plate.

He pushed the jam and clotted cream closer to me. "Help yourself. What would you like?"

"An answer to my question. And I'll take both, please."

His smile twisted and he gave me a knowing look. "What we'd like is your discretion. And to let Garrett handle this."

"Meaning?"

"Jamie was going through a rough patch after the election. He was taking antidepressants and he'd also started drinking more than he should have done, especially considering the medication," he said. "If we can keep that from getting out . . . well, Elena would be terribly grateful."

We'd been all over this yesterday. I dug my fork into a warm scone smothered in strawberry jam and a dollop of thick, golden-yellow cream. "Something was bothering him, Mick. Are you going to tell me what it was? Why would the last thing he said be to ask forgiveness of someone named Rick?"

Mick stirred milk and sugar into his coffee until I thought his spoon would melt. "I told Elena about that. She says it's someone who donated money to the campaign, a lot of money. He and Jamie had a falling-out, plus—like I said—Jamie felt he let down the people who helped him, both financially and as volunteers. Elena and Garrett will take care of talking to him, so you're off the hook."

"A campaign donor? Seriously?"

"There's some history there. It's complicated."

"Jamie asked me to do it, Mick. I gave him my promise. I'm kind of honor bound to keep it."

"Elena wants to handle this, Lucie. Besides, Rick wouldn't know you from Adam's house cat. It's already difficult enough for the family to deal with Jamie's death. The crash, the fire . . . please. I'm asking as a favor, but the family really wants to take care of this on their own. What difference does it make who tells him?"

He wasn't going to back down. "All right." I held up my hands, surrendering. "Tell me something, though. Do you think Jamie deliberately drove his car into my wall?"

Mick set down his plate and looked at me with a stare that could have pinned me to the opposite wall. "Jamie did not commit suicide." He enunciated each word as if I might not understand him otherwise. "He wasn't himself when he got behind the wheel of that car yesterday. You yourself said you smelled alcohol on his breath. Possibly mixed with drugs . . . medication."

"Yes."

"I can tell you for an absolute fact that Jamie had no intention of deliberately taking his own life. First of all, there was no note, no letter he left behind for his family. Second, he was on his way to a meeting with your cousin at the Goose Creek Inn to discuss the Jefferson Dinner. He was looking forward to that dinner, showing off the bottles of Norton from the shipwreck. What happened was an accident. There's no logical explanation otherwise for why his car hit that wall and he died in such a horrible way."

Unless it was because Jamie's real estate business was in trouble and he'd diverted campaign money for personal expenses, which Mick either didn't know or didn't know I knew. Had Rick—apparently a deep-pockets donor—found out about the misused money and threatened to expose Jamie?

"Maybe because he was depressed about losing the election," I said. "And he had some staggering campaign debts to repay." I wasn't giving away anything Kit had told me last night or that she had confronted Jamie about it the day before he died.

"Yes, but he was dealing with both of those things. That's why he was on medication. And the fund-raiser Saturday night is to start tackling the debts." Mick shook his head in frustration.

"Let it go, Lucie. Enough people have been hurt already. Don't make it worse. He had a life insurance policy in place for years, so the company is still going to pay out. The only situations they wouldn't cover are an act of terrorism or if Jamie had been in a war zone, neither of which happened."

Mick had doubled down on this, and I felt as if I'd been run over by a steamroller. Maybe it was time to change the subject.

"All right. You win. But I do plan to drop by and see Elena to express my condolences. Either today or tomorrow."

"I'm sure she'd appreciate that. I'll let her know."

I stood. "I ought to go. Thank you for the coffee and the scone."

He got up and his lips brushed my cheek. "I know I am asking a lot, Lucie. You're so bloody loyal to your friends and you want to do right by everyone. I've always admired that about you. So I appreciate you agreeing to let Garrett handle the press."

We both knew he wouldn't have relented until he wore me down and I gave in. I gave him a who-are-you-kidding look.

"I'm sure we'll see each other at the wake and the funeral," I said.

He nodded. "Elena asked me to be one of the eulogists. We all go back a long way together. It's going to be rough, this funeral. Come on, I'll walk you to your car."

I checked my rearview mirror as I drove away. Mick was leaning against one of the columns on his front veranda, his arms folded across his chest, watching me with a contemplative look on his face. He hadn't told me the whole truth about Jamie and there were missing pieces in his story. Was claim-

ing that Rick had been a campaign donor who'd had a falling-
out with Jamie one of them?

Something about that just didn't ring true. Mick and I
knew each other too well. I didn't believe him even though I'd
feigned agreement.

And he knew it, too.

AT THE BOTTOM MICK'S long, winding driveway, my phone
rang. The Bluetooth display showed "Home." Persia.

I pushed a button and said, "Hi, Persia. What's up?"

"My little lamb is having a bad day, Lucie. She knows something is going on and she's out of sorts. She's been fussing and
weepy all morning. It's so unlike her."

As much as we'd tried to shield Hope from what had
happened yesterday, she still had a child's uncanny sixth sense
for picking up—and absorbing—the tension of the adults
around her.

"She hasn't seen anything on television, has she?" I asked.
"Or overheard something on the radio?"

"She didn't need to. Apparently she heard the commotion
of all those trucks and reporters in the driveway this morning. I told her someone wanted to talk to you, is all, and now
they're gone and everything is okay. But she's not buying it."
Persia sounded perturbed. "So I was wondering if you might
run by the General Store and pick up a blueberry muffin for
her. Maybe two. I'm ready to resort to bribes."

The General Store was just about the last place on the
planet I wanted to go right now. Thelma Johnson, the sweet
grandmotherly-looking octogenarian who owned it and looked

as if she'd blow away in a mild breeze, could wangle information out of anyone who dropped by with the deft, relentless
skill of a military interrogator who needed to know the enemy's
plans. You never saw the blood until it was over. She even had
her own intelligence-gathering network known as the Romeos,
which stood for Retired Old Men Eating Out, a somewhat can-
tankerous group of senior citizens who swooped into every
watering hole and restaurant in two counties to not only sup-
plement her information but also spread the latest news—some
would call it gossip—far and wide. Like the kids' game of telephone, it usually meant stories changed, sometimes unrecog-
nizably, in the retelling.

Thelma would already know everything there was to know
about Jamie's accident, but I'd still get the third degree the
minute I walked through her front door. "Maybe I could get
Hope a couple of cow puddles from the Upper Crust instead,"
I said to Persia.

"She wants blueberry muffins. From the General Store."

I sighed. "Okay. She shall have them."

"And don't worry about Thelma," she said. "I'm sure you'll
do just fine."

"I'll bet someone said that to Napoleon just before Waterloo,"
I said, and heard her rich chuckle as we both disconnected.

TEN MINUTES LATER WHEN I walked into the General Store,
Thelma was standing behind the cash register counter, absorbed in a magazine that I knew would be one of her beloved
soap opera weeklies. Thelma always dressed with the va-va-
voom flair of a Broadway diva whose best days are behind her,

preferring colors strong enough to vibrate and outfits so pro-
vocative that, if she'd been a teenager, would have gotten her
grounded or at least sent to her room to change. Today was
no different. She wore a too-short, too-tight dress with stiletto
peep-toe heels, but what I didn't expect was that she was
dressed completely in black, the color of mourning.

"Why, Lucille," she said, her reedy voice more subdued than
usual, "come on over here, child. I've been expecting you."

I stopped in midstep. Mick had said the same thing. "Did
Persia call and ask you to save two blueberry muffins for
Hope?"

"No, she did not. You're in luck, though. I've got two left."
Thelma tapped her right temple with a bony index finger. "How
do you think I knew you were coming? It's my extraterres-
trial psychotic perception. The spirits from the Great Beyond
talk to me, Lucille, you know that. And today they've been
speaking to me loud and clear about you."

Thelma swore by the power of her Ouija board and claimed
she could communicate with those who'd gone over to the
other side, including my mother and Leland. I wondered if
she'd already had a chat with Jamie Vaughn. Then I decided
maybe I'd rather not know.

"About me? What exactly have they been saying?" Sometimes you didn't know whether to abandon reason and believe
what Thelma said or go with clear-eyed logic and common
sense. Maybe she was listening to voices inside her head that
only she could hear.

"It's a long story," she said. "Why don't you have a cup of
coffee with me and we can talk about it? I'm sure you're plumb
wrung out after what happened yesterday. I've been watching

the news, especially that reporter from Channel 3 flouncing around accusing you of hiding the truth about how Jamie died. Don't journalists have to abide by a code of ethnicity or something?"

"Uh . . . I don't think so," I said. "I think anyone's fair game. Especially someone like Jamie since he ran for president. He's a public person."

Thelma took off her thick trifocals and pulled a tissue out of a box on the counter, dabbing her eyes. For the first time I noticed that her makeup, which usually looked as if she applied it with a garden trowel, was blotchy and uneven and her mascara was smeared. This wasn't the first time today she'd been near tears.

"Oh, Thelma . . . are you okay?"

She sniffled. "That poor man. God rest his soul. It's just so turrible the way it happened. Folks should leave him his dignity, not prowl around like they're going through a trash bin." She blew her nose. "I don't blame you for not wanting to tell that woman what really happened."

Here it was. The slippery slope. "I'm not hiding anything," I said in a firm voice. "Just like I told Pippa O'Hara."

"Lucille, you're just like your sainted momma. She never could lie, either." Thelma gave me a knowing look. "Help yourself to a cup of coffee, child. On the house. Today's Fancy is Abracajava. Kind of peppy. I think you'll like it."

Thelma kept three coffeepots labeled "Plain," "Fancy," and "Decaf" on warming plates on a table next to the glass cabinet that held her fresh-baked muffins and doughnuts. A cup of coffee on the house meant she was definitely going to grill me.

"You know, I should probably just pay for the muffins and be on my way."

"I wouldn't if I were you." She gave me a severe look. "There's something you need to know. It'd go down a lot easier with a cup of coffee."

My stomach did an uneasy flip-flop. "About Jamie?"

"About you."

We fixed our coffees in silence, and I followed her to a small alcove where a couple of mismatched rocking chairs were pulled together in a semicircle around a small wood stove that warmed up the place in winter. Thelma took the Lincoln rocker, her usual seat, and I sat in the bentwood chair next to her.

She sipped her coffee and fixed her eyes on me. "So, tell me, what really happened yesterday?"

Thelma didn't beat around the bush. I wasn't going to get out of here until she heard something that sounded vaguely like the truth.

I shrugged. "Jamie was speeding. I think he must have lost control of his car because I had to swerve to avoid him. I was coming from the opposite direction when he crossed into my lane and I ended up on the shoulder on the other side of the road. The next thing I heard was him crashing into the pillar at the vineyard entrance."

Thelma's head bobbed gently as if she suffered from palsy, a faint uncontrollable tremor. Somehow I had a feeling she already knew this part of the story. "Then what?" she asked.

Past this point I would not go.

I drew in a ragged breath. "It's hard to talk about." Which was the truth.

Thelma set her coffee cup on top of the stove with a hand that shook. "Did he suffer?" Her voice shook, too.

Our eyes met. "Oh, my Lord," she whispered and pulled the crumpled tissue out of the sleeve of her dress as tears ran down her face. "Oh, my dear, sweet Lord."

"The fire was . . . almost instantaneous. So it was quick."

She nodded, the tissue now at her lips. "I suppose that's a small mercy."

"Yes."

I wasn't going to tell her anything else. Nothing about Jamie's dying request, no explanation why Mick and I couldn't—didn't—save him. Not one word about any of that, not even the slightest hint that I thought that crash was deliberate. Not an accident. I needed to change the subject fast because it felt like all the air was being sucked out of the room and I could barely catch my breath.

"Are you wearing black because of Jamie?" It was a peculiar thing to ask, but I'd never seen that color on her unless she'd been at someone's funeral.

She blinked. "I am."

"I didn't realize you two were so close."

"Not in the way you might think, not as if we were close friends," she said. "But I did it out of respect for a good man."

There seemed to be more to her story, so I waited.

"Years ago I needed to refinance the mortgage on this store," she said after a moment. "The roof was leaking and the heating system wasn't going to make it through the next winter. Jamie ran into me the day I was at the bank, Blue Ridge Federal, waiting for my appointment. We chatted and then he went his way and I went mine. Thing is, my application got turned down because I'd bought the store during the real estate bubble bath market when folks were crazy enough to pay a fortune for something that wasn't any bigger or sturdier than a kids' tree house. Now I was looking for money . . . what did that loan officer say . . . when I was upside down. I owed more on the store than it was worth."

"I didn't know this."

"No one knows. But Jamie found out . . . I have no idea how. So you know what he did? He sent one of his construction crews over and they not only fixed my roof, he had them put in a brand-new heating system. Wouldn't take a dime for it, either, and told me it had to be our secret."

"What a generous thing to do."

She picked up her coffee mug and rubbed at the ring it had left on the top of the stove with her other hand. "I have my ways of finding things out, Lucille. I'm not the only person around here he helped on the quiet."

Her chair creaked in a comforting rhythm as she started to rock back and forth. I finished my coffee. "I'm not sure what this has to do with me."

She stopped rocking and studied me. The look in her eyes told me that whatever she said next was going to be something I wasn't expecting to hear.

"I thought long and hard about telling you this, Lucille. Especially after Jamie's accident yesterday, and the spot where that crash took place. The same wall, the exact same place as you and Gregory Knight all those years ago," she said. "But if it was me, I'd rather know than not know."

My veins felt like ice water was congealing in them. Why was Thelma bringing up Greg? "Not know what?"

She folded her hands in her lap. "I had a visitor in here the other day . . . Friday, it was. Hunter Knight."

"Who's . . . Hunter Knight?" The question died on my lips. I'd heard what she'd said, but I didn't believe her. "Greg's older brother? He's a minister, I think. He lives somewhere in Central America or South America doing missionary work."

"He used to. And he worked for that organization that helps folks out when their inhuman rights have been violated. Amnesiac International. Anyway, now he's moved home to help his younger brother."

"I think you mean Amnesty International."

"That's what I said, didn't I?"

"Uh . . . yes. But how's Hunter going to help Greg?" I said. "He murdered a man. He's in jail."

"He was asking about you, Lucille. Hunter, that is. Wondering how you were doing."

"I hope you didn't tell him anything. I don't want to see him or his brother. Ever. I mean it, Thelma. *Ever.*"

"If he shows up again I'll make sure he knows."

"You do that." My voice quivered with anger. I didn't think hearing Greg's name or that a member of his family wanted to reach out to me would upset me this much. "Thelma, no and no and no."

"Oh, dear, I shouldn't have said anything to you, should I? I'm sorry I upset you so."

I wanted to tell her it was okay, to behave like a sane, rational person who could handle this like an adult. I had rebuilt my life knowing Greg was somewhere where I would never have to see him or hear from him for a very long time. But I never thought that his older brother would turn up and try to insert himself into this corner of Virginia, my home, where I wanted to feel safe again.

"What in the world was he doing here? What brought him to Atoka?"

"He said he came to visit someone. Clammed right up when I tried to find out who it might be. Just told me he was trying to help out a friend, is all. Him being a man of the cloth I suppose a body's got to respect what people tell him in confidential absolution." She gave me a sideways look. "So I guess the person he wanted to visit wasn't you?"

I glared at her, and she said, "I didn't think so. We'll discuss it no more, Lucille."

"Does anyone else know he dropped by?"

"I might have mentioned it to the Romeos."

She might as well have taken out an ad in the *Trib*. "So everyone in northern Virginia knows."

"Whoever he went to visit is still a mystery. The Romeos get around, you know," she said in a mild voice. "Aren't you the least bit curious to find out who it was, what brought him here?"

"No," I said. "I . . . I don't know."

"I thought you might be," she said. "I promise you, I'll find out, child. And when I do, you'll be the first to know."

I stood up. "I'd better be going. Thank you for the coffee, Thelma."

She walked me to the front door. "I stopped by the entrance to your vineyard last night," she said. "So many people leaving candles and flowers and whatnot. It was a lovely tribute to him. But you know what else?"

"What?"

"His spirit was there, too. Jamie still hasn't crossed over to the other side." She leaned close to me, her eyes boring into mine through her thick glasses. "And do you know why?"

Because I haven't fulfilled his dying request to ask forgiveness of a stranger named Rick. "No. I don't."

She wagged a finger, admonishing me. "He is not at peace, Lucille. Not at all at peace. He's going to haunt us all until he is. Mark my words."

I nodded, mute, and fled.

Eight

As much as I wanted to believe that what Thelma's Ouija board told her about Jamie's spirit having not crossed over yet was no more than her overactive imagination and a bit of wishful thinking, there were plenty of folks around here who swore by sightings of Colonel John Singleton Mosby, the Confederate guerrilla commander more famously known as the Gray Ghost. According to urban legend, Mosby—who, along with his rebel group of Partisan Rangers, led daring raids against Northern troops and supply trains—could still be seen roaming our area on moonless nights in search of Union soldiers. He wasn't the only local Civil War ghost that haunted the region, either.

So why couldn't Jamie's spirit still haunt us as well? Haunt *me*?

My phone rang as I was about to get into my car. The display read "Mick." I held my thumb over the call button and took a deep breath. Thought about letting it go to voice mail.

I punched the button. "Hi, Mick, what's up?"

"Lucie, I just spoke to Elena." He sounded businesslike and a bit brisk. "She was wondering if you could drop by the house for a few minutes. She's had friends and neighbors stopping by all day, but she'd especially like to see you. Anytime in the next hour would work best for her. After that she has an appointment with Hunt Funeral Home."

I wondered, and it made me feel disquieted, if "talk to Lucie" had been on their checklist of things to do as part of the funeral arrangements. Make sure I truly abided by the request to bow out and let Garrett Bateman take over media relations for the family.

I had planned to go by and see Elena anyway, to offer my condolences and to return Jamie's MedicAlert bracelet. The bracelet, however, was on my bedroom dresser in a bone china trinket box my mother had given me. After carrying it in my pocket, the bracelet had seemed to grow heavier, along with the weight of my conscience. Maybe it didn't matter if I didn't give it to Elena today. I could always slip it to her discreetly at the wake, or give it to her later. It wasn't as if Jamie needed it anymore.

"Lucie?" He sounded concerned. "Are you still there?"

"Yes, sorry. I was on my way home, but I can stop by now." Though Hope would have to wait to get her blueberry muffins.

"Good." I could tell he was pleased. "I'll text her and let her know."

I was beginning to see what Quinn meant about the vibe between Mick and Elena, but Mick had been friends with both Jamie and Elena when they'd met at UVA as students nearly thirty years ago. Plus Elena, a senior biochemist who worked for a medical research laboratory in Leesburg, had been a consultant to Dunne Pharmaceutical in Miami before Mick sold it for more than a billion dollars and moved to Atoka a few years ago.

It took less than ten minutes to drive over to Longview, the Vaughns' elegant redbrick home. The house sat about half a mile back from the main road on a bluff overlooking a sweep of rolling hills outlined by post-and-board fences and Civil War–era stacked stone walls that crisscrossed pale green meadows in lovely symmetry. In the distance, the red tin roofs and whitewashed buildings of a farmhouse with its adjoining barns, silos, and stables gleamed in the afternoon sunlight. A brown-and-gold Loudoun County sheriff's cruiser sat parked in front of the driveway entrance, a jarring addition to an otherwise peaceful scene. The officer waved me through once I identified myself and then moved his cruiser so it blocked the driveway once again.

The long private road to the house wound back and forth in a lazy zigzag past a man-made pond with a pier, Elena's large greenhouse, a putting green, and a swimming pool with an enormous pool house and terraced outdoor kitchen. Elena and Jamie employed a full-time staff to take care of the grounds and gardens, several of whom I passed cleaning beds, trimming hedges, and blowing leaves. When I finally parked in the circular drive in front of the house, the air smelled heavily of rich, peaty mulch.

I recognized Garrett Bateman's dark green Jaguar in the driveway, parked next to Elena's silver BMW. Mick hadn't said Garrett would be here, though it shouldn't have surprised me that he was.

A somber, unsmiling maid dressed in black opened the door when I rang the bell, and invited me in. "Mrs. Vaughn and Mr. Bateman are in the drawing room," she said. "They're expecting you."

Longview had been built during Prohibition and the Roaring Twenties when Jamie's grandfather moved to Virginia as part of a wave of Northerners—mostly from New York—who swept up land that was excellent for breeding horses along with grand plantations owned by Southerners impoverished by the Civil War, all for a pittance of their true value. The house's most ingenious feature was a lavish, well-stocked mirrored bar that took up a wall between two entrances to the drawing room. During Prohibition, anytime federal agents who suspected liquor was being served raided the house, a paneled wall hidden inside a concealed compartment could be pulled out like a pocket door and moved into place so the bar vanished like magic.

I knocked on the closed door and Garrett opened it. His dress shirt was wrinkled and untucked from his jeans, he was unshaven, and he looked like he hadn't slept in the last twenty-four hours, reminding me of Mick Dunne. The grief in his eyes behind horn-rimmed glasses was almost unbearable, and he smelled of alcohol.

I gave him a quick hug, and he said, "Come in, please, Lucie. Elena and I are about to have a drink. Can I fix you something, too?"

"Nothing for me, thanks."

Elena Vaughn, tiny and fragile looking in a black boatneck sweater and black trousers, sat on a white leather Art Deco sofa scrolling through something on her phone before quickly typing a text message. She punched Send, set the phone on a rosewood-and-glass coffee table, and looked up. Our eyes met. Her smile was sad.

"Lucie." She stood up and smoothed her trousers with the palms of her hands as if she were ill at ease or uncomfortable. "Thank you for coming."

I walked over and hugged her. "I'm so sorry," I said. "So very, very sorry."

Where Jamie had been tall, dark haired, broad shouldered, athletic, and outdoorsy, Elena was his opposite, a delicate beauty, fine boned with pale porcelainlike skin, flame-colored hair, and bewitching green eyes. Ironically, the reality was that she had a backbone of steel and gritty determination. Jamie was the easygoing one, a soft touch with a big heart.

She nodded and Garrett slipped something into her hand. A tissue. She wiped her eyes and blew her nose. "Every time I think about him being gone, I just lose it."

"There are so many tributes at the front entrance to the vineyard. He was so beloved—" I broke off. Maybe I was only making this harder for her to bear.

Elena nodded. "Sasha texted me photos. We're just completely overwhelmed. I'd like to try to get over there and see for myself, but the press—" She waved a hand as if she wanted to dismiss them all and said in a tired voice, "The calls haven't stopped. Thank God for Garrett."

Garrett handed Elena a martini glass. It didn't seem like her first of the day, either. "Won't you have a drink, Lucie?" She gestured to the bar. "We've got everything. And please, have a seat."

She sat back down on the sofa. I took a black-and-white-striped fan-shaped club chair across from her and sank into the plush upholstery. She was right. The bar was overfull with bottles of alcohol, mixers, and a couple of bottles of red wine.

"No drink for me, thanks," I said.

"How about a glass of wine?" Garrett asked. "We've got a great twenty-year-old Zinfandel from California."

"Twenty-year-old Zin? I'm tempted, but I really shouldn't," I said. "Elena, by the way, your flowers are beautiful. I saw your arrangements earlier when I stopped by Mick's place."

Though Longview hadn't been on the Historic Garden Week tour this year, this room was also filled with flowers. An enormous cut-glass vase of lilacs, snapdragons, curly willow, hydrangeas, and tulips that sat on a teak-and-ebony console table was obviously Elena's creative handiwork, but there were other, more staid and formal arrangements that I suspected had been sent in sympathy. The foyer had been filled with flowers as well.

"Speaking of the press," Garrett said, sitting down after pouring himself a brandy, "Elena and I saw that O'Hara woman maul you this morning, Lucie. She's a bully. You shouldn't have to endure that."

"She evidently thinks I'm hiding something."

Elena gave me shrewd look. "Let her think what she likes. You're not."

"Elena." I cleared my throat. "This is very hard for me to say, but Jamie didn't want me to help him get out of the car before the fire started."

"Mick told us," Garrett said in a smooth, take-charge voice, "that one of the pillars at the entrance to your vineyard toppled over, trapping Jamie with no possible way to get out before the car caught fire. I drove by last night very late and took a look for myself. Mick said Jamie knew it was impossible to escape and he wanted you out of the way where it was safe. Apparently, you very nearly didn't manage it before the car burst into flames."

They were backing Mick's version of what happened. "Jamie seemed very distressed when I spoke to him," I said. "He asked me to find someone named Rick and ask for his forgiveness."

"Jamie had a falling-out with a friend who donated a lot of money to the campaign," Garrett said. "Mick told you that. Elena and I will talk to him and take care of it. You don't need to worry about it anymore."

"But—"

Elena set her drink on a glass-topped coffee table. The martini glass made a sharp little click, amplifying her irritation. "Why are you pushing this? Why are you making this harder for me than it already is?"

"I'm not," I said. "I'm sorry."

"Lucie," Garrett said, "you really need to let me handle everything. It's what I do for a living. I'm good at it." He cleared his throat, and I caught the look that he and Elena exchanged. "There's something else."

"What?" I asked.

"Pippa O'Hara would like nothing better than to drag Jamie's name through the mud," he said. "She had a beef with him ever since the campaign and she's not over it."

"Then she shouldn't be covering the story if she can't be objective."

"Her boss calls her tenacious." Garrett sounded disgusted. "Look, we know Jamie was speeding, going way over the limit on Atoka Road."

"That's right. He nearly ran into me."

"And you swerved to avoid him so you didn't see the actual crash," Garrett went on. "Correct?"

"Yes." He already knew this was true, so why was he going over it with me?

"Look, Lucie." He took a hearty swig of his brandy.

I hate it when someone says "Look, Lucie" in that tone of voice. What comes next is never good.

"Right now everything points to what happened as a tragic accident. Jamie was speeding, it had been raining." Garrett caught Elena's eye again, and they exchanged another coded message. "Jamie was taking medication to deal with depression after that nasty campaign and he might have had a drink or two before he got behind the wheel. That's probably going to come out in the investigation."

Elena leaned forward, her arms resting on her knees, holding her hands together as if she were praying. "So as you can see, there's no need to get into anything else."

"Because if you do," Garrett said, "you're going to get dragged into something ugly."

I couldn't tell if it was a threat or a warning. "What are you saying?" I asked.

"Ten years ago you were in a car accident in exactly the same place," Elena said, her eyes straying to my cane, which I'd placed on the marble floor next to me. "It left you permanently disabled, changed your life forever."

"That's right," I said in an even voice.

"We think," Garrett said, "that your own deeply personal experience—how you were trapped in that car, just as Jamie was—might color what you saw . . . or believe you saw . . .

yesterday. Pippa O'Hara's already brought it up. She'll take you apart—shred you into pieces—if she thinks you're covering up something. What's worse is she'll make you out to be unreliable or unstable because of your own emotional connection to Jamie's accident."

I sat back in my chair, speechless and stunned.

"There's no need for that to happen," Elena said after a moment. "We're doing this to protect you as much as to protect Jamie and all the good that he did in his lifetime."

"I see."

"We also have a favor to ask," she said. "I hope you'll consider it. It would mean so much to Jamie. And me."

Garrett walked over to the bar. He picked up an envelope and handed it to me. The return address in the upper left-hand corner said "Vaughn/Tanner for America."

"Open it," he said.

Inside were two twenty-thousand-dollar tickets to Saturday night's Jefferson Dinner fund-raiser at the Goose Creek Inn. The tickets that included a tasting of the 1876 bottle of Norton.

"For you and Quinn," Elena said. "We'd like you to go as our guests. You're related to Daniel Norton, Lucie. I'd really like it if you could speak about him that evening, specifically the story of how the Lemosy family tried to take credit for the work Norton did now that Jamie won't be there to do it. Jamie loved that he was able to be part of restoring Norton's name to the native American grape he bred, how Daniel Norton persevered in spite of heartbreak and loss. Jamie was such a champion for the underdog."

"These tickets cost a fortune," I said. "I couldn't possibly accept your gift. We couldn't."

"You'd be giving the talk that Jamie won't be there to give," Elena said. "I'm sure you, of all people, understand how important it is, especially talking about the historical significance of the bottles of Norton that are being auctioned off. Oliver and Owen are going, but it would mean more for one of Daniel Norton's relatives to speak about the importance of reclaiming his reputation. And we'd like you and Quinn to taste the wine, of course."

"What about you?" I said. "It would be more appropriate for you to give your husband's speech, wouldn't it?"

She shook her head. "I won't be up for it. I won't be attending."

"I'll be there," Garrett said. "Because of the auction."

"Please," Elena said, "do it for Jamie."

Garrett gave me a sly wink. "Don't tell me you're not intrigued by the idea of sampling a bottle of Norton from 1876."

"I—I mean, well, yes, of course."

Elena stood up and pressed her hands together. "Then it's settled."

Garrett got up as well. "Let me walk you to the door, Lucie."

It was clear this discussion was over. I picked up my cane. "Thanks, but I can see myself out."

"Nonsense," he said. "Don't mean to rush you, but B. J. Hunt is due here at four to finalize the last of the arrangements for the wake and the burial. The cremation is . . . later today. We need a few minutes to get ourselves together."

Cremation. I caught my breath. I should have realized Jamie's remains would have to be cremated.

"Of course," I said. "Elena, is there anything else I can do?"

"Just let Garrett handle everything," she said. "That's more than enough."

I went over and hugged her goodbye. "I'll see you Thursday. And Friday. Take care of yourself, and if you need anything, you only have to call."

Elena took an unsteady breath. "We'll get through this," she said. "Somehow."

At the front door, Garrett slipped me his business card. "Any more calls or inquiries, just refer them to that number, you hear?"

I took the card. "What about all the mementos people are leaving at the vineyard entrance? Would you like me to . . . save them for you?"

"I can tell you right now that we don't want a death memorial," Garrett said. "You can dispose of everything, if you wouldn't mind. In my opinion, anything still there after the funeral borders on being maudlin."

"All right," I said. "We'll take care of it."

"Good."

"One more question," I said. "I don't really know how to ask this, but—"

"Then please don't." He cut me off. "Jamie had everything to live for, Lucie. A loving family, a successful business, financial security, a good life. Losing the presidency was tough, but he was dealing with it. I'm sure the Loudoun County Sheriff's Department is going to rule that what happened was a tragic accident once they finish their investigation. That's all there is to it."

"Of course. Goodbye, Garrett."

I walked to my car. Though I didn't turn around, I knew he was watching me through one of the windows in the foyer and didn't move away until he could no longer see my car.

Halfway down the driveway I realized I had forgotten to tell them about Jamie's MedicAlert bracelet. But as the brown-and-gold sheriff's department cruiser moved out of the way so I could turn onto the main road, it occurred to me that there was a lot Elena Vaughn and Garrett Bateman hadn't told me, either.

And they had just bought my complicity to go along with their version of what happened to Jamie with two tickets to a twenty-thousand-dollar dinner and the once-in-a-lifetime opportunity to drink a unicorn wine. I guess I'd just been bribed.

Nine

ope was sound asleep on the Aubusson carpet in the middle of the foyer by the time I arrived home with her blueberry muffins. Persia had covered her with a bubblegum-pink Cinderella blanket and now she lay tangled up in it next to the Barbie dollhouse Eli had built for her, surrounded by doll-sized furniture that had been strewn everywhere as though a tornado had blown through Barbie-land. A nearly naked Barbie lay on her back with both arms sticking straight up in the air, looking as if she'd surrendered any hope of trying to restore order to the chaos of her pink-and-white home.

"My little lamb collapsed about an hour ago, just wore herself out," Persia whispered when she met me at the front door. "I didn't have the heart to move her."

"Let her sleep." I handed Persia the bag with the muffins. "I'm sorry these are late. I stopped by to see Elena Vaughn."

"Sasha's over with Eli in the carriage house," she said.

"They got here a little while ago. He had some business thing he needed to do and then he's driving her home."

"How's she doing?"

Persia raised her eyebrows and gave a small one-shoulder shrug. "She's taking it hard. After all these years, she had finally reconciled with her father and now he's gone."

"I should go see her and offer my condolences. I've also got Jamie's MedicAlert bracelet. It's upstairs in the bedroom. I'll ask Sasha if she'd mind giving it to Elena since I didn't have it with me when I stopped by Longview." I glanced over at Hope, who had started to snore softly and was now murmuring something in her sleep. "Maybe I'll get it later. I don't want to wake her."

"If you want to tell me where it is, I'll get it," Persia said. "I don't think Eli and Sasha planned to be here long, so you ought to go over there now or you'll miss seeing her. Just stop by here before they leave and I'll have it for you."

"It's in the little bone china box on my dresser," I said. "Thanks."

MY PHONE DINGED WITH a text message as I walked across the driveway to the carriage house. Quinn and I had been going back and forth for the last twenty minutes after I texted him on my way home from Longview and told him I had a surprise for him when I saw him that evening. Ever since, he'd been teasing me to tell him what it might be.

Bigger than a bread box?

Definitely. Huge, in fact.

Animal, vegetable, or mineral?

Yes. Well, maybe not too much mineral.

Does it involve wild, passionate sex?

Only if you want an audience. Or we could wait until it's over.

His next text was a row of smiley faces with half a dozen exclamation marks. Wait until he saw the tickets . . . and learned how I'd come by them. As much as I was dying to attend the Jefferson Dinner and sample Norton wine from 1876, it still felt like I'd sold my silence in return for something I couldn't afford.

Through the mullioned French doors Eli had installed where the old wooden carriage doors used to be I could see my brother and Sasha facing each other, seated on the high stools Eli used when he was working on a set of drawings at his drafting table or building models that made ideas he dreamed up in his head into 3-D miniature reality. Late afternoon sunlight from a window behind them limned their profiles, turning them into silhouettes. Eli was leaning toward Sasha, his hands outstretched, holding hers, the body language of someone in earnest conversation. Sasha was nodding, her head bowed and her shoulders drooping. It was a haunting—and private— tableau of two people weighed down by sorrow and grief. I stopped walking, feeling guilty at having stumbled into such an intimate scene, but Eli caught sight of me and motioned that I should come in and join them.

Sasha's eyes were red rimmed when I walked into my brother's studio a moment later. "Hey, Luce." Eli's voice was sad and subdued.

Elena's twin sons, Owen and Oliver, had their mother's flame-colored hair and fair skin, but Sasha was Jamie through and through—shoulder-length brown hair, brown eyes, outdoorsy, athletic build, good-looking in a wholesome all-American way. Only her olive-skinned complexion wasn't Jamie's, and I guessed it came from her Italian-American mother.

I went straight to Sasha and hugged her. "I'm so sorry."

She sniffled, the remnants of earlier tears. "Thanks. I still can't believe he's gone."

"Me either. I just came from seeing Elena. She said you texted her pictures of the mementos and tributes at the vineyard entrance. You must know how much he was beloved by so many people. I hope it's a comfort."

"It is." She chewed her lip. "Lucie, I want you to tell me everything. You were the last person to see him. I want to know what happened."

I caught Eli's eye and saw an imperceptible shake of his head. *Don't do it. Don't tell her everything.*

"He was speeding," I said. "I'm sure you've heard that already. Plus it had been raining, so there were a lot of wet, slick spots, along with places that were flooded out. I think he lost control of the car. And he wasn't wearing a seat belt."

She groaned. "Dad always drove way too fast and he could be a real pain about wearing a seat belt. I tried telling him about clients I've worked with who became disabled as the result of a car accident . . ." Her hand flew to her mouth. "Oh, God, Lucie, I'm sorry . . . I didn't mean . . ."

"Don't worry about it," I told her with a rueful smile. "You're right. I'm sure Eli told you he crashed into the same spot where my accident happened." Might as well get it out in the open.

She nodded. "He also said you tried to help my father get

out of the car but he was trapped inside . . . and then the fire started."

"It's a little more complicated than that."

"What do you mean?"

"Sasha, he'd been drinking, and I think he might have mixed the alcohol with pills. He wasn't really himself."

Her lips tightened as she absorbed that information. I didn't look at my brother.

"Wow," she said as if the wind had been knocked out of her. "Wow."

"I'm so sorry."

"It's okay." She lifted her chin and gave me a determined look. "I told you I wanted to know everything. What happened after that?"

"He passed out. He'd lost consciousness by the time the fire started." I drew the line at telling her that I'd heard Jamie's last anguished scream.

"Did he say anything?"

Eli caught my eye again, blinking another coded message. *Watch what you tell her.*

"Yes," I said, "he did. He asked me to find someone named Rick and ask for his forgiveness. He said, 'Tell Rick I'm sorry.'"

Eli looked stunned. This was news to him.

"Rick?" Sasha frowned. "Who's Rick?"

"According to Elena and Garrett he's a wealthy campaign donor who had a falling-out with your father."

Her frown deepened and she shook her head. "I spent a lot of time around Dad during the campaign, and I don't remember anyone named Rick. No one he had a fight with and no one important enough that he would remember him right before he died."

Well, now. Wasn't that interesting. "Really?"

"Yes. Really."

"Then why would they say that's who Jamie was talking about?"

"I have no idea."

"I also have your dad's MedicAlert bracelet. He was holding it and it slipped out of his hand, so I picked it up. I was going to give it to the EMTs because . . ." I stumbled over that last sentence. We all knew what I meant. "I thought Elena might want it now."

Sasha gave me another curious look. "My dad didn't wear a MedicAlert bracelet," she said in a flat voice. "At least not that I knew of. What was it for?"

"An allergic reaction to Coumadin."

"What's Coumadin?" Eli spoke up for the first time.

"Blood thinner," Sasha and I said together.

"You have to worry about someone bleeding out if they're on Coumadin and they're injured or badly cut," Sasha told him. To me, she said, "He wasn't allergic to Coumadin. The only medication he took was for high blood pressure."

"Then whose bracelet is it?" I asked.

"Rick's?" Eli said, and I shot him a surprised look. What if he was right?

"You say you've still got it?" Sasha askcd.

"It's at the house."

"What did Elena say when you told her about it?" she asked.

"I didn't get around to mentioning it," I said. "It slipped my mind, especially since I didn't have it with me. That's why I asked if you would give it to her."

"Let's go take a look at it," Eli said. "Any other news you'd care to share, Luce? Something we don't know yet?"

"No," I said, and crossed my fingers behind my back. I still hadn't told them I thought the crash was no accident. One thing at a time.

By the time we got back to the house, Barbie, her dollhouse, and her furniture had been whisked out of sight and Hope was gone. Persia must have heard the front door open and close because she called from the kitchen, "Lucie, is that you? Your medallion is on the table next to the telephone."

I got it and handed it to Sasha, who turned it over, frowning some more as she checked it out. "I've never seen this before," she said. "It's old, by the look of it. Tarnished and banged up." She looked up at me. "Would you mind if I take it?"

"Of course not. You have more right to it than I do," I said. "Are you going to ask Elena about it?"

She closed her hand around the bracelet, and like me, I had the feeling that it was becoming heavier the longer she held on to it. A burden.

"Eventually," she said. "But first there's someone else I'm going to ask."

DINNER WAS JUST QUINN and me since Eli had taken Hope with him to have dinner with Sasha and Zach at Sasha's place. I waited until we finished the dishes before I handed him the envelope with the two Jefferson Dinner tickets. He slid them out, let out a long whistle, and gave me a puzzled look.

"No, I did not pay forty thousand dollars for these tickets."

"Good, because if you did we could kiss the money we've been putting aside for a destemmer goodbye," he said. "Where did you get them?"

"Elena and Garrett gave them to me when I was over there this afternoon. I think they're a bribe to let Garrett do all the talking for the family about Jamie and for mc to butt out."

He looked relieved. "One, that means you can tell Pippa O'Hara to take a hike the next time she tries to bait you, and two, Garrett ought to do all the talking for the family. It's what he does for a living," he said. "They didn't have to give you forty thousand dollars worth of tickets for that. But I'm not sorry they did . . . I'd gnaw off an arm to try that Norton wine. Now we both can."

"You don't seem too bothered by this," I said. "That they're bribing me."

"If there's an ulterior motive behind why Jamie drove his car into our stone wall yesterday, I think his family should decide how much they want the public to know," he said. "You don't have to take on that responsibility."

"Sasha thinks Elena and Garrett are lying about the identity of the mysterious Rick."

"Let the three of them work that out."

"I promised Jamie I'd find Rick and tell him Jamie asked for his forgiveness."

"You can't do anything about that right now. The ball is in their court. Sasha has the MedicAlert bracelet and it sounds like she is going to get to the bottom of things," he said, holding out his hand to me. "Come on. There's a pink moon tonight and it's also the apogee full moon. Let's take two glasses and the rest of the dinner wine and go have a drink at the summer-house so we can see it."

Why did he always have to be so damn logical and pragmatic? Much as I wanted to challenge what he said, I knew he was right.

"All right." I gave in and took his hand. Sasha wanted to find out who Rick was as much as I did, and she knew the people to ask. What bothered me, though, was that she seemed to imply that Elena and Garrett had lied earlier today. What I couldn't figure out was why: What were they hiding?

". . . or we could open a new bottle," Quinn was saying. "Which do you prefer . . . Lucie?"

"Um . . . which what do I prefer?"

"Are you listening to anything I'm saying?" he asked. "You're still stuck on this Rick guy. Let it go, sweetheart. You'll eventually find out from Sasha who he is."

"All right. I give up," I said. "Let's go look at the pink moon. It's the worst named moon of any of them, you know. It's always such a disappointment that it's not actually pink."

"Maybe," he said, "but it's still going to be pretty."

WE SAT BUNDLED IN blankets in two Adirondack chairs that we had dragged outside the summerhouse years ago and left near the edge of a bluff overlooking a sweep of farmland that ended at the foothills of the Blue Ridge Mountains. It was Leland, my father, who first suggested Quinn bring his telescope over here rather than the wooded area around the winemaker's cottage where he used to live because of the spectacular view of the night sky. Over the years, I'd often joined Quinn on starry nights while he slowly taught me to identify the planets and constellations, gave me my first look at the Perseids meteor shower that appeared every August, explained the stories behind the Native American names for all the full moons, grieved over Pluto being demoted as one of the nine planets.

"You remember what the apogee full moon is, right?" he asked. He had lit a cigar and the tip glowed comfortingly in the darkness like a tiny orange mini-moon of its own.

"The smallest moon of the year because the moon, which makes an elliptical orbit around Earth, is at its farthest distance from Earth," I said. "And the April full moon is always called the pink moon because the first flowers of the season are usually pink. If there are two full moons in a month, the second one is called the blue moon. Always."

"You get an A-plus. My star pupil," he said. "Want some more wine?"

"Yes, please." I held out my glass.

"Pretty night," he said. "Nice and clear."

I slid down in my chair and tilted my head so I could look up at the sky. Directly above us were the stars of Ursa Major. Though I'd known how to find it since I was a kid, it was Quinn who had informed me that it was visible in the northern hemisphere year-round and not a seasonal constellation like many others.

"There's something I need to tell you." I traced a finger around the stars in the bear's tail, which also made up the Big Dipper.

"Does it have to do with Jamie Vaughn?"

"No."

"What is it?" He leaned over and caressed my hair. "Your voice went funny just now, so whatever it is, you're upset."

He could read me so well. "Thelma told me she saw Hunter Knight a couple of days ago. He stopped by the General Store. Apparently he was in the area to visit someone. She said he asked about me."

After a moment he said, "Hunter Knight, as in Greg's brother, the one who's a priest? Lives in Guatemala or Honduras? That guy?"

He knew damn well who I meant. Even though I couldn't see his face, I knew it looked like thunder. By unspoken agreement, the subject of Greg Knight and my accident had been deemed ancient history, nothing either of us wanted to discuss. Among the reasons: because of my injuries I was told I could never have children.

"He's a missionary. Or was. And he's not a priest, he's some kind of minister and he worked for Amnesty International. He doesn't live in Central America anymore, either. He moved back here to help Greg."

Quinn puffed on his cigar and the tip glowed furiously. "Don't tell me Greg is out of jail. It's a little early for probation."

"Oh, God, I didn't even think of that. I have no idea where Greg is, but I thought they locked him up for life." The idea of Greg being able to walk around wherever he liked, being able to find me again, terrified me.

"What was Hunter Knight doing in Atoka?" Quinn asked.

"Thelma said he clammed up when she asked him," I said. "And the Romeos didn't turn up anything, either."

"If that crew couldn't find out what he was up to, the guy's better than any spy a foreign government could send over here. There's nothing Thelma doesn't know."

"She's planning to find out."

"I bet she is. Thelma leaves no stone unturned."

"She'll let me know when she does."

"Who does Hunter know around here that he'd want to see after all this time?"

"I have no idea. He doesn't have family or any relatives in the area anymore."

"Well," Quinn said, "it's a small town, as everyone always says. It won't take long before word gets out about what he was doing here."

My phone buzzed in my jacket pocket. Quinn heard it, too, because he said, "Let it go, honey. You've had enough on your plate for one day."

I pulled it out to turn it off, but then I saw the caller ID.

"It's Sasha," I said, and answered the call. "Hi, what's up?"

"Lucie." She sounded distracted and upset. "I just talked to my mother in Charlottesville. She was wondering if you'd be willing to drive down there to talk to her. She broke her leg a few weeks ago and it's still in a cast. Otherwise, she'd drive up here to see you."

"Why does she want to see me?" I asked.

"She wants to talk to you about what my dad said before he died. And she would like to see the MedicAlert bracelet. I'm giving it to Eli to bring back to you. That is, if you're willing to do this."

I sat up in my chair. "Absolutely. When can I visit her?"

"She said the sooner the better. Would tomorrow work?"

"Give me directions and I'll leave first thing in the morning," I said.

After I disconnected, Quinn said, "Let me guess. It has something to do with this Rick guy."

I nodded. "Sasha said her mother wants to talk to me. In person. I told you Rick's not some deep-pockets political donor who had a falling-out with Jamie. I bet he's someone from Jamie's past, someone worth forty thousand dollars to Elena and Garrett to keep me from trying to find out who he really is. What I don't know is why."

"But you're going to find out."

"Oh, yes. I am."

Ten

Whose side were they on? The question haunted me all night and from the moment I pulled out of my driveway on Wednesday morning until I arrived in Charlottesville just before ten thirty. Why didn't Elena and Garrett want me to pursue finding Rick? Who was he, anyway? Who were they trying to protect? Not Jamie . . . at least it didn't seem like it.

The drive south to Charlottesville took less than two hours down Route 29, a pretty two-lane road that wound past farmland and pastures and through small towns, always with the hazy, layered Blue Ridge Mountains as a backdrop. Down here, though, the mountains were more substantial and imposing than they were back home, and spring was further along by a couple of weeks. This was Thomas Jefferson's country; Monticello had always been the place he loved the most, where he had been the happiest. But over the years the neighboring town of Charlottesville, a pretty village founded in 1762, had gradually succumbed to urban sprawl—miles of strip malls and low-rise motels—that extended farther and farther up the highway each time I came here, just like Anyplace, USA. Route 29, in the middle of rush hour, could be as gridlocked as traffic in Washington, D.C., and that was crazy.

Vanessa Pensiero, Sasha's mother, lived in the Lewis Mountain section of town, a neighborhood almost entirely surrounded by land belonging to the University of Virginia and whose residents were mostly UVA professors and administrators. It was an older, established community of mature shade trees and plants, meandering lanes, and eclectic architecture. I found the address with no trouble and parked on the street. A white picket fence wrapped around a redbrick Colonial with well-cared-for landscaped gardens and the flowering trees that made Virginia so beautiful at this time of year. I let myself in through the front gate.

A dog that sounded truly ferocious barked when I rang the doorbell, and a moment later, a woman in her early fifties wearing a large gray orthopedic boot on her left leg opened the door with one hand and held on to Bruiser, as he looked like he should be called, with the other.

"Down, George," she said. "Hi, I'm Vanessa. You must be Lucie. His bark is really worse than his bite. He's actually a lovable old guy."

George? "Isn't he a rottweiler?"

"He won't hurt you, I promise. The worst he could do is jump up and try to give you a hug." Her eyes strayed to my cane. "Though in your case, he might knock you over. You're rather petite. I'll put him in the basement. Do come in."

Vanessa wrangled lover-boy George down the hall and

opened a door. "Get down there, buddy. We'll play later." I heard what sounded like a small militia descending a flight of stairs and George vanished.

She came back and joined me in the entryway. We studied each other and she said, "I've heard a lot about you from Sasha. She seems quite smitten by your brother."

"He seems equally smitten by her."

"So it's serious, then?" A mother asking questions. *What are his intentions with my daughter?*

"I think you'd have to ask her. As for Eli, we have a deal. He stays out of my love life and I stay out of his."

She smiled. "Touché. What can I get you to drink? Coffee? Tea? Iced tea?" She arched an eyebrow. "A Bloody Mary?"

"Iced tea would be lovely, if you have it made."

"I do," she said. "I put mint and lavender from my garden in my tea. And the honey, if you want it, is from my hive."

"Yes to everything, please."

I had seen the greenhouse in the side yard. So Vanessa, like Elena, was a gardener. I wondered what other qualities they had in common, because they looked and seemed nothing alike. Elena was delicate and fragile as spun glass. Vanessa was sturdy, solid, an Earth Mother.

"Good," she said. "We can fix our teas and then we can sit in the sunroom. It's going to be warm enough today to open the windows. I hope you don't have allergies. The pollen's already terrible. Everything in the house has a fine coating of yellowish-green dust all over it."

"Fortunately I don't. Eli's the one with allergies." I followed her down a paneled hallway that was a shrine to Sasha as she grew up. Framed photographs covered the walls: school chorale concerts, honor society award ceremonies, swim meets, soccer team pictures, first Communion, ballet recitals, a Sweet 16 birthday party, prom night, graduation, and all the other growing-up moments parents record, capturing awkwardness and puberty, acne and orthodontics.

Vanessa must have realized I was lingering to look at the photos because she came back and said, "She's the love of my life. I miss her every day."

"She's not that far away," I said. "It's only an hour and a half from here to Atoka."

"I lost her to her father when she moved up your way."

It sounded like a rebuke. "No, you didn't. She talks about you all the time."

"Jamie wasn't part of her life at all when she was growing up," Vanessa said. "I raised her by myself, a single mom with a little girl, until I finally married her stepfather when she was twelve. He died last year."

"I'm so sorry."

There was an ocean of bitterness welled up inside Vanessa Pensiero.

"Jamie had everything," she went on. "He didn't have to take my daughter, too. He charmed her, spoiled her with his money and everything he could offer her . . . Sasha wanted so badly for Jamie and me to make up and be friends."

I followed her into the kitchen. She took a pitcher of iced tea out of the refrigerator and got two tall glasses from a cabinet with jerky, automated movements.

"I'm sorry," I said again. "Divorce is never easy, especially when there are children involved."

"Divorce?" She spun around and gave me an incredulous

look. "We were barely married. Jamie did the honorable thing when he found out I was pregnant our senior year of college. Me, a nice Catholic girl, unmarried and expecting a baby. My parents practically disowned me. He married me the day after graduation, with just our immediate families as witnesses, and even before Sasha was born we both knew it was over. He'd already been bewitched by Elena and I lost him."

"That must have been rough."

"It was devastating. I loved him. Once."

Our eyes met, hers anguished. She still loved him, in spite of everything she'd just said. Jamie's death had been a devastating blow for her, too. She took a small ceramic pot that looked like a beehive out of a cabinet and pushed it toward me.

"I didn't mean to burden you with my problems or old grudges," she said, and I had the feeling she was suddenly embarrassed by her outburst. "Please, help yourself to some honey."

I used a wooden honey dipper to add a dollop of her honey to my tea and followed her to a cheery glassed-in room filled with comfortable well-worn furniture that said this was the heart of the home. A bird feeder hung on the branch of a still-bare oak tree in front of one of the open windows where a male and a female cardinal gorged themselves on sunflower seeds. A rectangular coffee table in front of the sofa had the battle scars and drink rings of dozens of board games that had been played and puzzles that had been assembled over the years, maybe over popcorn or hot chocolate or a glass of wine.

Vanessa sat on the chintz-covered sofa and indicated that I should join her. "Sasha told me Jamie said something to you before he died," she said. "And he gave you a MedicAlert bracelet."

"He didn't exactly give me the bracelet," I said. "It slipped out of his hand and I picked it up off the ground."

"May I see it?"

I took it out of the pocket of my jeans and handed it to her. She turned it over and sucked in her breath, running her thumb over the words written on the back.

"Oh, my God." Her voice dropped to a whisper. "You shouldn't have this. Really. You have no idea . . ."

She knew whose bracelet this was. I pounced on her words. "No idea about what? Tell me."

She set the bracelet on the coffee table as if it were glowing from some kind of otherworldly radiation. "First tell me what Jamie said to you."

"He asked me to tell someone named Rick that he was sorry. He said he wanted Rick to forgive him."

"No." Her voice was sharp. "Tell me exactly what he said to you. His *exact* words."

I thought for a moment. "He said, 'I'm sorry. Tell him I'm sorry.' So I asked him what he was talking about and he said, 'Tell Rick. Tell Rick I need him to forgive me.' And then he said he was sorry again. 'So very sorry,' he said. And he made me promise to tell him. He insisted."

Vanessa sat back on the sofa and propped her orthopedic boot on the coffee table as if she were dealing with the super-heavy gravity of Jupiter. For a long time she said nothing, just ran her thumb up and down the side of her iced tea glass, an unfocused look in her eyes.

"Vanessa," I said. "Who's Rick?"

She turned her head. Not only did she know who he was, but the answer scared her.

"Not Rick. Taurique. Tell-Rick. Tau-rique. Could he have said the name 'Taurique' to you? Could you have misheard what he said as 'Tell Rick'?"

I sounded it out. "Yes, I suppose he could have said Taurique. Who is he?"

"Taurique Youngblood. Age . . . by now, he's probably in his late fifties, maybe a bit younger. He's in jail. On death row, actually, though his execution keeps getting postponed. Charged with the murder of a UVA student named Webster Landau. Webb." She paused. "You're too young to know about this . . . it happened my senior year."

Jamie wanted forgiveness from a murderer on death row. Dear God. "Sorry. It doesn't ring a bell. Who was Webster Landau?"

"A doctoral student in the biochemistry department. A *brilliant* student. The kind every professor dreams of working with but almost never does. Webb was incredibly gifted, IQ off the charts . . . an amazing person. Unfortunately, he had an ego to match, but we all knew he was going places. A Nobel Prize someday wouldn't have been out of the question. Elena was his TA . . . teaching assistant. Of course, she was brilliant, too." She gave me a significant look. "She was also Webb's girlfriend."

"Oh."

"In those days, we were all friends. Jamie and me, Elena and Webb, and Mick Dunne, who'd usually bring along some freshman as his latest conquest. Mick's girlfriends never lasted. He had a wandering eye."

"He still does," I said. "You know he's my next-door neighbor?"

She nodded. "Why do you think he moved to Atoka after he sold his pharmaceutical business in Florida? Elena worked for him, you know. She was the director of development for Dunne Pharmaceutical's two most successful drugs. When we were in school, Elena and Webb—and Jamie—were always as thick as thieves. And Mick's still not married. Never will be. I think deep down he always carried a bit of a torch for Elena, but he just didn't want to get tied down."

I wasn't ready to tell Vanessa that Quinn, too, thought Mick still had feelings for Elena, or that I had been one of Mick's many conquests so I knew firsthand what he could be like. For that matter, I wasn't ready to tell her that I thought Jamie had intentionally driven into my wall and Mick hadn't tried to rescue him before his car caught fire.

"How were Jamie and Mick involved with Webb?" I asked.

"Jamie was a biology major and Mick was studying biochemistry, like Elena. I was the odd one out, the English major. Jamie wanted to be a doctor, a surgeon like his father. His family was really pushing him to go to med school."

"I didn't know that."

She sipped her iced tea. "After Webb died, the fire went out of Jamie. Plus all of a sudden he had a wife and child to support. So he gave up the idea of medical school and got a job in the construction business. Found out he was good at it, so he kept going, eventually bought the company he worked for, and on and on." She shrugged. "Mick went into the pharmaceutical business, started out in sales. And you know how that ended up."

I did. He renamed the mom-and-pop company he bought "Dunne Pharmaceutical" and took it from a little start-up to a major player. "So Jamie and Mick knew Webb because of Elena?"

"Yes, but they also volunteered to help Webb with his research. A lot of students did that for extra credit. Plus they ended up in the little club known as 'Dori's Darlings.' That's what the other students called them. It bred a lot of jealousy and ill will among those who were left out."

Before I could ask who Dori was, she said, "Professor Theodora Upshur. Webb's thesis adviser. She's the reason he came to UVA, to work with her. Another brilliant mind. Dori—as we called her—owned a farm a couple of miles from the school. It was a wonderful rambling old house with a lot of land that had been in her family for generations. Dori used to invite a select group of students for dinner on a regular basis—we all helped cook, of course. A lot of drinking went on, so usually we'd stay over, spend the night in one of the bedrooms or else sleep out in the barn since nobody wanted to walk back to their dormitory drunk. The discussions on those evenings were incredible . . . it made me think this was what the seventeenth-century European literary salons must have been like, where brilliant, educated people with great minds were passionate about ideas, saving the world, changing it. My God, we thought we were invincible. Those evenings were magical."

There was a dreamy, faraway wistfulness in her voice. I waited for her to go on because the story obviously didn't have a happy ending. "Until," she said, "they weren't. And things got out of control really fast."

"What happened?"

She raised an eyebrow again and propped her elbow on the arm of the sofa, leaning her head on her hand. "The perfect storm. Webb was working on a study that took him out to Cal—UC–Berkeley, that is. He'd gotten involved in a project to develop a drug that could . . . I don't remember exactly what it was . . . but it had something to do with multiple sclerosis. But I do remember that he hadn't told Dori he was taking on an additional research project—especially one that didn't involve UVA—which really upset her. Webb was her protégé. She didn't want someone in California poaching him, and she definitely didn't want him going rogue, and then maybe using her lab to conduct research on some potentially groundbreaking drug without her involvement, either. Credit where credit was due—with her."

Vanessa rattled the ice cubes in her glass. "So," she said, "by this time Elena was getting fed up with covering for him in Charlottesville, plus she felt she wasn't getting any recognition or acknowledgment of the extra work she'd taken on for him. And while Webb was gone—" She gave me a false, brittle smile. "Jamie and Elena slept together. Webb found out and went . . . oh, God, he just went absolutely nuts. It didn't do much for my relationship with Jamie, either. I'd just learned I was pregnant. He was in love with someone else."

She stood up and her boot hit the floor with a dull thud. "Would you like a splash of bourbon in your iced tea?"

"No, thanks. I've got to drive back to Atoka. You go ahead, though."

"I think I will. Otherwise I'll probably never get through telling you all this."

She clumped across the room to a long, low cabinet with an

enormous flat-screen television sitting on top and opened one of the doors. The bottle of bourbon was about a third full. Vanessa poured a liberal amount into her iced tea and I knew this wasn't the first time she'd done this.

She came back and joined me on the sofa. "Where was I?"

"Jamie slept with Elena."

"Right." She took a swig of her bourbon-laced tea. "It got worse. Webb accused Mick and Jamie of fudging some of their results in the data they'd been compiling for him. It was extra work, outside of their classwork, but UVA has an incredibly strict honor code. No cheating, lying, or stealing. A violation of any one of those—it's called a single-sanction rule—is an automatic expulsion. You're tried before a board of your peers. It's one of the oldest university honor codes in the country and, believe me, you don't want to go up in front of that board."

"Were they cheating? Had they faked their results?"

Vanessa squirmed and looked like she wanted to ask if she could take the Fifth. "Jamie was working flat out. He, Mick, and Elena were all Lawnies. It was their senior year. The three of them had so much going on. Lawnies were the elite; they were expected to take part in campus activities, be community leaders, set examples by their behavior. One of the conditions for accepting a room on the Lawn is that you agree to leave your door open as often as possible because of all the historic interest in Thomas Jefferson's original 'Academical Village.' The place is a UNESCO World Heritage site, for God's sake. Loads of people come to visit."

Though I hadn't attended UVA, I'd been there often enough to visit friends to know that the private rooms on the redbrick colonnaded Lawn were awarded only to students who had out-standing academic records and were considered by the faculty and staff to be leaders and individuals of high moral character. A charge of cheating would be a devastating blow to any student at the university. For a Lawnie, it was a death sentence. You were letting down centuries of tradition.

"So is that a yes, they did cheat?" I asked. "You didn't really say." Actually, it sounded like she was trying to make excuses for them.

She drank more iced tea and made a face as if it had turned bitter. "They ran out of time, so yes, they faked some of the results, extrapolating from what they already knew to be true. If Webb turned them over to the Honor Board, they'd both be expelled right before graduation."

"But he didn't turn them in."

"No."

"Because . . . ?"

"Because he disappeared that night and no one ever saw him again. Ever saw him alive, that is."

I set my glass on the ring-scarred coffee table and folded my hands in my lap. "What happened?"

She looked at me as though I'd just opened the box that let trouble out into the world.

"We were at Dori's for dinner. The usual Friday night drinking began. That night, though, Dori was pissed off with all of us and said we were squabbling like a bunch of kinder-gartners. She was so upset she left the house and drove off. After she was gone, things really went downhill. Webb and Elena were in the kitchen shouting at each other, and when Jamie stepped in to try to calm Webb down, Webb picked up a knife and went for Jamie." Her eyes grew wide at the memory. "It was crazy. Fortunately he was so drunk he missed, and by then Mick showed up and managed to get the knife away from Webb, although he ended up getting cut himself. It was a mess, blood everywhere. I bandaged his hand with the red bandanna Elena was wearing in her hair." Vanessa finished her iced tea and sat there, staring into her empty glass as though telling me this story had exhausted her.

I suspected this was the first time in a very long time that she had recounted what happened that night in so much detail. But I was also fairly certain that it lived in her head like a worm that had bored into her memory and hadn't ever given her a day's peace of mind. I wondered if Sasha knew this grisly tale about her father and guessed she might not.

"I know this must be hard for you, but I'd like to hear all of it," I said.

"I've told you this much so . . ." Vanessa shrugged. "Webb left . . . on foot. He just went crashing out of the house. Everyone disappeared after that. We all went our own ways—no one was talking to anyone else, the atmosphere was so volatile, like we were all ready to explode—sleeping on our own in different bedrooms. Jamie and I were barely speaking since I'd just found out about Elena. The next morning I had terrible morning sickness, and when I came downstairs to the kitchen, the only person there was Elena. Mick was upstairs sleeping, but Jamie had left sometime during the night. We had no idea where Dori was. Elena and I were on dreadful terms by that point. Somehow we managed to clean up without killing each other, and then Elena woke up Mick and she drove his car back to Grounds—campus, that is—because his hand was bothering him. He'd put another bandage on it to replace Elena's scarf, but you could still see where the cut had bled through."

"Then what?"

Vanessa shrugged. When she spoke, I could tell it was an effort to finish the story. "Webb didn't show up all day. He lived in the Range, the graduate student rooms on the other side of the Lawn. You have to compete for those rooms as well—be an exceptional student, a leader, involved in the university, that sort of thing. Anyway, Mick and Jamie went and checked out his room and Elena checked the lab, but it looked like he hadn't been to either place. By Sunday morning, everyone started getting really worried so Elena went to the head of security, who called the Charlottesville police." She stood up so abruptly that her boot whacked the coffee table and my drink glass rattled.

I reached out and grabbed it.

"Wait here," Vanessa said. "Would you like more iced tea?"

I wasn't going anywhere. Not now. "Yes, please."

She left the room and returned a moment later with a file folder, which she handed to me. "You may as well read these. It'll save a lot of time explaining everything. I'll get our iced teas."

I picked up the folder. The top article was a fragile, yellowed story from the *Charlottesville Daily Progress* with the headline "Massive Manhunt for Missing UVA Student." I skimmed it. After an intensive three-day search involving hundreds of volunteers including his fellow students, Webster

Landau's body had been discovered in a shallow grave in a wooded area on the farm of Dr. Theodora Upshur, the chair of the biochemistry department at UVA and Landau's dissertation adviser. Cause of death was blunt force trauma to the head. The last time he'd been seen . . . etc., etc., etc.

The next article said that twenty-five-year-old Taurique Youngblood, an African-American resident of the nearby town of Ivy, who had done yard work for Professor Upshur, had been arrested after he tried to use a credit card belonging to Webster Landau to buy cigarettes and Twinkies at a 7-Eleven. Webb Landau's bloodstained backpack was also discovered in a trash can in Youngblood's backyard. Youngblood claimed he had no idea how the backpack got there, but he had an arrest record for two instances of robbery and assault. Later, the police found Webb's car and Taurique's fingerprints on a jack in the trunk—possibly the murder weapon—which Taurique claimed were there because he'd helped Webb change a tire a few days earlier.

The rest of the articles followed the logical progression of Taurique Youngblood being charged with the murder of Webb Landau. The case had attracted national attention because of its sensational nature—white PhD student with a brilliant career ahead of him in science brutally murdered by a local black man who'd been so audacious and heartless as to use his victim's credit card to buy snacks and cigarettes.

It didn't take a jury long to find Taurique Youngblood guilty and even less time for the sentence to be handed down: death by lethal injection. A lot of people think of Texas or Oklahoma when they think of states that still execute their worst convicts, but the Commonwealth of Virginia is right up there—we're third in the number of prisoners we've put to death. Plus we got an early start: The first execution in the future United States took place in Virginia in 1608 at the Jamestown Settlement, a hanging for treason.

I went through the articles one more time, stopping to look at the photos. A candid of Elena, Mick, and Jamie, all so much younger, standing on the edge of a forest as they got ready to participate in the search for a friend who'd gone missing the night of an alcohol-fueled party that they'd all attended. It was hard to read their expressions in the grainy black-and-white photo. Scared? Guilty? Did one of them—or all of them—already know where to find Webb's body? I couldn't tell. The photo of Dori—Dr. Theodora A. Upshur—was her university head shot. Serious, studious, unsmiling, with shoulder-length dark hair, horn-rimmed glasses, and a distinctive beauty mark above her upper lip. The surprise was Webb's picture. After what Vanessa had told me about him, I'd pictured a short, slightly doughy guy with pale, soft skin and glasses with thick Coke-bottle lenses who spent all his time indoors in a laboratory. Webb looked nothing like that. Instead he was handsome and clean cut, with a mesmerizing smile, intelligent eyes, and the lean, well-muscled body of an athlete. Someone who stared at the camera with the cocky self-confidence that showed he knew that when the gods handed out the gifts and talents, he'd been abundantly blessed.

The police booking photo of Taurique Youngblood, looking disheveled and wild haired, with a bug-eyed, confused stare as if he didn't understand why he was being photographed, was disturbing. It was the kind of picture that screamed *guilty* every time you saw it in the newspaper. *Get this guy off the street. He's dangerous.*

I closed the folder and set it on the coffee table, haunted by the photo of Taurique. By then Vanessa had returned with our teas and was seated on the sofa watching me read.

"You said Jamie left Dori's house the night Webb disappeared," I said. "Where did he go? He was the only one—except Webb—who wasn't there the next morning. And Dori, too, of course."

"Jamie said he walked back to town and had a couple of beers in one of the bars on the Corner," she said. I knew the Corner. It was a stretch of bars, nightclubs, restaurants, and shops directly across from the main campus, a big student hangout. "Then he went back to his room on the Lawn and slept off the booze." Before I could ask, she said, "A couple of people said they saw him. So he had witnesses."

Now we were getting to the come-to-Jesus part of our conversation. The MedicAlert bracelet wasn't Jamie's, and Vanessa had been shocked and upset to see it, telling me I shouldn't have it. As far as I was concerned, that whittled down the list to just one person.

"Whose MedicAlert bracelet is this?" I asked. "It's Webb's, isn't it?"

"Yes."

"How did Jamie get hold of it?"

"I have no idea."

"Do you have any idea who killed Webb Landau?" I asked. "Assuming it wasn't Taurique Youngblood, that is."

"No." She gave me a defiant look. "I know I didn't."

"That's a big endorsement for the others who were with him that last night," I said. "Jamie, Mick, Elena. Even Dr. Upshur, Dori."

"Don't judge me. You have no idea what those three days were like while we were looking for him." Her anger flashed unexpectedly. "My God, we were all so tense we were barely eating and sleeping. I was sure I was going to lose the baby from all the stress. I kept throwing up . . . in fact I wished I would lose it because it would have solved so many problems. It was April, nearly the end of term, and everyone had papers due, exams to study for . . . graduation coming up." She clapped a hand over her mouth and looked horrified. "Oh, my God, I can't believe I told you that. Sasha can't ever know what I said about wishing I'd lose my baby. I love her more than any- thing in the world. I'd do anything for her."

I figured Sasha wasn't aware of this turbulent part of her parents' history. "I won't say anything," I said, "but I'm con- fused. I thought Taurique was sentenced to die by lethal injec- tion thirty years ago. Why would Jamie want me to find him and ask his forgiveness now?"

"Because he's still alive. His lawyer keeps filing appeals, so his case has gone through the entire Virginia courts system. Now it's in some federal court and that could drag on for years. His lawyer claims Taurique's Sixth Amendment rights were violated, that he never got a fair trial with an impartial jury."

Vanessa had given me a long answer to the obvious ques- tion. What I wanted to know was something different. So I asked it.

"Do you think Jamie killed Webb? He certainly had a

motive. Webb was going to turn him in for cheating, and that could have gotten him expelled just weeks before he graduated."

"Mick was as guilty as Jamie was," she said, avoiding my eyes.

Once again she hadn't answered the question. "What happened to Professor Upshur? Dori."

Vanessa shrugged. "She quit her job, left the university, and no one ever heard from her again. Eventually the farm was sold to a young couple, who turned it into a vineyard. You probably know it—Skyline Winery."

"I do," I said. "I know the owners, but I had no idea about its history."

"I always thought . . ." Vanessa began and then stopped herself.

"What?"

"That Dori was a little in love with Webb. I mean, there was a big age difference between them and she was his dissertation adviser, but . . ."

"You said she disappeared that night because she was so upset with all of you. Do you think she could have murdered Webb?"

"No one knew her farm as well as she did. He was buried in the middle of the woods. You'd really have to know your way around to find the place."

That sounded like a yes. "So maybe Jamie knew who really killed Webb. Dori Upshur."

"It's possible. Good Lord, anything's possible. You're talking thirty years ago. Memories get fuzzy after all that time."

I'd bet no memory got fuzzy for Taurique Youngblood on death row. My money would be on him reliving those days over and over and over again so that he could tell the story backward if he needed to.

"Why would Elena and Garrett Bateman tell me 'Rick' was a donor who gave a lot of money to Jamie's presidential campaign?" I asked. "Do you think they knew Jamie was talking about Taurique Youngblood?"

"You'd have to ask them. Maybe there was someone named Rick and he and Jamie did have a falling-out . . . though it does seem hard to believe the two of them wouldn't have reached the same conclusion I did. And now they're trying to protect Jamie. Keep you from asking questions about things they'd prefer not to have come up." She shook her head. "Garrett Bateman. I'd nearly forgotten about him."

"You know him?"

"Of course I do. Garrett and Jamie were fraternity brothers. Jamie was Garrett's big brother. Garrett worshipped the ground Jamie walked on. He would have done anything for Jamie."

"Would he cover up for Jamie now if he thought he was guilty of murder?"

She gave me a steely look that unnerved me. "He wouldn't think twice about it. He's Jamie's right-hand business partner, you know. Or was."

The MedicAlert bracelet lay on the coffee table where Vanessa had set it down. "I'm surprised neither Elena nor Garrett said anything when you showed them that bracelet," she went on. "They must have known it was Webb's, the same as I did."

"I didn't show it to them," I said. "I didn't have it with me when I stopped by Elena's place and I forgot to mention it."

"Are you saying they don't know you have it?"

"That's right. I gave it to Sasha figuring she'd give it to Elena, but she gave it back to me. Instead she called you and here I am."

Vanessa sat back on the sofa and folded her arms across her chest. "Well, well, well. You do realize you've got a key piece of missing evidence that's part of a murder investigation that put a man on death row? Anybody who cares about Jamie Vaughn would sure hate to have that bracelet resurface after all this time because it's only going to make Jamie look like he had something to do with Webb Landau's murder."

"I can see that."

She gave me a conspiratorial look. "Right now you and I are the only two people who know who it really belongs to. You could just toss it in a Dumpster somewhere or get rid of it some other way and that would be the end of it. Or leave it with me. I'd dispose of it."

"I suppose I could, couldn't I?"

She leaned forward, and before she could do anything, I picked up the bracelet and slipped it in my pocket.

"But you're not going to do that, are you?" she said.

"I don't think so."

"Why? Why make trouble after all these years? Taurique Youngblood had already been arrested for robbery and assault. He was no Boy Scout."

She had turned the tables and now suddenly I was a troublemaker. I gave her a clear-eyed look and she flinched.

"Taurique is on death row for murder," I said. "He says he's not guilty and obviously there are judges who believe him enough to keep postponing his execution."

"Don't do this," she said. "You don't have to. You'll destroy Sasha if you do. No one will thank you for it."

"I made your daughter's father a promise before he died that I would ask Taurique Youngblood to forgive him."

"You don't know what you're getting into." Her voice turned sharp with anger and frustration.

"No, I don't. But now I know there are two people I can't let down. Jamie Vaughn." I looked her in the eye. "And Taurique Youngblood."

Eleven

Vanessa Pensiero and I didn't part company on the best of terms. In fact, I had barely closed the gate at the entrance to her yard when George came bounding out of the house, barking furiously and scaring the hell out of me. He stopped at the gate, panting and showing his big teeth while he watched me on the other side of it.

I said, "Good doggy, you just stay right there," a couple of times as I made my way to the Jeep without taking my eyes off him. Then I got in the car and cursed Vanessa. She'd let George out on purpose.

There might be no love lost between her and Elena, but I wondered if, after our tense conversation, Jamie's first wife might call his second wife and fill her in on our little chat. Of course if she did that, she'd also be ratting out Sasha, who was the one who set up the meeting. I really hoped Vanessa would say nothing, that using George to vent her anger on me for stirring up the past would be enough.

My GPS got me out of the Lewis Mountain neighborhood and back on Route 29. As soon as I left the strip mall traffic congestion behind and 29 became a pretty country road again, I called Kit and told her about Jamie's bracelet and my visit with Vanessa Pensiero.

Kit was sucking on a drink through a straw, probably finishing her lunchtime Diet Coke—I could hear the gurgling noise that meant she was at the bottom with only ice left—and then she banged the cup down. After that all I could hear was the lightning-fast clicking of her computer keys.

"Taurique . . . spell it again?" she said.

I did.

More clicking. "Yup, here it is. We covered it in the *Trib*. The search for Webster Landau and the arrest and trial of Taurique Youngblood." Silence on her end because I knew she was reading.

"Talk to me," I said finally. "Do any of the articles mention Jamie and the others? Elena, Mick Dunne, Vanessa?"

"There's a lot of stuff to go through," she said, "including a bunch of trials and appeals. Why don't we meet when you get back here and I'll have everything printed out for you? Plus I'll have read all of it by then."

"Any surprises?"

"Yes," she said. "But probably not what you're thinking. Now that Jamie's dead, my source has dried up. No more envelopes left at the bureau with my name on them."

"I wonder why."

"I've been trying to figure that out myself," she said. "Maybe *because* Jamie's dead. Now that you just told me about Webb Landau and Taurique Youngblood being convicted as

his killer, I'm wondering if it's because dead men tell no tales—
Jamie. Because it sounds like he had a tale he wanted to tell.
Or a wrong he wanted to right."

"I don't get it. Why would that make someone stop sending
you information about Jamie's campaign's financial problems?"

"Because there's no more reason to. I bet my source also
knew about Webb's murder and the fact that Jamie was trou-
bled by Taurique Youngblood being on death row. Now Jamie's
not going to talk. It makes sense, don't you think?"

"I guess so." It seemed logical that the two would be related, but it still bothered me. Why, after all these years, was
the murder of Webb Landau coming up again? "I should be
back by three. Where do you want to meet?"

"It's a nice day," she said. "How about the Goose Creek
Bridge?"

"The last time you were there was with Jamie."

"I know," she said. "It just feels like the right place to have
this conversation. Because you know what else I think?"

"Someone else knew Jamie was upset, and that person
doesn't want the murder of Webb Landau brought up again,"
I said. "And unlike Jamie, he or she is willing to let the wrong
man do time for killing him."

"Exactly."

"You realize you're talking about Jamie's family and closest friends, Kit. People he loved the most. Elena Vaughn, Mick
Dunne, and Garrett Bateman."

"I'd also add Vanessa Pensiero and the professor, Dori
Upshur, to that list," she said. "And what about Jamie's kids?
Owen, Oliver . . . Sasha?"

"They weren't even born when Webb was murdered. And definitely not Sasha."

"Maybe one of the twins is trying to protect their father," she said. "Oops . . . my boss is waving at me. I'm being summoned. See you at the bridge at three."

We disconnected and I thought about our conversation as I headed north. Whatever happened, I knew one thing was true: The game was still afoot. It hadn't ended with Jamie's death.

MY NEXT CALL WAS to Quinn, who was in the barrel room cleaning barrels. A lot of people have the mistaken idea that owning a vineyard is glamorous and not really work because all we do is spend our days swilling wine and wandering through the vineyard admiring God's handiwork as the grapes ripen perfectly on their own before our eyes. Don't get me wrong. I love what I do, but it's true that what they say about the fastest way to make a small fortune owning a vineyard: You start with a large one.

And here's the other thing that's true: We are always, always doing everything we can to make sure our equipment is as clean as it can possibly be. Ninety-nine percent of what worries any winery about the business of growing grapes and making wine is that something in some part of the process is not sterile or becomes contaminated—a bottle, a barrel, a hose— and you end up with bacteria in your wine. So we are constantly cleaning, sanitizing, sterilizing, wiping down surfaces.

One way to clean barrels is by burning sulfur disks inside them, which kills bacteria, but Quinn and I had embraced the technology of using ozone, O_3, a pale blue gas with a pungent smell that occurs when oxygen and electricity interact. If you've ever smelled fresh, clean air after a thunderstorm, you've smelled ozone. It's also possible to fabricate. Ozone is a toxic, unstable, and dangerous gas, but at least you don't have to use sulfur, which leaves a flavor behind in the wine barrel.

"How's the barrel cleaning coming?" I asked.

"We should finish by tonight," he said. "Where are you? Are you coming home? How did it go with the first Mrs. Vaughn?"

"Madison County, not right away, and I might have made an enemy."

I heard a sound like air being let out of a tire. "You turned on the old Montgomery charm, huh? What happened?"

"It's a long story," I said, "that has to do with the murder of a friend of Jamie's when he was at UVA nearly thirty years ago. The *Trib* covered it, so I'm meeting Kit, who's going to give me copies of the articles. I'll be home after that."

"A murder?" he said. "Jesus, Lucie. Do you think it has something to do with Jamie's death?"

"I do. Right now the only people who know I know anything about this are you, Kit, and Vanessa Pensiero. I'd like to keep it that way as long as possible."

"In other words, don't say anything to Eli and Sasha."

"Right."

"Don't you think Vanessa will tell her daughter what you talked about?"

"I think she—and Elena and Mick Dunne and possibly Garrett Bateman—have covered this up for so long that I doubt she'd say anything now."

"Those three are involved, too?"

"Elena and Mick for sure. I don't know about Garrett, but it wouldn't surprise me if he was."

He let out a long, low whistle. "I don't have a good feeling about this," he said.

"I know," I said. "Me neither."

KIT AND I HAD been coming to the Goose Creek Stone Bridge since we were teenagers to talk over problems large and small, and—although alcohol was prohibited and downright illegal if you were underage—to drink unlabeled bottles of wine I used to filch from Jacques, our first winemaker. It wasn't until years later that I discovered Jacques had wised up to me and watered down the bottles he left for me to conveniently "find."

The bridge was one of the Civil War sites around here where you felt certain the spirits of the past still lingered, along with the slightly creepy feeling that there were eyes you could not see watching you from behind trees and through tangled vegetation. The road was now overgrown with bushes, brambles, and weeds, and by summer the honeysuckle would fill the air with its intoxicating sweet scent.

I arrived before Kit and parked my car next to the rusty old gate. Today it felt as if an eerie stillness had settled over the place; I sensed it immediately in the warm breeze that stirred the tall grass and rustled the trees and bushes, as though a gust of wind had blown through earlier and left behind dust or sand that didn't belong here. Something foreign. Alien.

I got out of the Jeep and started walking down the dirt and gravel path toward the bridge and Goose Creek. A few invisible birds called to each other in the woods and a woodpecker rat-a-tatted on a nearby tree. But the overwhelming silence was so unnatural and unsettling that I kept glancing over my shoulder, which spooked me even more.

In just over two months it would be the anniversary of the Battle of Upperville, which had been fought here. Maybe that was what I was sensing: old ghosts. Or maybe something lingering from Kit's meeting with Jamie right here less than forty-eight hours before his fiery death. I heard a car engine on Lemmons Bottom Road and saw, with some relief, a flash of fire-engine red that was Kit's new SUV. I went back to meet her.

Today she was dressed in a bright yellow sweater and black jeans, along with faux-alligator-skin ankle boots. A file folder stuck out of her *Washington Tribune* tote bag, which I guessed contained the collection of newspaper articles she had printed out for me on Webb Landau's death and Taurique Youngblood's trial.

She gave me an air kiss and a quick hug and we walked together to the bridge. "That trial," she said, "was something else. Wham, bam, thank you ma'am. It didn't take them long to try Taurique and for a jury to convict him of murder. I talked to Bobby about it, and he asked for a set of copies of these stories so he could read them as well."

"Is Bobby working on the investigation into Jamie's crash?" I asked.

We had reached the bridge. Kit set down her tote and the two of us sat side by side, our legs dangling over the stone parapet, looking down on Goose Creek as we had done so often in the past. With all the rain the day before yesterday, the creek had swelled over its banks so that the water now flowed swiftly, sparkling in patches of afternoon sunlight that filtered through the green-tinged trees.

Kit frowned. "You know Bobby. He can't really talk about what he's doing, but I'm not entirely sure there is an active investigation anymore."

"What do you mean?"

"I . . . uh think it's going to be ruled an accident. You didn't hear that from me, okay? My marriage might be in jeopardy otherwise."

"An accident? Just like that? That's *crazy*." I gave the word all the withering outrage I could summon. Too many secrets. Too many things being swept under carpets. Two days ago. Thirty years ago. What was going on? Was this a conspiracy to protect . . . who?

Kit held up her hands in mock surrender. "Hey, don't shoot the messenger. Come on, Luce."

"Sorry. But you can't be serious."

"This might surprise you, but Bobby isn't the big enchilada who runs the sheriff's department. He doesn't get to call all the shots. He takes orders from someone, too, you know."

"So the ruling of accidental death is coming from higher up?"

"I didn't say that. I also didn't not say that. But one thing weighing heavily in this is that it was a single-vehicle crash when the roads were wet and slick. And there was no note or letter. Most suicides want to explain why they did it. So can we stop right here, please? You get the drift, okay?"

I did. "So who is calling the shots?"

"The answer to that is above Bobby's pay grade." She made a zipping motion across her lips. "Let it go."

"I can't. I promised Jamie I'd find Taurique and ask for his forgiveness."

"Do you know what it would take to get to that guy? He's in a maximum-security prison in southern Virginia. You can't just waltz in there and smack down your driver's license and let them wand you. You'd need clearances up the ying-yang before you could go near the place, and then he'd have to agree to see you."

"So I'd get the clearances. As for seeing me, do you think Taurique might have other plans? Too busy to fit me in?"

"Lucie, come on. Besides, what are you going to say to him? That Jamie asked for his forgiveness before he died—and then what?"

"I don't know."

"That MedicAlert bracelet doesn't prove anything. It could have fallen off Webb Landau's wrist anytime—there's no chain of custody after all these years, or even any forensic evidence that would be useful. The bracelet doesn't prove that Jamie killed Webb Landau or even that he knew who did."

"It at least casts doubt on Taurique's guilt."

"Says you. Jamie's dead. Look, if you push too hard on this, it could boomerang back on you. You and that wall Jamie hit have some common history, as I don't need to remind you. Don't go there."

"What are you getting at?"

She shrugged. "Look at Pippa O'Hara. She's already tried to tie you and Jamie together because you both had accidents in the exact same spot. He died and you—" She paused and I knew she caught herself before she said it.

"Became disabled."

Her cheeks flushed pink. "All right, became disabled. So you've got some emotional baggage here and maybe you can't be objective."

"That sounds just like what Elena Vaughn and Garrett Bateman said to me yesterday," I said. "Are you telling me it's a political decision to say the crash was an accident? Elena and Garrett are putting pressure on people who will determine how this goes down? Otherwise, just imagine the headlines and the tabloid speculation. 'Has Jamie Vaughn Always Been Suicidal?' or 'What Demons Drove Jamie Vaughn to the Brink?' or 'Jamie, We Hardly Knew Ye.' The guy we almost trusted with the nuclear codes."

"Okay, okay," she said. "But does it matter? It won't change anything. Jamie's still dead."

I stared at her. "For Taurique Youngblood it might matter a hell of a lot. He'd get his life back."

She gave me an exasperated look. "If Jamie had any new evidence or wanted to make a confession about Webb Landau's death, he picked a hell of a way to go about it. Crash into a wall and deputize you to tell Taurique he's sorry. What good is that going to do anyone?"

"There's still the MedicAlert bracelet."

"Which means nothing," she said in a patient voice. "Look, I read those articles. It was an open-and-shut case as far as they were concerned. Taurique got caught using Webb's credit card, Webb's backpack was in his trash can, and his prints were all over a tire jack handle, which was found in Webb's car. The handle also happened to fit the bill for the murder weapon."

I slid away from her on the parapet and turned so I could get a better look at her, make sure she had not morphed into some stranger I didn't recognize. "Which isn't the same as murder, Kit. And don't tell me you think race didn't enter into what happened to Taurique. Virginia. Southern Virginia. Thirty years ago. What about all those appeals?"

"Not one court has overturned the verdict."

"So far. I think there's something else, something more. Jamie did, too."

"And he let it fester all these years until just now? All of a sudden his conscience bothered him?" She looked at me as if I'd just admitted to believing in Santa Claus or the tooth fairy. "Okay," she said, sounding weary. "If you want to see this thing through, then there's someone you should talk to. There's a group called the St. Leonard Project that has an office in the basement of St. Patrick's Catholic Church in downtown D.C. not far from the *Trib* building. They're one of many groups that work with prisoners who claim they've been wrongly incarcerated based on corrupted evidence, false testimony, the new availability of DNA, things like that."

"They've taken on Taurique's case?" I asked, sounding hopeful.

"That's right."

"Have you talked to them?"

"Not me," she said. "A colleague of mine in Metro has. I put their phone number on a Post-it in the folder of articles I copied for you, if you want to call them."

"I will. And thanks."

"Don't mention it." She made a face as if she'd just swallowed something nasty. "Really. Don't. I wish you'd just let it go."

"Why are you so upset about this?" I said. "You still don't think confronting Jamie about his business problems the other day pushed him over the edge, do you? You're not feeling guilty about that?"

"I don't think it helped his state of mind when he got into his car that last day."

"It's not your fault, Kit. Are you giving up on the story you were writing?"

"It's on hold temporarily because of the accident."

"Is that your decision?"

"My boss's."

"And if it were your decision?"

"It isn't." She pulled the folder with the copies of the newspaper articles out of her tote and handed it to me. "Bedtime reading," she said, changing the subject. "Call me after you've read it all and let me know what you think."

"I will. What about you? You've read everything already. You really think Taurique was guilty, don't you?"

"The Charlottesville police were under a lot of pressure to wrap up this case as soon as possible. You had parents calling the university asking if their kids were safe, kids freaking out, the story—because it was so sensational—making national news, giving Charlottesville and the university some very unflattering publicity." Kit shrugged. "Taurique got caught red-handed with Webb's credit card. Then there's the rest of the evidence, and as far as the police—and the jury—were concerned, it was an open-and-shut case."

"I know all that. And you keep avoiding the question."

She raised her eyebrows and shook her head, still exasperated with me. "You know one thing I've learned since I married Bobby? The saying 'Where you stand depends on where you sit' is so true. You wonder how the other guy can be so dumb or wrong until something happens and you *are* the other guy. Now I'm a detective's wife and I see things through that filter. When you get someone like Taurique Youngblood as a suspect in a murder case, a guy who rings all the bells, then you stop looking. Nobody says, 'Hey, let's keep going and see if we find someone else.' They say, 'We're done,' and move on to the next case."

I knew she was right. About almost everything. If Jamie Vaughn suddenly had a crisis of conscience because he'd murdered Webb Landau rather than be expelled from school for cheating weeks before graduation, then maybe that's why he'd crashed into the vineyard wall and killed himself. Because he couldn't face admitting to Taurique Youngblood that he'd let an innocent man go to jail for a crime he'd committed.

And now Jamie had left me to finish the job he couldn't handle. Ask Taurique Youngblood to forgive him. Kit was trying to warn me to stay away, not to get involved. There was a missing part of this puzzle that I still didn't understand: Why now? What had happened to push Jamie over the edge to revisit a murder that had happened so long ago?

If I could figure out what it was, then maybe some of this would start to make sense.

Twelve

My plan after Kit and I split up at the Goose Creek Bridge was to go home, start reading Kit's collection of articles, and call the St. Leonard Project if it wasn't already too late in the day. I didn't know whether a group like that kept nine-to-five business hours; somehow I thought their altruism would involve late nights, gallons of coffee, and volunteers who occasionally crashed on cots in the office so they could keep their crusade going, keep fighting the good fight for justice against a system that had grievously wronged someone and sent an innocent person to jail. Instead I got no farther than the end of Lemmons Bottom Road when Quinn called to say there was a change of plans for the evening.

"I made reservations for us for dinner at the Inn," he said. "Persia's taking care of Hope and Zach. He came home from preschool with Hopie this afternoon. Persia's fixing spaghetti with homemade Bolognese sauce for them. Eli said Sasha wanted to talk to you about your visit with her mother, so we figured it was best to do that without the kids around. Eli said they could meet us for drinks and then they'll take off."

"Do you know if Sasha talked to her mother?" I asked.

"She did."

"Do you have any idea what Vanessa said to her?"

"As a matter of fact, I do. She said—and I quote—'Get Lucie to tell you what we talked about.'"

Great. Now there were two people who had passed the buck to me. First Jamie, then Vanessa.

"What are you going to tell her?" he asked.

"If she really wants to know, I'm going to tell her something her mother kept from her all these years. The truth," I said. "That her father got caught cheating at UVA and was one of the last people to see the friend who planned to turn him in before the guy was found murdered on the property of a university professor. And that Jamie asked forgiveness of the man whose now on death row accused of that crime."

Quinn groaned. "It's a good thing we're drinking," he said. "This is going to be a hell of an evening."

THE GOOSE CREEK INN sits tucked away in a bend on Sam Fred Road on the outskirts of Middleburg. If you are not expecting it, the half-timbered building surrounded by flowering cherry trees, dogwoods, and magnolias can surprise you, especially after dark when it suddenly appears out of nowhere, softly bathed in floodlights and fairy lights woven through the trees like an enchanted cottage in the middle of a forest. At this time of year with the trees in bloom, the whitewashed building looks as if it's enveloped by a pink-and-white cloud and is so lovely it can take your breath away.

I had gone home so Quinn and I could drive together in one car, plus it gave me time to start reading Kit's articles aloud to him. The stories about the intensive search for Webb Landau included interviews with Jamie, Mick, and Elena, all sounding frantic with worry, as well as an appeal from his parents, and a longer interview with Dori Upshur about what a brilliant student he was. Just as in the Charlottesville papers, the headlines grew bleaker as the assumption shifted from Webb being a missing person—possibly injured—to the new reality that he was likely the victim of foul play. The party at Dori Upshur's farm where things got out of hand had been on a Friday; by Saturday, as Vanessa told me this morning, his friends had checked the laboratory where he worked as well as his room on the Range and found no clues anywhere. By Sunday, the Charlottesville police were called in and the search for Webster Landau began in earnest.

Once again I couldn't help staring at the photographs. Especially that mug shot of Taurique and the golden boy photos of Webb.

"Hey," Quinn said. "Earth to Lucie. Are you going to finish the article you were reading? You keep staring at that picture of Webb Landau. What is it?"

"Sorry. Nothing. I just didn't expect him to look like that."

"Like what?" He glanced at the photo before flicking his eyes back to the road.

"To be so good-looking. Vanessa never mentioned that. Elena was Webb's girlfriend, but she cheated on him with Jamie, which is what started the argument that night," I said.

Quinn shrugged. "So the guy's a handsome hunk and he's brilliant. Maybe someone was jealous of him, and his murder had to do with envy. Get a rival out of the way."

"The only person who fits that description is Jamie. He wanted Webb's girlfriend and ultimately he married Elena after he split up with Vanessa."

"It could be a professional rivalry," he said. "What about the professor? Dori? Didn't Vanessa say she thought Dori had a crush on him, but she was also annoyed that he was working on some research project he didn't share with her?"

"If she had a crush on him, then why kill him?"

"Unrequited love."

"Maybe," I said. "I wonder what happened to her."

Quinn pulled in to the parking lot. "Come on, it's showtime. Maybe Sasha knows something about this already, something she picked up as a kid." He gave me a knowing look. "Or maybe her dad confided something to her right before he died, dropped some hint that she didn't realize was important at the time."

A gust of wind stirred up dry leaves under our feet and riffed through the wind chimes hanging from the branch of a Japanese maple in the center of a small courtyard. The chimes gave off a musical sound that reminded me of a waterfall.

"I didn't think of that," I said. "You could be right."

He slipped his arm around me as we walked up to the front door. "That," he said, sounding smug, "is why you have me around."

Inside, the Inn smelled, as it always did, of the fragrant aromas of cooking. One of the many reasons the Goose Creek Inn was so popular and well loved was that dining here was like

THE VINEYARD VICTIMS   169

eating at the home of a good friend who was not only a fabulous cook but also always remembered your drink preference
or that you liked butter for your homemade baguette or your
salad dressing on the side. I got a friendly kiss on both cheeks
from the maître d', who also had a warm greeting for Quinn
before he informed us that Dominique had taken care of us,
reserving a table for four in one of the smaller dining rooms
where we'd have more privacy. Sasha and Eli were already
waiting for us.

My brother stood up when a waiter led us to our table and
brushed my cheek with a kiss. In a breath so soft I could barely
hear him he said, "Take it easy, okay? She's pretty fragile."

I squeezed his arm to let him know that I got his message
before I leaned over and gave Sasha a hug. Quinn hugged her,
too, and we all sat down. Eli and Sasha had already ordered
drinks—Chardonnay for her and a Sam Adams for him. Quinn
and I told the waiter that we'd have the same, so as not to pro-
long the awkward interlude before we got down to it.

There wasn't any good way to start this conversation, especially after Eli's warning that Sasha was still in rough shape.
Until I finished reading all of Kit's newspaper articles, I already
knew I wasn't going to share them with her or my brother, so
I'd left the folder in the car. One thing at a time. Maybe the
best way was just to start talking and see what happened.

Sasha was a physical therapist with her own practice in a
historic building in downtown Leesburg, specializing in patients with neurological disorders, some of the toughest cases
to rehabilitate. She also worked with children, who were some
of the most heartbreaking cases. Eli told me that she had two
long-term young patients whose parents owed her for hours

and hours of sessions, but when she found out they couldn't afford to pay, she figured out a barter system—one of them had an uncle who did all her yard work and the other took care of her website and advertising—plus she wrote off some of their debt when it became too onerous.

I wondered if someone with Sasha's mental toughness, not to mention the physical strength she needed to manipulate patients—lifting and moving limbs or people who were dead weight—could be as delicate as Eli seemed to think she was. She told me once that she had gone into physical therapy as a wounded healer: someone whose own injuries—usually invisible and psychological—were made better or whole because she helped others. A bitter divorce and an absent father met those criteria perfectly. That she had the courage to reconcile with her father was, to me, another testament to how strong she really was.

"I met George today," I said to her. "And your mother."

Sasha's face cracked into a smile. "I hope she put him in the basement while you were there. He can be a bit rambunctious."

"Who's George?" Quinn asked.

"Mom's rottweiler," she said. "She adores him."

"We had iced tea with lavender and mint from her garden and honey from her beehive."

"Your mom has a rottweiler?" Quinn asked.

Sasha nodded, still smiling. "She does. And she loves gardening."

"One of these days I'd like to meet her," Eli said. "And, of course, George, too."

"You'll get a chance," Sasha said. "She told me today she's coming to Dad's funeral. She made her decision after talking to you, Lucie." To Eli and Quinn she added, "George will stay home with the pet sitter."

"We didn't discuss the wake or the funeral," I said. "But we talked a lot about the past, when your mom and dad and Elena and Mick Dunne were all students at UVA. Do you know much about those years?"

The waiter arrived with our drinks, along with a platter of crackers, cheeses, pâté, and black, garlicky olives. "Compliments of Dominique," he said. He lit the small votive candle on our table next to a bud vase with two pale pink tulips in it. "*Bon appétit.*"

After he left, Sasha said, "Mom was pretty bitter about Dad leaving us for Elena. It took her a long time to get over it."

It wasn't lost on me that she said "us." Vanessa had made it clear that Jamie had abandoned Sasha, too, for most of the time she was growing up.

"Then why is she coming to the funeral?" Quinn asked.

Sasha folded her hands on the table. "Closure. She's seen all the stories on television and the Internet about what a shrine his accident site has become. But she knows a different person and she needs to make peace with the past. That's what any funeral is about. Letting go."

Eli had been busy fixing Sasha a plate of crackers with cheese and pâté. He slid it over to her. "You need to eat something, Sash."

Make it better with comfort food, or try to. Eli really wanted to shield her from what was coming. Sasha flashed a sweet smile at him and then looked directly at me. "So, are you going to tell me what my mom told you?"

I cut my eyes over to my brother, and Sasha laid a hand on

his arm. "I heard what you said to Lucie, Eli. I love you, but you don't need to protect me. I can handle this. I need to know."

"Are you sure?" I asked.

"Positive."

Her face grew pale and her expression increasingly strained as I talked, but she didn't interrupt. Like I'd told Quinn, if she asked, I was going to tell her the unvarnished truth. But that didn't mean I wasn't aware that I was taking a sledgehammer to her world, the gossamer-filamented relationship she'd rewoven with her father. At least I knew how she must feel. So did Eli.

Leland, our father, had been a total washout as far as loving and caring for his three children was concerned. That job fell completely to our beloved mother. But that didn't mean it didn't open an old wound if someone maligned him in front of one of us or remembered him badly and let us know about it. There was something intensely primal about family relationships: You don't want someone you are related to by blood, genetics, heredity, and a common history to be bad or cruel. Or a murderer.

"I'm sorry, Sasha," I said when I was finished. "Really, really sorry."

Eli put his arm around her and pulled her close. "You okay?" he asked.

She let out a ragged breath and then seemed to steady herself. "I don't know. I need some time to . . . take all this in."

"I know it must be a shock," I said. "Right now neither Elena nor Garrett knows I have that MedicAlert bracelet, and they don't know any of this story . . . unless you or your mother told them."

"I didn't. And Mom won't say an unnecessary word to Elena." She looked up. "So if I got this right, my father feels guilty about Taurique Youngblood going to jail for the murder of Webb Landau. And it was the last thing he said before he died."

Her unspoken question lay there like a ticking bomb. Did he kill Webb?

"Maybe he knows who killed Webb and kept someone else's secret for all these years," I suggested.

"That's certainly possible," Eli spoke up. "I just don't think Jamie's guilty. It's not in his character."

It half sounded as if he were trying to convince us. Which was the problem: Deep down, everyone at this table wondered if Jamie did it. Including his daughter.

"Did he say anything or give you any hint that he was worried about something before he died?" I asked Sasha.

What I hadn't told her—or anyone else—was what Kit discovered: Jamie's real estate development company was massively in debt and he had used campaign funds for personal expenses, many checks written to Elena and the vineyard. Though as near as I could tell his financial problems seemed unrelated to what had happened thirty years ago.

Sasha picked up her wineglass and drained it. "Something was bothering my dad terribly. Not just that he lost the election, but something else. He was a good driver, you know," she said. "Sure he drove too fast, but he could navigate the roads around here with his eyes closed. I just don't understand how he could have lost control of his car like he did."

It was a question, not a statement. I owed her the truth on this as well.

"I'm not sure it was an accident," I said, and now she looked like she was about to cry. Eli pulled her tighter to him.

"Lucie—" he said in a warning voice.

"It's okay, Eli." Sasha brushed the back of her hand across her eyes. "I asked."

"Mick Dunne said your father was on antidepressants and he might have been drinking more than he should have," I said. "He probably shouldn't have been behind the wheel that day. I smelled alcohol on his breath, Sasha."

"That's so unlike him."

"If it's any comfort, I'm pretty sure the sheriff's department is going to rule it an accident," I said.

"Even so, I'm surprised that he was drinking before he got in the car. Dad was on his way here—to the Inn—to talk to your cousin about the Jefferson Dinner on Saturday night. He wouldn't show up drunk. I wonder if Webb Landau's death was what was on his mind." She looked pained. "I also wonder why it came up now, after so many years. Now that he's gone, I guess we won't find out."

"That's not entirely true," I said. "There's a nonprofit organization in Washington that is working on Taurique Youngblood's behalf, claiming he was wrongly convicted of killing Webb Landau. It's called the St. Leonard Project."

Eli's eyes focused on me like a laser and Sasha's head jerked up. "How'd you find that out?" Eli asked.

I gave him an unflinching gaze. "From Kit."

"So she knows about all this? Jesus, Lucie. She's a damn journalist." Eli sounded irritated, but it went beyond that. He and Kit had once dated and it had been serious, until a spectacular, acrimonious breakup that, even now, still festered between them.

"I thought I might give the St. Leonard Project a call and see if I can set up a meeting with whoever is working on the case," I said, ignoring the daggers in Eli's eyes that he was throwing my way. "I promised your father I'd do this, that I'd make sure someone told Taurique that Jamie asked for his forgiveness."

"You want to show them the bracelet?" Her voice had suddenly become toneless, and I nodded.

"Look, Luce, maybe we should just drop it," Eli said.

Quinn had been silent during this entire conversation, drinking his beer, his eyes darting between Eli, Sasha, and me. "Then Jamie's death would be for nothing," he said. "You can't do that. Everyone here knows it. It would be wrong."

Sasha's voice trembled. "What if he's a murderer? Then what?"

"Do you think he is?" Quinn asked her.

"No." She took a deep breath. "Dear God, I hope not."

"So if you walked away from this, let it go?" he asked. "Then what?"

She didn't answer. Then she said in a soft voice, "I couldn't live with myself."

"Sasha," I said, "let me talk to someone at the St. Leonard Project and see what they have to say, okay?"

"All right." She sounded resigned. "If I walk in there, it will attract a lot of attention to my dad. It's a different story if you do it."

"It's going to be okay, honey," Eli said. "You wait and see."

He kicked me under the table and I kicked him back. I

knew he wasn't happy about this one little bit. Especially my bringing Kit into it. If only he knew it was the other way around, but I wasn't going to say anything about Jamie's business problems just now.

"We should probably be going," Eli said, reaching for his wallet in his back pocket. "Time to get the kids."

"This is on us." Quinn waved a hand at him.

Sasha pushed back her chair to stand up, accidentally bumping into my cane where it had been propped against the back of my chair. It clattered to the ground, startling a waiter and another table of guests who'd just sat down.

"Sorry," Sasha and I said together.

"I should have left it somewhere else," I added.

She picked it up and leaned it against the wall. "One of these days, I want you to come see me. I know a surgeon who might be able to do something about your foot. Make it like new again. At the least we could work on your balance, straighten your gait, and help you walk better." She gave me a sharp look. "Promise me?"

"Sure," I said, but I knew I wasn't going to do it. It would be a cold day in hell before I let anyone take a knife to me again. Ever. I'd had enough surgeries just to get my bad foot to where it was now, and doctors who'd told me I'd never walk after the accident. What if I had more surgery and things turned out worse? It could happen. Then what?

She hugged me and said in my ear, "I've worked with clients who are a lot more stubborn than you are, so don't think you can get rid of me so easily. I'm trusting you with my father's memory, his legacy. The least you can do is have a little faith in me." She said in a louder voice for the benefit of the guys, "You'll keep me posted about the St. Leonard Project, right?"

"I will," I said.

"See you home," Eli said to Quinn and me. He cut me a look that said he still hadn't forgiven me, and I knew we'd talk about this later.

"Wait," I said. "I nearly forgot something. Yesterday when I talked to Elena and Garrett, they told me 'Rick' was a campaign donor with deep pockets who'd had a falling-out with Jamie. Mick Dunne told me the same thing. When I mentioned that to your mother, she said she couldn't believe they wouldn't make the connection that 'Tell Rick' was really 'Taurique' just like she had."

Eli's eyes narrowed. "So what are you saying?"

"You think they're hiding something," Sasha said, "don't you?"

"They've got a reason for not wanting the murder of Webb Landau to be brought up again," I said, and looked at Sasha. "Unlike your father, who seemed like he was trying to face his demons."

"Jesus," Eli said. "This just gets worse and worse. I don't have a good feeling about any of it."

Sasha's eyes met mine. "Unless you figure that the good news could be that maybe my father isn't a murderer. Instead it could be my stepmother or one of my dad's best friends." She shook her head. "Wow," she said in a voice heavy with irony, "wouldn't that be a lucky break?"

Thirteen

Quinn and I ordered dinner, though it turned out that neither of us had much of an appetite after that grim conversation.

"Do you think Jamie killed Webb?" Quinn asked. Our waiter had brought our entrées, Virginia rainbow trout for Quinn, Gâteau de Légumes Napoléon—roasted layered vegetables with tomato coulis—for me. Quinn had ordered a bottle of white Bordeaux to go with the meal. We barely touched our food, but we were doing a bang-up job with the Bordeaux.

"I hope he didn't do it."

"That's not a 'no.'"

"All of them had motives," I said. "Jamie and Mick were caught cheating and Webb threatened to turn them in, which guaranteed expulsion right before they graduated. Elena . . . I don't know . . . she slept with Jamie."

"So she'd kill Webb? She was his teaching assistant, remember? Besides, he'd be more likely to kill her for cheating

THE VINEYARD VICTIMS   179

on him. You told me that Vanessa said Webb practically went nuclear at that party. And that he went at Jamie with a knife."

"Okay, so scratch Elena off the list."

"What about the professor? Dori."

I set my fork down on my plate and thought about it. "You don't kill the goose that lays the golden egg. He was Dori's protégé."

"Who didn't seem very loyal if he was doing research on some multiple sclerosis drug he didn't tell her about. Plus he was working with someone at Berkeley as well."

"I still don't think that's enough of a reason to drive someone to murder. Unless there was more to this unrequited love thing that you brought up."

"There's still Taurique," Quinn said. "The occasional handyman gardener who worked for Dori Upshur. His fingerprints were on Webb's tire jack, he used Webb's credit card, and Webb's backpack was found in Taurique's trash. How much more damning evidence do you want?"

"I wonder what makes the St. Leonard Project believe he's innocent?" I said. "All of a sudden."

"I guess you'll find out," Quinn said, "won't you?"

WE DECIDED TO SKIP dessert and we'd asked our waiter to box up our barely touched dinners when Dominique walked into the small dining room. She caught my eye from the doorway.

"Dominique looks like she's headed our way." Quinn had noticed her, too. "You're not going to tell her anything, are you?"

"No. But I'm sure she's wondering about Sasha, how she's holding up. Plus she's probably already seen our names as late additions to the guest list for the Jefferson Dinner. She might be a bit curious about how we came up with forty thousand dollars."

By now, all the tables in the room were occupied, and the place had come alive with the pleasant buzz of conversations, the clink of china and silverware, and the occasional pop of a cork being pulled from a bottle of wine. Dominique took her time making her way across the room, stopping for a laugh and a chat with other guests, calling everyone by their first name. I'd bet good money ours was the only table where the topic of conversation had been murder and who, among our friends and neighbors, might have killed a man thirty years ago. Everyone else around us seemed so normal.

Her arrival coincided with the waiter showing up with our to-go boxes and a plastic bag with the Inn's logo on it. My cousin looked horrified.

"*Mon Dieu*," she said. "Was your meal as bad as that? You've eaten nothing."

"Of course not," I said in a rush. "It was fabulous as usual. We're taking it home because we need to get back to finish some . . . uh . . ."

"Work in the barrel room," Quinn said.

"That can't wait," I added.

She gave us a look like a teacher who'd just been told the dog ate our homework. Then she turned serious. "I'm sorry I haven't called or come by since Jamie's accident . . . I saw the pictures of the vineyard entrance on television, all the flowers and candles and photographs. *Quelle tragédie*. But ever since then we have been completely booked. I think it's the people who are coming to Atoka because they want to see where it happened, where he died, like it's some kind of pilgrimage. And there have been so many phone calls about the Jefferson Dinner, especially journalists. Can they cover the event now that it's going to be a dedication to Jamie's memory? I finally called Garrett Bateman, who told me to refer all the calls to him."

"Are you going to let in the press now?" I asked. "Some of the guests don't want to be named publicly since they donate to both political parties. Then there's whoever buys the Norton. That person or persons might not want any publicity, either."

She gave a weary shrug. "The fire marshal will close the place down if one more person sets foot in here that night. It will be the straw that cooked the golden goose. I told that to Garrett."

Even though my petite, diminutive cousin looked so fragile a strong gust of wind could blow her away, she had the stamina of a workhorse, the stubbornness of a mule, and the workaholic habits of the Energizer Bunny without an Off switch. Anything to do with the Goose Creek Inn came first. And in spite of twelve years in the United States, American idioms still baffled her. Get her upset or agitated and the English sometimes went completely out the window.

"We've been overrun with visitors, too," I said. "The same gawkers you get who feel like they need to physically be at the scene of the crash and then stop by for a glass or two of wine to make what they just saw easier to take. Eli's trying to find a stonemason who can start the repair work on the wall and the pillar once the funeral is over, so we can begin to get back to normal."

"Are you going to the funeral?" she asked.

Quinn and I nodded. "Are you?" he asked.

"I hope so." She blew out a breath that made her spiky bangs puff out. "This dinner is going to be something to pull off—all the special china and silverware and the menu. It's the day after the funeral, so I don't know if I'll be able to get away. Then, of course, there's the wine and all the logistics involved with the auction. Everything needs to be perfect."

"Apparently Jamie was on his way here to meet with you the day he . . . the day of the accident," I said. "Mick Dunne told me he wanted to discuss the Jefferson Dinner."

Quinn pulled out a chair. "Can you join us? There's still some wine."

Dominique perched on the edge of the seat, mobile phone in one hand, ready to take flight the instant someone needed her. "I can only stay a moment and no wine for me, thanks. But you're right. He called and arranged the meeting that morning. He said he had something to tell me."

Quinn and I exchanged glances. "Did he say why he wanted to see you?" he asked.

"To talk about the Norton. Not only the bottle we would offer for the tasting but also the two that are going to be auctioned afterward."

"What about them?" I said.

"I don't know. He didn't go into any detail."

"How did he seem?" I asked. "Was he upset?"

She thought for a moment. "I was in the kitchen so it was

hard to hear him. But now that you mention it, I thought he sounded agitated."

"Where is the Norton?" Quinn asked. "Here, I presume. Those bottles should have been moved from Jamie's wine cellar weeks ago so the sediment settles to the bottom again. And treated with kid gloves."

"The bottles have been here for two weeks," she said. "Jamie had a special case built that controls the temperature and humidity so it's the same as it was in his wine cellar. And of course, it doesn't let in any light. Oliver brought it over from Longview."

"Longview?" Quinn gave her an astonished look. "Why move it there and make an extra stop? Are you sure?"

Dominique nodded.

"What in the world was that wine doing at Longview?" I asked. "I thought those bottles were under lock and key at Vaughn Vineyards."

"I don't know. Maybe because the house is halfway between the vineyard and the Inn, so Jamie decided to leave it there for a while."

"Did anyone else know what Jamie wanted to talk to you about that day? Oliver, Elena, Owen, Garrett?" I ticked them off on my fingers. It seemed unlikely any of them did, since Sasha hadn't known, but I still had to ask.

"Not that I know of. They've been too busy planning the funeral. To be honest, I was surprised they're still going through with this dinner. You'd think they would have postponed it under the circumstances."

"It might be because the wine is here already," Quinn said.

"And they don't want to move it one more time. It's too fragile. And of course it's not a bad idea to have a birthday party honoring Thomas Jefferson on his actual birthday."

"Or maybe," my cousin said in a tart voice, "because the Vaughns can't give back the money they've already received for the tickets. They still owe me quite a bit."

"You mean it's already been spent?" I said.

"I have a feeling it might be. Elena's been putting me off about paying some of the bills they owe. I think they're counting on a lot of money from the auction."

"That's going to depend on what the bottle the dinner guests sample tastes like," Quinn said. "Even if it's not that great—if it's gone off after all these years at the bottom of the Atlantic Ocean—you're still buying history, so selling the other two bottles will bring in some money. But if, by some chance, it has aged well, it could be worth a fortune. There aren't any other one-hundred-and-forty-year-old bottles of Norton anywhere in the world."

There would be something magical about owning one of those bottles. Especially if the wine was still good. It was risky to sample it just before the auction, but Jamie had always been a gambler, willing to bet big and audaciously. He could have just as easily auctioned off all three bottles and then nobody would know if they were getting a once-in-a-lifetime vintage or something that tasted like bilge water. Not to mention that opening one of the three bottles set the stakes higher, which was the reason for the twenty-thousand-dollar price tag for the dinner tickets and the chance to sample the Norton. Like Quinn said, you were drinking history.

"Oliver Vaughn is going to candle and decant it an hour

before they serve it," Dominique said. "Now that Jamie won't be there to do it."

Decanting wine helps eliminate any sediment in the bottle—particles like yeast and wine skins—which is especially important for red wine. Candling means just what it sounds like: The neck of the wine bottle is backlit by the light of a candle to make it easier to see whether there is any sediment before the wine is poured into the decanter.

Decanting wine isn't the same as uncorking a bottle and letting it breathe. Old wines like the Norton, and very fine wines, need to be decanted in glass vessels shaped like carafes, which have more surface area than wine bottles, to allow the aromas or flavors to be released. But it's also a guessing game when it's the right moment to drink the wine. As with everything in the business of growing grapes and making wine, timing things for the perfect moment between decanting and drinking such an old vintage as the 1876 Norton was a crapshoot based on your best guess. How long before it started to go bad—or whether you drank too early before it reached its peak flavors—was a roll of the dice.

"I wonder what it's going to taste like," I said.

"It seems you'll get a chance to find out," my cousin said. "I saw your names added to the guest list."

"The tickets were a gift," I said. "I was . . . with Jamie at the end. Between the destruction caused by the accident and all the visitors we've had to deal with, Elena and Garrett thought we should have them."

And they bought my silence in return for not admitting to anyone that I thought Jamie deliberately crashed his car into the wall and committed suicide.

"I'm glad you'll both be here, chérie." Dominique fiddled with her phone, looking uncomfortable. "Lately I haven't had a good feeling about that evening."

"Because it's the day after Jamie's funeral?" Quinn asked. "Bad karma, maybe?"

"Maybe. I wish I knew what he wanted to tell me. You know me, I always try to give people the shadow of a doubt, but I have a feeling something went wrong and Jamie never got to let me know what it was." She shrugged and stood up. "Unless we all find out on Saturday night."

I DIDN'T TAKE QUINN'S sleeping pill that night and the old nightmare came back, where I relived my accident, though this time it was mashed up with Jamie's, so Greg's car caught fire, just as Jamie's had done. Greg left me there as he did ten years ago, but this time we both could see that the car was on fire—and I couldn't get out. The next thing I knew Quinn was shaking me gently and pulling me into his arms. Moonlight flooded the bedroom. We hadn't closed the curtains and his face looked like white granite in the pale light. He bent and kissed me.

"It's okay, baby," he said. "It's okay. You're all right. Nothing happened. I've got you."

I heard a high-pitched wail, followed by footsteps, and my brother's soothing voice calming my niece. A moment later he knocked on our door, cracking it open. "Hey," he said in a soft voice, "is everything all right?"

"Lucie had a bad dream," Quinn said. "Is Hope okay?"

"I woke her up, didn't I?" I said, my heart still rabbiting in my chest. "Oh, Eli, I'm so sorry. Should I go see her?"

"Don't worry, she'll be fine," Eli said. "I'll stay with her until she falls asleep again."

The door clicked shut, and I said to Quinn, "I woke everyone up, didn't I?"

"It's okay. You want to talk about it?"

"I dreamed about my accident. It's the first time in years. But this one was different because Greg's car caught fire like Jamie's did."

I heard Quinn's sharp intake of breath. Then he said, "It's going to be okay, sweetheart."

"What did I say?"

"Nothing, really."

"Quinn."

He sighed. "Okay. You screamed and then you said, 'Don't leave me, Greg. Please don't let me die.'" He wrapped his arms tighter around me. "He's in jail, Lucie. He can't hurt you. And you're with me. You're fine . . . Jamie's accident brought all this back. You should have taken that sleeping pill."

"I don't want to start needing sleeping pills again. It was hard enough getting off them last time."

"It doesn't have to be for a long time. Just until you get past this."

He lay down again and pulled me with him so my head was resting on his chest. I could feel his breathing, slow and steady. "What if I don't get past it?" I asked.

"You will."

"How do you know?"

"Because I know you. You're strong and you can do anything you put your mind to."

"I'm not so sure about that. I keep thinking I'm over what

happened to me, ready to move on and not look back or think about what-if. Then I have this nightmare."

"Sasha says she knows a doctor who might be able to do surgery on your foot, rebuild it so you can walk properly again. Be almost as good as it was before the accident."

Sasha had whispered that in my ear like it was our secret. So how did Quinn know about it?

"Has she been talking to you? Or has Eli?"

"Yup. Both of them." He sounded upbeat. I should have guessed they were conspiring behind my back. "Before you go getting on your high horse," he said, "maybe you ought to give her a chance. Hear her out."

"What if I did have that surgery and the doctor screwed up and I ended up worse off than I am now?"

"Sasha doesn't seem to think that's what will happen." He stroked my hair, tucking a loose strand behind my ear. "You don't have to make any decisions tonight, Lucie. You have all the time in the world." He half sat up and looked at the clock on his bedside table. "It's three A.M. We should try to go back to sleep. Do you think you'll be okay?"

"I'll be fine." I leaned over and kissed him. "I love you. Thank you."

"I love you, too."

He fell back asleep long before I did. Downstairs, the grand-father clock in the foyer chimed four, and then what seemed like only minutes later I heard it chime five. In an hour we would be getting up. I slipped out of Quinn's arms and went into the bathroom for a drink of water. He didn't move. In the darkened glass of the medicine cabinet mirror, I could see an eerie gleam where the light reflected off the whites of my eyes. Everything else was a shadowy outline.

The old nightmare had come back with a new twist because I still wasn't over my accident. Even though I had accepted my disability, I was still angry at Gregory Knight who walked away—crawled, actually—and left me alone in the car. That's what had haunted me so much about Jamie. I knew what it felt like to watch someone leave when you believe you're going to die.

After all this time, I still couldn't forgive Greg, and it was eating away at me. I knew I needed to move on, get past this, or I would never be free of the nightmare. But how could I ever forgive someone who had not only murdered my godfather, a man I adored, but also left me permanently disabled?

There wasn't enough mercy or compassion in my heart to do that, give him absolution for what he did to me and to my godfather, how he changed my life.

Right now I didn't care if he rotted in jail. Until the day he died.

Fourteen

called the St. Leonard Project several times the next morning and kept getting their answering machine, a female voice that said no one was available to take my call, but if I left my name, number, and a brief message, someone would try to get back to me within twenty-four to forty-eight hours. Maybe they had to screen their calls. What kind of person would call a place whose mission was to try to get prisoners who were perhaps wrongfully convicted released from jail? Desperate family members clinging to the unwavering belief that their loved one really didn't do it or that it was an accident, that's who. The St. Leonard Project was probably inundated with requests.

I didn't have twenty-four to forty-eight hours to wait for someone to try to get back to me. Jamie's wake was tonight, the funeral was tomorrow, and the Jefferson Dinner was the next day, Saturday, April 13, Thomas Jefferson's birthday.

"Why don't you just drive in to D.C. and see if you can meet with someone?" Quinn said. We were still at the house, getting ready to head over to the vineyard. "I can cover every-thing here, and Frankie says we've still got people showing up for drinks after they've visited Jamie's shrine. You'd be better off somewhere else. Besides, the minute you say you've got a message that Jamie Vaughn asked you to deliver to Taurique Youngblood, you're going to get someone's attention fast. Not to mention you've got Webb Landau's MedicAlert bracelet."

"Maybe I'll do that," I said. "The St. Leonard Project is in the basement of St. Patrick's Catholic Church downtown on Tenth Street. It'll probably take me a good hour and a half to get there, especially once I hit D.C. traffic, but at least it's right in the middle of the city."

"I wonder where they got their name."

"I looked it up. St. Leonard was the patron saint of prisoners—prisoners of war, political prisoners, anyone in jail. His godfather was a Frankish king who, according to legend, promised to set free every prisoner St. Leonard visited."

"Huh. I didn't know that. Do you know anything else about this group?"

"Nope. I think they're fairly new. But I guess I'm about to find out."

ST. PATRICK'S WAS A beautiful old Gothic Revival church of turrets, towers, and a large rose window that was dwarfed by the high-rise hotels and office buildings surrounding it on the corner of 10th and G Streets in northwest Washington. It looked as if it belonged somewhere set off by itself, so its elab-orate tracery, embellishments, and the lovely symmetry of dark and light blocks of stone and marble could be admired appropriately, or maybe it just belonged in another century. Instead it was sandwiched between modern buildings that loomed over it, casting their shadows across its ornate façade.

I parked the Jeep in a nearby garage and walked down 10th Street to a set of steps that led up to the main entrance. Two African-American men, both white haired and grizzled, lounged on the steps, and I could feel them following me with their eyes as I climbed the stairs. A mounted plaque on a pillar outside the main door read "ERECTED ABOUT 1792. FIRST CHURCH TO BE ERECTED IN THE "FEDERAL CITY" OUTSIDE THE LIMITS OF "GEORGE TOWNE." FIRST PASTOR, REV. ANTHONY CAF-FREY, BROUGHT FROM DUBLIN AT SUGGESTION OF JAMES HOBAN, ARCHITECT OF THE "PRESIDENTIAL PALACE."

So the White House architect, James Hoban, had been affiliated with this church. At the top of the stairs I pulled on a handle of one of the heavy double doors in the arched doorway. It didn't budge, so I tried the other one.

"Don't bother. Church is locked up, miss. They open it for services and meetings."

I turned around. One of the men sitting on the stairs had spoken.

"Why is it locked?" I asked.

"Lady, this is D.C.," he said, as if that were enough of an explanation.

"I'm looking for the St. Leonard Project," I said. "It's supposed to be here in this church."

"Door on the left," he said. "They got an office downstairs."

"Thank you."

"Hey!" I turned around. The other man was pointing at

me, or rather, at my cane. "Just wonderin'. Where'd you get the stick?"

I looked at him in surprise. Most people weren't nervy enough to ask about it. Especially not total strangers. "Car accident."

He nodded. "That's rough. You're young. You here to volunteer?"

I wanted to tell him it was none of his business. Instead I said, "I promised someone who was dying that I'd get a message to a prisoner on death row."

"You come to the right place," he said. "They help the ones no one else wants. People call 'em the last resort before you gotta ride the lightning."

Ride the lightning. My stomach turned over. "Thanks," I said. "I didn't know that."

The second set of doors I pulled on opened with a creak. I stepped into a gloomy entryway that felt like I was in a tunnel after the bright sunlight outside. A cramped hall and a narrow staircase that led downstairs smelled of the mustiness and history of an old building and it pricked at my nose. There had been a church on this site since before Washington had been incorporated as a city, which meant it had witnessed the assassinations of four presidents, a civil war, two world wars, a devastating depression, racial riots that nearly destroyed D.C., and terrorism. In other words, the church had been here for the better part of our history as a nation.

The staircase led to a small corridor on the lower level where a half-open door with a white sign with black lettering on it read THE ST. LEONARD PROJECT. HOURS M–F, 10–4. The only phone number listed was the one I'd been calling. Below that sign was another sign, homemade, with a quote from the French philosopher Voltaire: "It is better to risk saving a guilty man than to condemn an innocent one."

Inside, a slender young woman with skin the color of café latte was talking on the telephone at a desk. There were three other desks in the windowless room, all unoccupied. Her back was to me, but I could tell she was deeply engrossed in a conversation, her hand flying across a yellow legal pad as she spoke and took notes. Her jet-black cornrows were streaked with purple, and she wore a brilliantly colored dashiki over skinny black leggings. Finally, she hung up and I knocked on the door.

I think she'd been aware of my presence all along. "Can I help you?" Her accent was soft and lilting.

"I'd like to talk to whoever is handling Taurique Young-blood's case, please."

Her eyebrows went up. This time I noticed her fingernails, long talons painted a vivid shade of purple to match her hair. "And you are?"

"Lucie Montgomery."

She stared at me and my cane as if she were trying to place me. Then her face cleared. "I thought you looked familiar. I saw you on television the other day. You're the one who witnessed the car crash that killed Jamie Vaughn."

"That's right."

Quinn had been right. The woman sat up straighter and her interest in me went up visibly. "May I ask what brings you here?"

I had a feeling she already knew, or at least she had an idea.

"I'd really rather discuss that with the person who is working on Taurique's case," I said.

"I see." She stood up. "Please wait here."

She walked past me to a closed door across the hall. No sign on that door. A man's voice said, "Come in," after she knocked, and she disappeared inside. I heard a murmur of voices and then she opened the door again. "Won't you come in, Ms. Montgomery?"

She opened the door wider to let me in, and I froze in midstep.

Hunter Knight stood behind a desk in a cramped office heaped with papers, law books, and accordion file folders. Hunter Knight, Greg's older brother, who, Thelma told me, had left his missionary work in Central America and returned to the States. She hadn't known what he was doing in Atoka, whom he'd come to visit, but I would bet my life as of right this moment that Hunter had paid a call on Jamie Vaughn a few days before he drove his car into my wall. Thelma also said Hunter was helping his brother in prison, and I'd taken that literally.

They help the ones no one else wants. Hunter's brother Greg and Taurique Youngblood. I wondered if there was a connection between them.

"Hello, Lucie," Hunter said. "It's been a long time. Please come in." He glanced at the young woman and said, "Thank you, Dasha . . . unless . . . can we offer you a cup of coffee, Lucie? The coffeepot is in the other room. It's not Starbucks, but it's got caffeine."

I licked my lips, not sure I would be able to speak. "No. No, thank you." My voice came out like a croak.

Hunter glanced at Dasha and nodded that she was dismissed. "Do come in," he said again to me.

Dasha closed the door with such a loud click that I wondered if she'd locked the two of us in here together.

"Dasha is one of our legal volunteers. She's getting her law degree at Howard and she's absolutely brilliant." Hunter cleared his throat. "Please take a seat. Make yourself comfortable."

There were two worn-out upholstered chairs in front of his beat-up metal desk. I took the less shabby one and glanced around his office. Hunter sat down, too. A coffee mug with LAWYERS NEVER LOSE THEIR APPEAL stenciled on it sat on top of a pile of papers in front of him. Behind his desk, more files and papers were stacked on a credenza underneath a poster with a photo of Nelson Mandela and the quote: "It is said that no one truly knows a nation until one has been inside its jails. A nation should not be judged by how it treats its highest citizens, but its lowest ones."

Then there was the framed photograph I didn't want to see, sitting on the credenza: the two Knight brothers, Hunter and Greg, obviously in happier times. Younger. Both with scruffy summer beards and bronzed golden tans, as devastatingly good-looking as Greek gods. At a beach somewhere, arms around each other's shoulders, grinning for the camera. Another photo of the whole family that looked like the kind of posed candid you'd send in a Christmas card where everyone was dressed in matching clothes: khaki pants and navy polo shirts. I'd forgotten there was a younger sister.

"Those pictures were taken a long time ago," Hunter said, half turning around in his chair to look at them. "I keep them to remember what's lost. My parents are divorced now. My sister moved to Canada after Greg's trial. And Greg, well, you know where he is. We're all scattered to the four winds."

I didn't say anything, though I wanted to ask him why. Why keep such painful reminders?

"I'm surprised to see you," he said after a moment. "I'm glad you came."

"I'm surprised to see you, too," I said. "I had no idea you worked here."

"You didn't?" He swiveled his chair around to face me again. "Then what are you doing here? Dasha said you've come about Taurique Youngblood. I saw that interview where Pippa O'Hara beat you up on television the other day. That woman would torture her own mother if she thought there was something newsworthy in it. There's obviously more to the story of Jamie Vaughn's death than you were willing to say to her. Do you want to tell me about it?"

I hadn't known Hunter well at all, just what Greg had told me about his beloved older brother, and once at a party at a house in Virginia Beach, Hunter showed up unexpectedly. Greg and I already had too much to drink, so I have a hazy memory of that night, and Hunter probably had a less-than-flattering memory of me. It was the only time we'd met, since I hadn't gone to Greg's trial. Hunter went, though, and so did his father—at least, that's what I'd heard. But I'd been told I wasn't needed as a witness, and by then, I never wanted to see Greg again.

What I'd forgotten was how much he and Greg looked alike. Hunter was Greg in five years' time, though I suspected prison had changed Greg so that by now he might have lost that all-American golden boy wholesomeness.

"First," I said, "before I say anything, I have a few questions."

Hunter leaned forward and folded his hands together on his desk. "Lucie, I'm not the enemy. I'm not Greg. But if I can, I'll try to answer your questions as long as they don't compromise Taurique's privacy. And then maybe you can help me. Deal?"

I had my hands folded together on my lap, too, but that was so Hunter wouldn't see how badly they were shaking. "I don't know," I said. "Don't ask me to make a bargain for someone's life."

His face reddened. "You misunderstand. I want to help. But here's what I believe: An innocent man is on death row for a crime he did not commit. Murder. And if you're here because of something to do with Jamie Vaughn, then I believe you might be able to help prove that Taurique Youngblood is innocent."

Webb Landau's MedicAlert bracelet felt as if it were burning a hole in the pocket of my jeans. Pretty soon I was sure it would start to glow red-hot and Hunter would surely notice it.

"Who did you visit when you came out to Atoka the other day?" I asked. "And why?"

Hunter's face cracked into a small smile. "Ah. I see you've been speaking to the woman who owns the General Store. She's quite a character. Thelma, isn't that right?"

"Yes."

"I went to see Jamie," he said. "I met him at his office and asked him what he remembered about the murder of Webster Landau."

"Why now? Why bring it up after all these years?"

"Before I answer that, tell me how is it you know about Webb. Did you find out from Jamie?"

"No."

"Then from whom?" He waited. "Lucie. Come on. You came here. You wanted to talk to the person who was in charge of Taurique's case. So talk to me. Please."

"I found out from Vanessa Pensiero. Jamie's first wife. Sasha Vaughn, Vanessa and Jamie's daughter, is dating my brother."

Hunter's eyebrows went up at that, but he said, "What made you seek out Vanessa? Does Sasha know about Webb and Taurique?"

"She does now. As of last night. Before that she had no clue about any of this, either from Jamie or Vanessa. For the record, she believes her father is innocent. So do I. I don't believe Jamie killed Webb Landau."

"Everyone is innocent until proven guilty," Hunter said in a mild voice, but his eyes were steely. "That's the law. But when the wrong person is convicted on bad or flawed evidence, there is an obligation—a moral imperative—to right a grievous injustice. Not to mention that it's part of our Constitution, the Sixth Amendment, to be precise. Everyone has a right to a fair trial."

"Are you that sure Taurique is innocent?"

He gave me an unflinching look. "Sure enough for the St. Leonard Project to take on his appeal and plenty sure that not only did he have a biased jury, the judge allowed sloppy evidence to be submitted that eventually convicted Taurique. And trust me, we don't waste our time."

So Hunter had gone straight to Jamie after taking on Taurique's case. "What did Jamie tell you when you spoke to him?" I asked.

"That he didn't kill Webb. And that he had no idea who

did," he said. "The latter statement, I'm certain, was a lie. Jamie does know . . . or did. And I'm not necessarily convinced he's innocent, either."

Hunter Knight was right. He didn't pull his punches. Hunter was obviously in touch with Taurique. If I told him what Jamie said to me and he conveyed Jamie's message, would that be one more nail in the coffin to convince Hunter that Jamie murdered Webb?

"I think," Hunter said to me, "you're here because you have some information relevant to the murder of Webb Landau. You didn't drive all the way into D.C. for nothing. I'd really like to know what it is you know."

"Okay," I said. "I'll tell you, because I promised Jamie. He asked me to tell Taurique that he was sorry. He wanted to ask Taurique to forgive him. It was the last thing he said before he died. So perhaps you can convey that message for him, since I gather you'll be seeing Taurique."

I started to get up to leave, and Hunter rose from his chair as if he meant to stop me. "Please don't go," he said. "I know how hard this must be for you. I know Jamie's car crashed in exactly the same place—"

"Stop right there. Don't even think of bringing that up." My voice rose in anger. "I saw Jamie before he died. I heard him scream as his car went up in flames. Do you know what I think? I think your visit contributed to pushing him over the edge, that it was one more factor that made him decide to crash his car into my wall. Here's what I didn't tell Pippa O'Hara, what Jamie's wife and his business partner don't want anyone to know: I think Jamie committed suicide. Jamie Vaughn died because he was consumed by guilt. What do you think about the moral imperative of righting that injustice?"

Hunter's face went pale and he sat back down in his chair. For a long moment the two of us just stared at each other, and I wished to hell I could get out of there. As for Webb's MedicAlert bracelet, I had no intention of showing it to him now. Not when he seemed so convinced Jamie had murdered Webb.

"Okay. Let's slow this down." Hunter placed his palms on his desk as if the room had tilted sideways and he needed to steady himself. "Maybe we should just take a break for today."

"Fine by me. I'm through, anyway."

"I appreciate what you've done, Lucie. Really."

"What, exactly, have I done? Made a more convincing case for why Jamie Vaughn is guilty of murdering Webb Landau?"

He shook his head. "It would take a lot more than your statement about what Jamie said to you before he died—which is hearsay, by the way—to get a judge to consider granting Taurique a new trial."

"Something must have happened to convince you to look into it all of a sudden," I said. "Webb Landau was murdered thirty years ago."

He sat back and considered me. "You're right. Greg asked me to help Taurique."

"Greg?"

"He's changed, Lucie. He lives every day with what he did to you and the knowledge that he took a good man's life. He knows he's guilty and he's serving his time, but in prison he has been taking correspondence legal courses. He's also begun advocating for fellow inmates, especially men who don't know how to read or write. He's also . . . found a place for God in his life."

"Good for him." I folded my arms across my chest, as much because it was chilly in his office as to shield myself from his words. "Why are you telling me this? Forgive me if I find it hard to believe your brother's sincerity and newfound compassion. Anyone can find God when he's walking down a one-way street with no way out. Or in a prison cell. Especially if he's trying to convince someone—like maybe a parole board—that he's changed."

"You don't have to believe Greg's faith is genuine," he said. "I'd hardly expect you to. Nor does he. Though just as Jamie asked for Taurique's forgiveness, I can tell you that Greg prays for you every day and hopes with all his heart that someday you might be able to forgive what he did."

I stood up, so furious with him for telling me this that my voice shook. "I came here to deliver a message from Jamie Vaughn and I have done that. That's *all*. You have no right to bring up Greg to me, to ask my forgiveness, to expect me to believe the fact that he's in prison doesn't have anything to do with his righteous conversion. And now I think we're through. I'm through. There's nothing more to talk about."

Hunter stood up, too. "I'm sorry, Lucie. I had no intention of upsetting you like this. It was unfair of me to bring up Greg to you under the circumstances, but you asked how I came to know about Taurique and I answered honestly. I appreciate what you've done today, but I think you're wrong about there being nothing more to talk about." He pulled open a desk drawer and took out his business card, scribbling something on the back. "Please take this. I wrote my private cell number on it and I don't give that out very often. I'm fairly certain we'll see each other again."

He held out the card and I shook my head. "I don't need your card. Because I'm equally certain that we won't see each other again."

"Please," he said. "You can tear it up when you leave if you want. But we're in this together now, you and me. I want to help Taurique and I think you want to help Jamie, for his daughter's sake if for no one else's. I need you . . . and you're going to need me."

I took the card. "Tell Greg," I said, enunciating each word with precise care, "to stop praying for me. I don't need his prayers and I sure as hell don't want them. I will never believe he's sincere, that he's had a religious transformation that isn't motivated by anything other than a desire to convince some judge to grant him early parole. You're his brother, Hunter. Of course you're going to believe him. But I don't."

I turned and walked out, slamming his door behind me, before he could say anything. Dasha's door was still open and she looked up from her desk as I flew past it.

"Lucie? Is everything okay?" she called after me.

"No," I said over my shoulder. "It's not."

Because the one thing I hadn't told Hunter—that I now knew to be immutably true—was that I would never, ever forgive Greg. No matter how much he prayed for me to have a little conversion in my own heart.

Fifteen

I got caught in Washington's horrendous rush-hour traffic—which seemed to begin earlier and earlier each time I drove into the city—so I knew Quinn and I were going to end up being late for Jamie's wake. Quinn had left two phone messages and three texts asking how had it gone and then, more urgently, *are you okay? where are you?* After that last exchange with Hunter, I was afraid I'd completely lose it—explode, cry, yell, do something—if I spoke to him, so I sent a text saying I was fine and that I'd fill him in on what happened when I got home.

When I walked into the house, Quinn was upstairs in our bedroom frowning at a dark suit he'd just taken out of the closet. I recognized that helpless look men get when they're going to ask you to choose a shirt and tie that go with the suit because they haven't got a clue what to wear, even though everything goes with black. I suppose the expression on my own face was why the fashion advice question died before he could get it out because in one smooth move he threw the suit on the bed and pulled me into his arms.

"What happened, sweetheart? Are you okay?"

I told him. When I was done, he said, "Look, maybe you should skip the wake tonight. I can make excuses, say you're under the weather."

"Thanks, but no. I'm going. I have to go. You know that."

"Are you sure?"

I nodded. "Yes. And we'd better get moving. It's already after six. I'm sorry I was so late. Traffic was a nightmare."

Quinn hung his suit on the closet door. He sat down on the bed, unlacing his work boots and pulling them off. "I can't believe Greg Knight—of all people—is the one pushing to get a judge to take another look at Taurique Youngblood's conviction." He stood up and unzipped his jeans. "My God, what are the odds? And Hunter Knight runs the St. Leonard Project? It's just crazy."

"Yeah, well, speaking of God, according to Hunter, Greg's become very devout in prison. Apparently he's found Jesus." I stepped out of my jeans and pulled my shirt off over my head. "I wonder if I have time for a shower?"

"Sure you do. No one's going to notice if we're not there at seven sharp. I didn't know Jesus was lost."

"I guess I asked for that."

He came up behind me and unhooked my bra. "We could shower together," he said, sliding his arms around me. "Save a little water."

"I'd like that."

"I wish I'd come with you today." He kissed my neck. "I should have been there."

There's no way I would have wanted Quinn to see the look on my face when I realized Hunter Knight was the one championing Taurique's appeal. And then sitting there listening to him talk about what a model prisoner and a saint Greg had become helping his fellow inmates.

"It's better that you didn't," I said. "Hunter doesn't need to know that you're involved in this, too. Anyway, I'm done with him, with the St. Leonard Project, with the whole thing. I said my piece and I won't be seeing him again."

Quinn gave me a long, assessing look. "Would you have gone today if you'd known you were going to run into Hunter?"

I walked into the bathroom without answering, and he followed me.

"Lucie?"

I turned on the taps and faced him. "I don't know. I'd like to think I would have. For Jamie's sake," I said, and my voice faltered. "But when Hunter brought up Greg and told me he was praying for me every night, asking for my forgiveness . . ."

Quinn pulled me into the shower with him and kissed me. "There's something I want to say to you. *Need* to say to you." His voice was gentle as we stood together under the spray of warm water. "I know you're not ready for this now—especially after what happened today—or maybe anytime soon. But someday, you're going to have to forgive Greg, Lucie. Not for his sake, but for yours. It's the only thing that's going to set you free, give you peace. Trust me. I know about this. If you don't, it will eat you from the inside out."

It was just about the last thing I'd expected to hear from him. Certainly not today and maybe not ever. If anything, I thought

Quinn nursed even more bitterness toward Greg than I did. Because of that accident I can never have children.

"I don't know if I can," I said, and now the tears I'd been fighting back slid down my face. "I don't know if I even want to."

He held me without saying anything and let me cry myself out as the water sluiced over both of us. Finally I wiped my nose with the back of my hand. "I'm done. I'm okay. I'll be okay."

"I know you will," he said. "But promise me you'll at least think about it, all right? I hate seeing you torn up like this."

"I can't do it right now. I need time."

"It's okay. Take all the time you want."

I nodded, and we finished our shower in silence. Later, as we were drying ourselves off, he said to me, "One more thing."

I gave him a wary look. "What is it?"

"Do you think you could pick out a shirt and tie that go with my suit?"

I smiled and kissed him. "That I could manage."

BY THE TIME WE were dressed and ready to leave for Hunt Funeral Home, it was after seven o'clock. Eli had already left with Sasha, since she needed to be there early. Persia, who was again babysitting Hope and Zach, had made dinner for Quinn and me, which she'd left in the kitchen. When I stopped into the parlor to say goodbye to them, I told Persia that we were so late we'd have to eat when we got home. My last meal had been breakfast, since I'd forgotten about lunch with everything that had happened in D.C., but my stomach was still doing flip-flops, so postponing dinner was fine by me.

We took the Jeep and left through the south gate, which had become the only way in or out since Jamie's accident. Normally we didn't let visitors use this entrance—it's in the middle of the vineyard and too easy for someone to take a little detour to explore the vines, which are strictly off-limits, but for now we had no choice. The headlights swept across the dark rows of bare, skeletal vines aligned like rows of soldiers.

"We'll have bud break over the weekend," Quinn said as we drove past the Chardonnay block. "These vines are going to be first."

"As long as we don't get a late-spring surprise freeze," I said. "I've had enough flame-filled nights to last me awhile."

We'd done everything from hiring a helicopter that would fly low over the vineyard to burning bales of hay or brush to keep the vines from freezing when the temperature dropped below thirty-two degrees. One year we were so desperate—and caught off guard—that we resorted to burning old car and tractor tires. Saving the grapes from a freeze was a headache that was either outrageously expensive or, in the case of the tires, horribly dirty. That year I needed to have temporary amnesia about us being good stewards of the land as the sky filled with black, noxious smoke.

"Maybe we'll be lucky this year," Quinn said as he stopped the car in front of the gate. "Hang on a sec. I'll get the gate."

"I'll do it. It'll be faster and we're late."

"No, sit tight. You're all dressed up."

He unlocked the gate, swinging it open so we could drive through. After he'd closed and locked it behind us, he said, "While I was driving around checking the vines today, I found a beer can in the Norton block. You'd think whoever did it would at least have the decency to leave a wine bottle since they were at a vineyard. One of ours, too. No disrespect to Jamie's memory, but I'll be glad when the front wall is rebuilt and we start using the main entrance again. There's too much access to the vines when customers drive through here."

"Are you serious? A beer can? What were they doing all the way over in the Norton block? That's not just littering, it's serious trespassing."

"It was more than one person. I also found a condom." He glanced over at me. "Used."

"Oh, God."

"If I catch whoever did it, they'll be sorry." He shook his head and said, without looking at me, "Next time I do the rounds, I might get one of Leland's hunting rifles out of his gun cabinet and take it with me for company."

"Hey, hold it right there, buddy. We don't shoot trespassers. Don't even joke about it."

"Who said I was joking? We ought to be able to protect what's ours. The Second Amendment says so."

We were on Atoka Road now, driving past the main entrance to the vineyard. A breeze fluttered the yellow crime scene tape and rustled the plastic sleeves on the hundreds of bouquets of flowers that had been left at Jamie's shrine, which now extended almost to the edge of the road and completely blocked Sycamore Lane. The lone lantern on the pillar that hadn't been demolished in the crash shone on the expanding memorial, which for once was deserted.

"Apparently they're expecting a big crowd tonight," Quinn said, changing the subject before we could get into a discussion of the right to keep and bear arms. "Eli said the afternoon viewing was crowded, but tonight it's really going to be packed. The entire Virginia Fever team is supposed to be coming, along with some big shots from the NBA. Eli said the president might even show up."

"Of the NBA?"

He raised an eyebrow. "Of the United States."

"Wow. That's quite a tribute to Jamie."

"His ashes will be there in an urn, and there are going to be a lot of photos from the family archives and the presidential campaign. Elena put the whole thing together."

"I'm glad they decided on cremation," I said. "After the fire, there . . . I . . . well . . . the car was nothing but a charred hulk."

"It might be a small urn."

"Don't."

"Sorry." He reached over and patted my hand as we turned onto Mosby's Highway. "You okay?"

"I can't stop thinking about my meeting today with Hunter."

"You never told me what he said when you showed him Webb Landau's MedicAlert bracelet."

"I didn't show it to him."

His turned his head and stared at me. "I thought that's why you went to see him. At least that's what you told Sasha last night."

"That was before I realized I'd be dealing with Hunter Knight, who already has some preconceived ideas about me. As it is, when I told him about Jamie asking for Taurique's forgiveness, I felt like I was hammering more nails into Jamie's coffin . . . oh, God, that was a terrible analogy."

His lips curved into a smile. "Don't worry. I knew what you meant."

"What I'm trying to say is that Hunter's so certain Taurique isn't guilty, it means he's convinced someone else murdered Webb and got away with it," I said. "I just made it easier for him to put two and two together that it was Jamie."

"He still has to prove it."

"What about the fact that Jamie drove his car into our wall? That doesn't make him look any less innocent, either."

"That story isn't going to hold up, Lucie," Quinn said. "Even if you swear that's what happened. Frankie told me she heard from Thelma when she stopped by the General Store this morning that it's official. Jamie's death is going to be ruled an accident. So that's the end of it."

"Hunter is not going to drop Taurique's appeal just because Jamie's dead. He's still going to try to find out who really killed Webb Landau. He wants to gather enough evidence to convince a judge to reopen the case."

"Do you think Elena knows anything about the St. Leonard Project? I wonder if Jamie told her about Hunter paying him a visit."

"I don't know, but something tells me he didn't. Hunter said the only person he visited when he came to Atoka was Jamie. I bet Jamie kept the whole thing as quiet as possible . . . maybe he was trying to figure out how to deal with it."

"And driving into our wall was dealing with it?"

"That's harsh."

"Look, he didn't leave a suicide note. They always leave notes, don't they?"

"Maybe he didn't really plan it. Don't forget, there were also no skid marks, so he didn't try to brake, either."

"You know what? We're just going around in circles," Quinn said. "We don't know what was going through Jamie's head. Whether he did it deliberately or if he was in the middle of texting someone and lost control of his car. Or even why. Guilt? Remorse? Who knows?"

"Remorse," I said right away. "I don't think Jamie killed Webb. Neither do you. But maybe he knew who did."

"And kept his mouth shut all these years? Man, that would eat at me, knowing the wrong person was taking the rap."

"What if you knew I killed someone? Would you turn me in? Or Eli? Would you turn in someone you loved, send them to jail instead of a guy who already had a criminal record and was convicted for the crime instead? Hey, Your Honor and people of the jury, you got the wrong person . . . my fiancée did it. Or her brother did."

He thought for a moment. "You wouldn't be you if you killed someone. You'd be someone else. It would change everything."

"All right, what if you found out about it after you married me? Would you still keep my secret?"

"Husbands can't testify against their wives."

"You're avoiding the question."

"I don't know if I could live with myself," he said. "Either way." We were nearly at the turn-off for the funeral home. "So now what's the plan?"

We were about to pay our respects to the family of a man who had just run for president of the United States. Already Loudoun County Sheriff's Department cruisers lined the highway and were clustered at the entrance, along with several large black SUVs. A couple of officers were directing traffic, a sure sign that Important People who traveled in motorcades were here. People who had security details. Half a dozen vans with logos of the major television networks were spread out in a long line like they were caravanning on the edge of Mosby's Highway. Apparently that was as near as the press was going to get to the funeral home, so there would be no filming guests entering and leaving unless it was in a car. What I was going to do was watch and listen and see if I could figure out who, among the closest friends of the deceased, might have committed a murder that they had managed to cover up for more than a quarter of a century.

"If Jamie didn't kill Webb and Taurique didn't kill him, then someone else did," I said. "My money is on whoever was at that final dinner party at Dori Upshur's house the night Webb disappeared. And in about five minutes, we're going to meet most of them."

"Yeah, well as they say, dead men tell no tales," Quinn said. "Now there's one less person alive who might really know what happened to Webb. If the murderer's there tonight, he or she might actually be relieved. Especially if Jamie was looking for forgiveness from the guy who's doing time for the crime."

I stared at him. "I never thought of it that way. But you might be right."

QUINN WAS RIGHT ABOUT the wake being mobbed. Lights blazed from every window of Hunt & Sons Funeral Home, a Victorian mansion of gingerbread frills and ornate architectural flourishes, as a long line of people waited their turn outside before they could even walk through the front door. The parking lot had already filled up, so the funeral home staff had opened the gates to a meadow next door for the overflow cars. A teenager wearing a black armband and holding a neon glow stick directed us through the gate to the meadow. We followed the queue of cars bumping over the rutted terrain until another man wearing mud boots used another glow stick to line us up in long rows.

The grass was still damp after all the rain we had the other day, but at least someone had mowed it recently. I tried to pick my way to avoid sinking into the mud in my best pair of black shoes, but my feet already felt cold and wet so I knew it was too late to save the shoes. Quinn and I walked past two limousines with D.C. license plates parked near the main entrance. More sheriff's department cruisers and three black SUVs—the escort convoy—were parked nearby on the lawn. A couple of men in dark suits wearing earpieces with wires that snaked inside their collars watched over the guests who came and went.

"I wonder if that's the president's limousine," I said to Quinn.

"He rides in that big tank they call 'the Beast,' but this one is definitely somebody's," he said. "They've got a metal detector at the front door."

A gloved man in a suit inspected my purse and then Quinn and I passed through the metal detector. A lot of friends and neighbors were among the crowd that milled around us, but there were just as many I didn't recognize, people from other parts of Jamie's multitextured, complex life. B. J. Hunt, who owned the funeral home, was off in a corner speaking to a man and woman I'd never seen before.

The murderer is someone I know.

It had been playing in my head like the refrain to a bad country music song for the last half hour. If it wasn't Jamie, who were the other possibilities? Elena, Mick, Dori Upshur. Maybe even Vanessa Pensiero, who could have been coy and clever enough to point me in the wrong direction by telling me only part of the story the night Webb Landau disappeared. What about Garrett Bateman, Jamie's fraternity "little brother" and current Mr. Fix-It-of-All-Things who had idolized Jamie?

Vanessa said she would be at the funeral but not the wake, and Dori Upshur had apparently vanished without a trace after she sold her farm. But the others would be here tonight, all friends, good people who were generous, kindhearted, well-respected members of our community. Then there was Mick, with whom I'd had a romantic relationship in the days when Quinn and I were in one of our cycles of dating other people. I especially didn't want to consider the possibility that it could be Mick. As for Taurique Youngblood, I genuinely believed he was innocent—Greg and Hunter Knight notwithstanding—because of Jamie's dying wish for Taurique to forgive him.

The one thing I didn't understand was why, after all this time, Jamie had held on to Webb's MedicAlert bracelet. It was one more reason I didn't think he murdered Webb. If I'd been the killer, that bracelet would have been the second thing I got rid of—after the murder weapon. So why did Jamie keep it? Blackmail? Would he blackmail his wife or his best friend or the trusted number two person in his company?

Quinn's arm slipped around my waist. "You seem like you're in your own world. You totally ignored two people who said hello to you and, in case you haven't noticed, you've got the attention of about half a dozen people who are staring at us. Including B.J., who is heading our way."

Quinn was right. I'd already overheard snatches of conversation and caught the swiveled heads.

". . . the last one to see him before . . ."

". . . you know where it happened, don't you, the exact same place . . ."

"Pippa O'Hara, that's who."

I lifted my chin. "I'm okay. Let 'em stare."

"Lucie, Quinn. How are you?" B. J. Hunt shook Quinn's hand and leaned in for a kiss for me. "You've had a rough time of it, haven't you, my dear? I stopped by the vineyard entrance to pay my respects yesterday. My God, there were so many tributes . . ." B.J.'s voice faltered as he pressed his lips together and shook his head. "This kind of loss just breaks your heart. It's one thing when a person has lived a long, full life. That's something you can celebrate and honor. There can even be some joy. But Jamie is gone too soon. It's such a tragedy."

Some careers in life are just not for me—podiatrist, air traffic controller, being the voice of those annoying canned telephone responses that keep you from talking to a live human—and B.J.'s is among them. The for-profit business of death: compassion and sympathy balanced with selling the complete package to the bereaved family. In B.J.'s case it had been the family business since the 1890s and, for all intents and purposes, everyone in Atoka and Middleburg who had passed away in the last 130 years or so had come here as a next-to-last final resting place. B.J. or his father or grandfather or one of his uncles had been the last person to say goodbye.

"Looks like a lot of people have come to pay their respects," Quinn was saying to B.J. "I'm sure that's a comfort to Elena and Jamie's family."

"You just missed the vice president," B.J. said. "That was his limo out front. He slipped out the back a moment ago after he spoke to Elena and the kids. The election may have been a nasty, brutal war between the two parties, but when there's a tragedy like this it's good to see some compassion and human kindness in Washington for a change, instead of attacks and insults." He covered his mouth with a hand. "You didn't hear that, understand?"

"Of course not," Quinn said.

"Hear what?" I asked.

B.J. placed a hand on my shoulder as his eyes wandered to someone behind me. I knew that well-practiced expression. Time to move on, greet the next guest, and appear gracious without seeming to ignore his duties to Quinn and me as he shifted his concern to someone else.

"Please excuse us," Quinn said. "We ought to go pay our respects."

B.J. nodded and gave my shoulder a sympathetic squeeze. "Of course. Don't let me keep you. And Lucie, you can always slip into my office if you need a moment. I realize this evening might be particularly difficult for you, honey."

I nodded over a sudden lump in my throat.

The rambling multistory house was large enough for several wakes to be held simultaneously, but tonight the Vaughn wake, with its substantial crowd and security presence, took over the entire funeral home. Quinn and I moved slowly through the congested rooms, greeting friends and neighbors until we reached a line that snaked through a double doorway and extended into the room where we were now standing.

"Shall we visit Jamie first and then see Elena and everyone else?" Quinn said in my ear.

Visit Jamie. It sounded so weird.

We joined the end of the line behind three young men who towered over us. Basketball players from the Virginia Fever, Jamie's team, immaculately dressed in suits and ties. I eavesdropped on their quiet chatter as the line inched forward. Sports, girls, food, tomorrow's practice, Saturday's game. Normal everyday things, which only made the unreality of Jamie's death seem more heartbreaking. Fifteen minutes later, Quinn and I stood before Jamie's urn and a display of photographs documenting his fifty-one years on earth, as beautifully curated as if it were for a magazine layout. There were a few early pictures of him growing up, but most of them focused on Jamie's life from the time he'd met and married Elena through the presidential campaign last fall.

Though there had been dozens of photographs of Jamie on television and in the media, especially when he ran for president, these were different: intimate moments out of the public eye when he could let his guard down and be himself. Goofing off juggling water bottles backstage before a campaign speech, muddy and grass-stained as he groomed his favorite horse after a charity polo match, dressed in a frilly floral apron ladling stew into bowls at a soup kitchen, drinking a beer in the Fever locker room with a tall, sweaty player's arm draped around him. And lots of pictures with Elena, his twin sons, and—I was happy to see—a few with Sasha. The sense of what was lost—what never would be anymore—was palpable.

Quinn squeezed my hand. "So sad," he said in a quiet voice. "So damned sad."

"I know." I stopped. "Hang on just a second, okay?"

I wasn't expecting it, but there it was. A photo of Jamie, Elena, and Mick lounging on the Lawn at UVA, books spread out around them, the colonnaded pavilions of Jefferson's Academical Village blurred in the background as they mugged for the camera. The guys scruffy in jeans, T-shirts, and long hair, Elena with her flaming red hair pulled up in a disheveled bun, an embroidered peasant blouse sliding off one bare shoulder, an arm resting on Jamie's knee in an unmistakable gesture of familiarity and intimacy. The picture had obviously been cropped at an awkward angle, and I wondered who had been left out. Webb? Vanessa? Both of them?

"What?" Quinn asked.

"I'll tell you later."

"Hey," he said. "Look at this."

I looked at the photo he was pointing at and caught my breath. Jamie's twenty-first birthday party, also with Elena and Mick, and a young-looking Garrett Bateman, whose long frizzy hair looked like he'd just stuck his finger in an electrical outlet. The three of them stood behind Jamie, who sat at a candlelit dinner table littered with dishes, wineglasses, and empty bottles, preparing to blow out more candles on a cake with HAPPY 21ST BIRTHDAY, JAMIE written on it. I leaned down and squinted at the picture. In the background out of the range of the flash was a shadowy figure who looked a lot like the newspaper photo I'd seen of Dori Upshur.

Would Elena really include a photo of Dori's Darlings at one of the dinners Dori had hosted at her farmhouse, with all the heartache and pain those memories must evoke? I hadn't realized Garrett had been at some of those evenings. There was no Webb or Vanessa in this shot, either, so Elena was rewriting history, but after the newspaper photos I'd seen, I knew the woman in the shadows was Dori, who couldn't have been cropped without spoiling the scene. Here, relaxed at home, she looked nothing like her serious official university photo. She was taller than I'd realized and reed slender. In this photo, the horn-rimmed glasses that made her look so professorial were pushed up on her head to keep her hair off her face. Her most noticeable feature was the beauty mark above her upper lip. Not a beautiful woman, but striking—you'd notice her if you walked past her on the street. She was probably in her midthirties back then; somehow I kept expecting her to be older, maybe gray haired, in her fifties. Though she probably was well in her sixties now.

Still I could see why Elena had chosen that picture. The photographer had caught them all in a moment of sweet intimacy, laughing uproariously at some shared joke, arms around each other, a merry band of friends. Even Dori, one hand at her throat, was laughing just as hard at the hilarity as the others were as she hoisted a tilted wineglass in the air. The camaraderie was unmistakable and mesmerizing. Until I saw this photograph I wouldn't have understood how they could have stuck together, no one betraying anyone else as Taurique Youngblood was convicted of murdering Webb. Now I knew. Webb's death must have devastated them all, but still they protected one another with oath-signed-in-blood loyalty.

"That's Dori Upshur," I said to Quinn. "I recognize her from the newspaper photos and her university picture."

"I wonder what happened to her." Quinn said.

"Vanessa said she sold her farm and disappeared after Webb died."

"Maybe she's on the run because she murdered Webb and got away with it," he said in my ear.

"I'd like to think she's guilty, because that would mean Elena, Mick, and Garrett aren't. Or Vanessa, either. And certainly not Taurique or Jamie."

Quinn took my hand. "Come on. Let's find Elena and the others."

THE LINE OF PEOPLE waiting to express condolences to Elena, her sons, and the rest of Jamie's family wound down one side of a large drawing room filled with groupings of sofas and comfortable chairs pulled together, a place where you could sit and have a quiet talk with someone or take a break from the raw grief that hung in the air like a fog. Boxes of tissues had been placed on every table or console, and a large bouquet of lacy spring flowers on the mantel of a stone fireplace looked like the artistic handiwork of Elena's garden club. Every so often during a lull in the quiet buzz of muted conversations I heard music through the sound system, something classical and subdued.

I spotted Elena before I caught sight of the others, mostly because her sunny yellow silk blouse, the color of Jamie's lucky tie, stood out in a sea of funereal black. Owen and Oliver, who were on either side of their mother, looking pale and stoic, both wore bright yellow ties. A grief-stricken older couple that I guessed were Jamie's parents stood at the beginning of the line. A dark-haired woman who resembled Jamie—his younger sister—and her husband were at the end. I'd seen both Mick Dunne and Garrett Bateman when we walked in. Though neither was in the receiving line, they both kept an eye on Elena as they moved around and greeted guests, Mick especially. Quinn said he'd picked up a vibe between Mick and Elena the other day. Maybe there was more to their relationship than I'd thought.

"Where's Sasha?" Quinn asked.

"Next to Jamie's sister and brother-in-law," I said. "Eli's with her but they're kind of on their own like an island."

Quinn tugged on the collar of his dress shirt. "I wish somebody would open a window or turn down the heat. It's like a damn oven in here. Are you okay, Lucie? You look as if you're about to pass out."

"I'm fine, though I wish I'd eaten something. Breakfast was a long time ago."

"Do you want to take a break in B.J.'s office?"

"No, that's okay. We're almost there. I might step outside on the porch for a minute after we're through just to get some air."

"We don't have to stick around until this is over," Quinn said. "We can take off after we pay our respects to the family."

"And leave Sasha and Eli on their own? They look like they could use an ally. Eli said Elena's already begun putting distance between her family and Sasha now that Jamie isn't there to stick up for her."

A muscle in Quinn's jaw twitched. "That's the one thing weddings and funerals have in common."

"What is?"

"They're the only times everyone in the family is expected to show up and pretend they get along even if they don't. I'm always surprised how many dysfunctional families there are. People you'd never expect."

We hadn't really talked about our own wedding in the few weeks since we'd gotten engaged, nor had we set a date. With our tumultuous history, by tacit mutual agreement we were both content to spend some time being engaged. Move in together and get used to living with each other. It was enough for now.

"That wouldn't be your way of telling me you'd rather elope, would it?" I gave him a sideways look.

"Uh . . ." The impact of what he'd said appeared to dawn on him and he turned red. "Of course not. I mean . . . no. I wasn't thinking about us. I know we haven't talked much about a wedding, but I always figured you wanted the real thing. You know, a big deal."

I did want the real thing. But I also wanted something that would be uniquely ours, something different. "I'm just teasing you," I said. "Anyway, this may not be the ideal moment to have that discussion."

The man ahead of us in line turned around and glared at the two of us. Quinn gave him a polite nod, which earned us another disapproving look. The line slowly moved forward, and then it was our turn.

Speaking to Jamie's parents was painful, especially once I told them my name and they realized who I was. His father thanked me for being with Jamie at the end and his mother gave me the glassy-eyed look of someone on tranquilizers who wasn't going to remember any of this after it was over.

The surprise was Elena, who seemed composed and in control. After we exchanged hugs, she said, "I hope no one from the press has bothered you anymore, Lucie, and you're letting Garrett handle anything to do with my family."

"Of course," I said. "And no, no one from the press has contacted me."

"Good. I don't know if you've heard, but the sheriff's department is going to rule the crash an accident. So that should be the end of any media interest."

Until Hunter Knight and the St. Leonard Project stirred the pot when they tried to reopen the case against Taurique Youngblood. Did Elena and Garrett have enough influence to stop that investigation as well? Elena gave me a long, steady look that made me wonder if she'd found out I knew about Webb Landau. If she had, only two people could have told her: Sasha or Vanessa.

"Yes," I said, "that should be the end of it."

"I certainly hope so," she said. "Things could be so unpleasant otherwise."

Was she warning me, or was that a threat?

I wanted to ask "for whom?" Instead I said, "The photographs of Jamie are wonderful, Elena. They capture him so well. I especially liked some of the old photos when you both were students at UVA. You have a lot of memories together."

Her eyelids flickered, and I knew she had read between the lines of what I'd just said. "Yes," she said. "We do." She turned to the woman in line behind me and put out her hand. "Marisa, thank you so much for coming."

Elena's curt dismissal was deliberate, and she nearly managed to pull it off except that her hand shook slightly as she held it out. I'd baited the hook with that comment about the old photographs and memories. Now I was almost certain Elena realized I knew something, which was why she'd just cut me off.

Did she know who killed Webb and had Jamie told her about Hunter Knight's visit before he died? Elena had just warned me not to stick my nose into anything more to do with Jamie's accident, or things could be so unpleasant. It was probably a safe bet that I wasn't going to learn the answers to those questions from her.

WHEN QUINN AND I joined Sasha and Eli, Sasha immediately wanted to know what happened during my visit to the St. Leonard Project. I knew this was coming.

"They're looking into Taurique Youngblood's conviction," I said. "And trying to get an appeal. A guy named Hunter Knight visited your father recently, but Jamie was the only one he's spoken to so far."

"Why only my dad?" Sasha asked. "Why not anyone else?"

Eli gave me a suspicious look. "Hunter Knight. That name rings a bell."

"He's Greg Knight's brother," I said in a calm voice. "He runs the St. Leonard Project."

"You've got to be kidding me."

"Afraid not." To Sasha, I added, "I don't know why he was the only one. We didn't get into that."

"Does he think my dad's guilty?" She glanced around and lowered her voice. "Of murder?"

"I don't know, Sasha. Honest."

"Didn't you *tell* him he's innocent?" She was tired and grieving and overwrought. "You should have said something."

"I did," I said. "But what I think doesn't matter. You know that. And it's not going to stop them trying to get the case reopened."

"Lucie—" Eli gave me a warning look. "Maybe we should drop this subject, okay?"

I didn't want to say that I wasn't the one who had brought it up. "Sure," I said. "It's warm in here. I think I need some air. Will you all excuse me?"

"I'll come with you," Quinn said.

"No, please stay here. I just want to clear my head. I'll be right back."

I heard Eli say, "Let her go," under his breath, and I fled the room.

The night had turned chilly, and the fat, nearly full moon that was visible above the tree line lit up the wraparound porch with a silvery white light that was almost as bright as daytime. I leaned against the railing and watched guests leave Jamie's wake and melt into the darkness of the parking lot and the field beyond. I had fulfilled my promise to Jamie, and Elena had just warned me to stay out of her family's business. If I got involved any deeper with the St. Leonard Project, it was practically a given that Greg Knight would find his way back into my life. Why go through that heartache?

Maybe it was better to let it all go.

"Do you need some help, miss? Are you all right?"

A white-haired man in a dark suit with the lapel pin of a funeral home employee stood behind me, holding an unlit cigarette in one hand. He must have floated across the porch because I hadn't heard footsteps.

"Didn't mean to scare you," he said.

"It's okay. I'm fine, thank you," I said. "I just needed some fresh air. It's warm in there."

"We turned the heat down," he said. "You should find it a bit cooler. You'll catch your death out here if you're not careful. No coat and all."

"I was just on my way back inside," I said. "Good night."

"Good night, miss."

The metal detector at the front door was gone now that the vice president had departed. More people were leaving than arriving, and the foyer, which had been so crowded when Quinn and I had met B.J. here earlier, was nearly empty. The line waiting to pay respects to Jamie had vanished. I stopped in the doorway to the room where his urn sat surrounded by Elena's photo gallery. Only one person was there, her back to me, as she bent down, apparently staring intently at the photographs as I had done. Heavyset, wearing a Burberry raincoat with a red silk scarf wrapped around her neck.

She straightened up, turned around, and walked directly toward me. Our eyes met. "Good evening," she said. "It's all yours. I'm just leaving."

"Thank you," I said. "Do I know you?"

"I'm sure you don't. I'm not from around here."

"Sorry. You look familiar."

She averted her eyes and kept walking.

Behind me I heard a man's voice say, "The family is receiving guests on the second floor in the Dominion Room if you'd like to go upstairs, madam. Or there's an elevator around the corner if that would be more convenient."

I turned as the woman headed straight for the front door without acknowledging him, bypassing the staircase to the second floor as she left the funeral home. The man who had spoken to her looked startled by the snub. Then he noticed me watching and shrugged.

"How did you know she didn't already go upstairs to pay her respects?" I asked.

"I saw her arrive," he said. "She went straight to the viewing room. Been there the whole time."

"Do you know how long she spent there?"

"Ten, fifteen minutes." Another shrug. "Didn't talk to anybody. Except you. Why do you ask?"

"I . . . don't know. She looked like someone I recognized."

The woman who had walked past me and straight out the door without paying her respects to Jamie's family was Dori Upshur. She was heavier, and the sleek dark hair was now silver, but she wore it in the same way I recognized from the photos—a short bob that fell just below her ears. Eyeglasses pushed on top of her head like a headband. And there was that distinctive beauty mark just above her upper lip. It was Dori Upshur, all right. I'd bet my life on it.

And she'd come to pay her respects to Jamie. But not to Elena.

Sixteen

told Quinn I'd seen Dori Upshur at Jamie's wake as we were driving home. Out here where we live, the country lanes are dark, deserted, and seldom lit by streetlamps. There's usually no white dividing line painted down the middle, which keeps you slightly off balance because you don't want to end up on the soft verge or the wrong side of the road. All you see is what unspools directly in front of you as your headlights pick out the road bit by bit. Maybe a couple of startled deer will dart in front of your car or a raccoon's eyes will gleam like a madman's, but you're unlikely to see another vehicle—and certainly not another person. The world seems far away, remote. Either your troubles and worries recede and fade as well, or they fill up the silence and play games inside your head.

Mine clanged like a noisy, dissonant symphony.

"Are you sure it was Dori Upshur?" Quinn asked. "All you have to go by are a couple of really old newspaper photos."

"And those pictures at the funeral home."

"Which are thirty years old. How could you tell it was the same woman?"

"I don't know," I said. "I just knew it was her. Especially that beauty mark."

"If you're right, I wonder what she was doing there."

"I am right. She was paying her respects to Jamie, just like the rest of us were."

"I meant, after all this time. Didn't you say she disappeared after Webb Landau was murdered?"

"That's what everyone I've spoken to said. I wish I'd been able to talk to her."

"And say what? Ask her if she knew who killed Webb? You might not get very far."

"Such a cynic," I said. "Though you're probably right."

"I thought you were going to walk away from this, Lucie," Quinn said.

"I am," I said. "I am."

He gave me a look like he only half believed me. But he didn't say a word either way and we let the subject drop.

PERSIA HAD BEEN ASLEEP on the sofa in the parlor when Quinn and I got home a few minutes later. She showed up in the foyer, one hand over her mouth stifling a yawn, a crease on her cheek from where she'd been lying on one of the throw pillows.

"Sorry," she said, yawning again as she tucked a hairpin back into her coiled braids. "I fell asleep after Zachary's grandmother came to pick him up and Hope went to bed."

Quinn gave her a puzzled look. "What are you talking about? His grandmother was at the wake tonight."

"Persia means his other grandmother," I said, though no-body had said a word to me about Vanessa Pensiero dropping by here to pick up her grandson. "Did she just show up?"

"Not exactly," Persia said. "Sasha called and said there was a change of plans. Then a few minutes later someone rang the doorbell. Vanessa somebody-or-other. I was still feeding the children, so we weren't ready for her. She seemed a bit put out, but I wasn't going to let Zachary leave without dinner, don't you know. So she offered to gather up his things because I think she was in a hurry. I told her where they were and she skedaddled off to find them."

"I thought Vanessa wasn't driving because of the cast on her foot," I said.

"She seemed to get around just fine. I didn't realize you didn't know she came by."

"It must have slipped Sasha's mind to mention it to me," I said.

"Maybe," she said. "Speaking of dinner, yours is waiting for you in the refrigerator. It won't take long to reheat."

"You're an angel," I told her. "I don't know what we'd do without you."

She smiled. "You're about to find out. I'm going straight home to my cozy little apartment."

"I'll walk you back to your place," Quinn said.

"You'll do no such thing." Persia drew herself up to her full four foot eleven inches. "Don't you go treating me like an old lady, Mr. Quinn. I can walk myself home just fine, thank you very much. You can spit from here to my front door. What do you think is going to happen between here and there? Some-one's going to jump out of a bush and rob me?"

"No, no, nothing like that," Quinn said, turning red. "And of course you're not an old lady. It's just . . ."

"Just what?"

"Better quit while you're ahead, Quinn," I told him with a grin. "Good night, Persia. We'll see you in the morning. Thanks for dinner."

"That's more like it," she said. "Good night, you two."

In the kitchen I reheated Persia's homemade beef stew and Quinn uncorked a bottle of our Norton. "Getting ready for Saturday," he said, as he poured wine into two glasses. "Wonder what Jamie's one-hundred-and-forty-year-old wine will taste like compared to ours?"

Later, when we were upstairs after changing for bed, I said to Quinn, "Did you move Webb Landau's MedicAlert bracelet? I'm sure I left it on my dresser when I got back from Washington this afternoon."

"I didn't touch it," he said. "Actually, I didn't see it. Maybe it's still in your jacket pocket or your purse."

"It can't be, or I would have set off the metal detector at the funeral home. No, I'm positive I left it here. There was no reason to take it with me."

He walked over to my dresser and lifted the lid of the heart-shaped Limoges box my mother had given me. "It's not there."

"I know it's not there."

"What about your jewelry box?"

"Nope. I checked."

He got down on his hands and knees and peered under the dresser. "Not here, either."

"You don't suppose—" I said and stopped.

"What?"

"I wonder if Vanessa Pensiero came in here while Persia was downstairs with the kids."

"You think she took it?"

"She knew I had it. Maybe she saw it on my dresser and decided to swipe it."

"What are you going to do? Confront her? Ask her to give it back? That's kind of tough because it's not yours."

"It's not hers, either. She had no business snooping around in our bedroom."

Quinn placed his hands on my shoulders and massaged them with his thumbs. "Calm down, sweetheart. It's late, we're both dead tired, and it's been an emotional day. Maybe you didn't leave it on your dresser. I mean it, I didn't see it there. Maybe it's somewhere else and you'll find it in the morning. There's nothing you can do about it now, anyway. Let's go to bed."

With one hand he threw back the quilt and the blankets and pulled me down with him onto the soft white sheets. "I wish I could make the memories that haunt you go away," he said into my hair. "I'd do anything."

I sat up and knelt next to him, pulling my nightgown over my head and dropping it on the floor. "Do you mean that? Anything?"

He looked surprised, but then he smiled. "Want me to prove it?"

We had taken awhile to get to this place, watched each other fall in and out of love with the wrong person in relationships that had left scar tissue on the heart. Now it was finally our turn, and making love with him was sweeter and more satisfying than anything I'd ever known. Quinn filled all the empty places in my heart and my life, and he let me know—in no uncertain terms—that I filled those places in his.

The last remaining ghost between us—the one we both wanted to banish—was my accident. That it had reared its ugly head after all this time with Greg unexpectedly inserting himself into my life had unnerved me, and Quinn knew it.

An hour later, when we were both lying exhausted and spent next to each other in bed, he said in a quiet voice, "A man can always tell when a woman has something on her mind in the middle of sex, sweetheart. Or some*one*."

"I'll get over this," I said. "I promise."

He turned on his side and ran a finger from the hollow of my neck all the way down my body as though he were dissecting me into two halves. I shivered.

"Now it's your turn to prove it," he said. The soft wash of moonlight that streamed in through the windows had turned his profile to silver, like an old coin. I could just make out the challenging look in his eyes.

I pushed him back down and straddled him. "You're a sex maniac, do you know that?"

He reached up and brought my mouth to his, kissing me long and deep. "Aren't you glad that I am?" he said in a drowsy voice. "So are you."

QUINN FELL ASLEEP ALMOST instantly after our lovemaking, but sleep still wouldn't come for me as my mind revved up again. Once I let the thoughts back in they wouldn't leave me alone . . . whether Vanessa Pensiero might have taken Webb's MedicAlert bracelet, the mysterious reappearance of Dori

Upshur—who wouldn't pay her respects to Elena—and Elena's veiled threat to me to stay out of what she called "family business." Jamie's death had been the catalyst for all of these events, and tomorrow at his funeral, I suspected everyone involved would want the door closed again—slammed shut—on the murder of Webster Landau so that the past would stay buried as it had been for thirty years.

Except Jamie, who had pried it opened with his final request for forgiveness. And I was his only witness. If someone in Jamie Vaughn's closest circle of friends had committed murder, how far would that person go to keep the truth from coming out now?

If it were me, I'd want to shut up anyone who was a threat, since there was no statute of limitations on murder. That might even include silencing Jamie himself. Which meant it was possible that Jamie's accident wasn't a suicide. Or an accident as the Loudoun County Sheriff's Office was going to officially claim. Maybe someone had tampered with his car or he'd gotten behind the wheel after taking a lethal combination of drugs and alcohol that someone had given him. Mick said Jamie had been drinking too much and it was known he was on antidepressants.

If that were true, then we were talking about murder.

And then, of course, there was me. I'd have to be silenced as well.

Wouldn't I?

ON FRIDAY MORNING IT poured the kind of rain that made you think about building an ark. The sweet spring air of the last few days had turned raw and chilly and the sky was the depressing color of dingy laundry. The rain wreaked havoc on the traffic for Jamie's funeral since Trinity Episcopal Church, which looked like it had been plucked out of twelfth-century France, sat right on the edge of Mosby's Highway. By the time we reached the village of Upperville, where the little sandstone church was located, the highway had become two narrow lanes and the speed limit dropped to twenty-five, slowing traffic to a crawl. Even though Quinn and I were early, two sheriff's department officers in rain gear directed us to drive on and park elsewhere since the church and overflow lots were already full. As a result, cars had started parking on the shoulders up and down the road, turning it into a single lane so you needed to play chicken with oncoming traffic. By the time we found an empty spot, we were a good half mile away. We started hiking back to the church, and within minutes, my other pair of good black shoes was soaked through. I was running out of shoes to ruin.

On days like this when the weather was damp and cold, my bad foot bothered me more than usual. I did my best to keep up with Quinn as we followed everyone else walking single file along the side of the road, but it didn't take long for him to notice I was falling behind.

He stopped and turned around. "Are you okay?"

"Yup, fine. Just a bit slow today."

"You're limping worse than you normally do," he said. "It's your foot, isn't it? Does it hurt?"

"A little. You go ahead and save me a place. I'll catch up."

"I'm not going anywhere without you." He took my hand.

For the longest time I hadn't wanted anyone—especially

Quinn—to see my deformed foot, which I'd hidden under full-length dresses when I had to dress up, or jeans and boots when I was working in the vineyard. The first time we made love, he spent a long time massaging my oddly shaped foot, telling me it was my best and most beautiful feature because it showed just how gritty and determined I could be—learning to walk again when doctors had predicted I would be in a wheelchair for the rest of my life. To Quinn, my bad foot represented my inner strength and courage.

I knew then that I would love this man forever with all my heart.

"Have you done any more thinking about what Sasha said to you the other night?" he asked me now. "About that doctor who might be able to do surgery on your foot, make it better?"

"I've had enough surgery in my life for two people. No more doctors and knives."

"Would you at least talk to her about it? Please? For me?"

It was rare that Quinn asked me to do something, especially when he knew I was so adamantly against it.

"I'll talk to her," I said. "But it won't change my mind."

"Thank you. I'd like to be there when you do."

"Maybe after Jamie's funeral is over and things get back to normal," I said. "Though that might not be for a while, especially if Hunter Knight is going ahead with his campaign to appeal Taurique Youngblood's conviction."

"Which doesn't involve you anymore," he said. "Right?"

We had reached the church. It looked like the Secret Service was on hand again as a couple of black SUVs drove past us down Mosby's Highway, having discharged their official passengers.

"Look," I said, avoiding Quinn's question, "the funeral procession is arriving."

A hearse and three limousines from Hunt Funeral Home pulled into the parking lot as traffic stopped in both directions. The limo drivers opened car doors as Jamie's family slowly emerged and began making their way to the cobblestone courtyard. I spotted Sasha and Vanessa, each holding one of Zach's hands. Eli followed a few paces behind. Once Zach glanced over his shoulder as he trotted along, glancing at my brother with a scared, uncertain look on his face. Eli reached out and patted the little boy's shoulder, and my heart twisted. This was going to be rough.

The funeral was a full Anglican burial service with Holy Communion and a choir that sang all the traditional hymns. Oliver and Owen each did one of the readings before the Gospel and I couldn't help thinking it was ironic that Oliver stumbled over his passage from the Book of Wisdom: *The souls of the righteous are in the hand of God, and no torment will ever touch them . . . they are at peace.* Jamie Vaughn—I was sure of it—was not at peace. That would have to wait until—and if— Taurique Youngblood got justice, and even if he did, I suspected the implications for those Jamie loved the most would be life altering.

What he had set in motion was not finished. I craned my neck without trying to look too obvious to see whether Dori Upshur had come to Jamie's funeral, whether she needed to be there to witness this final goodbye after walking out of his wake last night.

"What are you doing?" Quinn finally whispered in my ear.

"Looking for Dori," I said. "You're taller than I am. Do you see her?"

"If she's wearing black, she's going to be tough to pick out of the crowd."

"Very funny."

Someone behind us shushed us as Mick Dunne got up to deliver the first eulogy. He got through it, by turns funny, serious, somber, and emotional with a voice that cracked once or twice, but he didn't break down. Neither did Garrett Bateman, who gave the second eulogy, although there were audible sniffles throughout the church when he told two deeply moving stories of people Jamie had helped on the quiet, and I remembered Thelma, teary eyed and wearing black as a tribute to him the other day. I had seen her in the crowd a few rows in front of us, and when we'd driven by the General Store this morning, the neon sign that read OPE was dark and a handwritten sign on the door read WE ARE NOT OPEN DUE TO TEMPORARILY BEING CLOSED FOR A FUNERAL.

Just before the Dismissal and the final hymn, the grayhaired female rector asked everyone to please stand for the Committal. As we rose, I caught sight of Hunter Knight leaning against a wall on the other side of the church near the back, dressed in a dark suit underneath a raincoat. What was he doing here? He certainly wouldn't be welcome if anyone from Jamie's family knew who he was and his recent history with the deceased.

"We have but a short time to live," the rector was saying. "Like a flower we blossom and then wither; like a shadow we flee and never stay."

I couldn't take my eyes off Hunter, who must have felt my gaze on him because he suddenly looked straight at me and our eyes met. He nodded, acknowledging me, before he turned and quietly walked out of the church. Had he been here for the entire service? How had I not noticed him?

The prayer ended, and the organ began the introduction to the final hymn, "O God Beyond All Praising." An English hymn, but my French mother had always loved the soaring melody. The choir would sing one full verse before the rector began to walk down the aisle, with Jamie's family following her. I'd never be able to get out of here and catch up with Hunter, who I suspected would have vanished by then. There was a reception afterward in the parish hall, but I doubted he would be there.

"Damn."

Quinn looked up from his hymnbook. "What?"

"I'll tell you later."

By the time we left the church and followed everyone else outside to the courtyard, I felt like I was standing in a crowded D.C. Metro train at rush hour. Hunter Knight had vanished and I didn't see Dori Upshur, either. It had started to drizzle as we slowly made our way toward the parish hall under the covered walkway.

"We're going to be packed like sardines at this reception," Quinn said. "That hall can't hold everyone who was in the church."

"It won't have to. A lot of people are leaving."

It was true. Small groups were peeling off from the crowd, walking toward Mosby's Highway like they were at a sports event or a concert and wanted to avoid a scrum in the parking lot more than they wanted to see who won or hear the last en-core. The parish hall was still crowded and noisy, though, and it wasn't long before Quinn and I got separated near the buffet table.

I accepted a glass of ginger ale and cranberry juice punch from a woman standing at a punch bowl and scanned the room. No Dori, no Hunter.

"Lucie." I turned around. Sasha, looking more pale and wan than she had last night, held a crumpled handkerchief in one hand and a cup of black coffee in the other. "I've been look-ing for you. I didn't see you in the church."

"We were sitting in the back. Where are Eli and Zach?"

"They went in search of cookies."

"I didn't realize Zach was coming."

"He's the only grandchild. A grandson. My mother and Elena thought it was important for him to be there. The next generation." Her smile was twisted.

"Is he okay?"

She shrugged. "Thank goodness for your brother. I don't think I could have gotten through this without him. He's so good with Zach." Her eyes met mine. "I'm sorry I snapped at you last night. I shouldn't have done it."

"It's okay."

Someone jostled Sasha so she nearly spilled her coffee. "Let's find somewhere that's not in the middle of traffic," she said. "Or I'll have hot coffee all over myself."

We ended up near the door that led to the bathrooms at the far end of the room. "Your foot must be really bothering you," she said. "You're limping. Are you all right?"

"It's the weather."

"Why don't you come see me next week? Let me take a look at it. I still think you should talk to Charles Quillian. He's a miracle worker."

"Your doctor friend?"

She nodded. "He's good, Lucie. I met Charlie at a conference two years ago on disease-modifying therapies for patients with multiple sclerosis."

"There were two women with MS who had physical therapy with me at the hospital after my surgeries," I said. "I didn't think there was much you could do once you were diagnosed with it."

"PT can do a lot to help certain kinds of MS," Sasha said. "And drug research has come a long way since Mick Dunne's company developed that immunosuppressant drug that was supposed to help stop relapses. I'm sure you've heard of it. It was the only drug on the market for years. He made a fortune from it."

"What drug—?"

"We're back." Eli and Zach appeared, each holding a chocolate-chip cookie the size of a small plate. Eli took Sasha's empty coffee cup and gave her his cookie. "Here, sweetheart. Hey, Luce. I would have brought a cookie for you if I'd known you were going to be here."

"She can have half of mine." Sasha broke hers in two and handed me the larger half.

"Thanks. This thing is huge," I said. To my brother I added, "I don't suppose you've seen Quinn?"

"He's talking to Oliver Vaughn. Trying to pick his brain about the Norton they're going to serve tomorrow. And your mother is talking to Owen and his girlfriend, Sash. I asked her if she wanted a chair because of her boot and she said she was fine." He picked up Zach in his arms. "Is that a good cookie, buddy?"

Zach nodded. "Yup."

"Mom's a real stoic," Sasha said, giving Eli a grateful smile.

"I understand she came over to the house last night when she got in from Charlottesville to pick up Zach," I said.

"That was her idea," Sasha said. "She said it would save me a trip, plus she could get the Cookie Monster here home earlier and put him to bed." She dabbed at the chocolate on Zach's face.

"More cookies," Zach said. "Please."

"No." Sasha said. "You'll get sick."

Eli raised an eyebrow.

She relented. "Okay, just one more. Any more than that, Eli, and he'll explode."

Zach giggled, probably imagining an explosion of chocolate chip cookies as his version of heaven, and then he and Eli left.

"Sasha," I said. "I'm not sure how to say this, but last night I discovered that Webb Landau's MedicAlert bracelet is missing. I'm sure it was on my bedroom dresser before I left for the wake."

"Missing? How did . . . Wait a minute." She gave me an incredulous look. "You're not implying that my mother took it, are you? Because she would never do anything like that."

"I don't know what to say. It was there when I left and I couldn't find it when I came home."

"Lucie . . . no. There must be some explanation other than my mother stealing it." Sasha sounded distraught. "In fact, why don't you ask her yourself? Here she is now."

Vanessa Pensiero and I had not parted on the best of terms the other day. This wasn't going to improve our relationship. "Hello, Lucie," she said in a cool voice. "Ask me what?"

"Lucie says the MedicAlert bracelet Dad gave her the day of the accident is missing," Sasha said before I could speak. "She left it in her bedroom last night before she went to the wake and when she got home it was gone."

Vanessa's eyes narrowed and she focused on me. "What are you saying?"

"Did you take it, Mom, when you were there to pick up Zach?"

Vanessa's head snapped back in surprise. "Of course not. Why would I do that?" She turned to me, a look of distaste on her face. "Are you accusing me of stealing?"

"I just wondered if you knew anything about it going missing."

"You have a housekeeper," she said, the chilliness now a deep freeze. "I met her. A woman of . . . color. Did you ask her? Or maybe your niece, who saw something she thought was jewelry sitting on your dresser and wanted to play with it?"

I felt as if I'd been slapped hard across the face. "Persia would never . . ."

"Did you ask her?"

"No."

"Then I suggest you do. Today is difficult enough as it is," she said. "For so many reasons. You just made it even more heartbreaking. Excuse me. I need to get some fresh air." She turned and stomped away, her heavy boot clumping as she left.

Sasha gave me an anguished look. "I shouldn't have brought it up. Look how upset she is."

"Sasha," I said, "I told you the bracelet was on my bedroom dresser. You only told your mother it was in my bedroom."

There was a long moment of silence before she said in a shocked voice, "She knew it was on your dresser."

"That's right," I said. "She did."

Seventeen

'll talk to her," Sasha said. "Maybe she was trying to protect my father by taking it . . . protect Zach and me. What good is it now to anyone, anyway?"

"I'm not sure it's the bracelet itself," I said, trying to think this through. "What really matters is why your father held on to it for all these years. If he murdered Webb Landau, you'd think he'd want to get rid of it. If he didn't, maybe he knew who the killer was and the bracelet was some kind of insurance. Or leverage."

"Against whom?" She gave me a wild-eyed look as the weight of my words sank in. "Do you realize who the other suspects are?"

I did. "Sasha—"

"No." She held out a hand, palm facing me like a shield. Or a warning. "Just stop right here. This has gone far enough. I won't allow my family and the people my dad loved the most to have their lives ripped apart."

I didn't want to say, "You can't play God. It's not your choice." Instead I said, "What about Taurique Youngblood's life being ripped apart?"

"A jury thought he was guilty and convicted him of killing Webb. He already had a criminal record. They found evidence, Lucie." I wondered whether she was trying to convince me—or herself.

"Now he's on death row. Maybe wrongly. And your father's last words were to ask for his forgiveness."

She flinched, but she didn't back down. "Look, no one knows why Dad had that MedicAlert bracelet or why he said what he said. Now we're never going to know. There's nothing more anyone can do. And you need to drop this. It has nothing to do with you."

"The St. Leonard Project is not going to drop it. It's not over, Sasha."

Her eyes grew stormy. "It is as far as I'm concerned. My mother was right. You picked a hell of a day to have this conversation. Excuse me. I'm going to find Eli and Zach."

She left, stiff-necked and angrier than I'd ever seen her. It was time to find Quinn and get out of here. Sasha was wrong: This wasn't over. Neither she nor Vanessa could make it so; they couldn't put the genie back in the bottle. It was too late for that.

Besides, maybe Hunter Knight wasn't the only person looking for answers to who really killed Webb. Why had Dori Upshur returned after all these years? Where had she been and what brought her back to Virginia? Did Jamie's death trip a switch that had something to do with Webb Landau's murder? That fiery accident had been all over the national and international news. Dori couldn't have missed hearing about it unless she lived in a cave.

Just because I hadn't seen her at the funeral this morning didn't mean she hadn't been there. She could have kept a low profile, just like she'd done last night. As far as I knew, no one who had been one of Dori's Darlings seemed aware that she was in town. Maybe she was still around.

And I knew just who could answer that question.

I TOLD QUINN ON the drive back to the vineyard that I'd caught Vanessa in a lie about taking the MedicAlert bracelet and about the unpleasant conversation I had with Sasha afterward.

"What are you going to do?" he'd asked. "You can't steal it back. For all you know, Vanessa's probably gotten rid of it by now. That's what I'd do, anyway."

"Probably. I was surprised by Sasha's reaction, though."

"If someone other than Taurique Youngblood killed Webb, and Sasha's mother and father either know—or, in Jamie's case, knew—something about who did it, or maybe one of them is guilty of murder, then why would you be surprised that she wants this whole thing to go away? You think she wants someone she loves and cares about to go to jail?"

" 'Every guilty person is his own hangman.' I don't remember who said that, but I read it somewhere once. And if you keep someone else's guilty secret, then you're guilty, too."

"What about your brother? What if he gets mixed up in this because of Sasha? Would you feel any different if someone from your family got involved?"

"You really know how to twist the knife."

"See." He nodded. "It's not so easy, is it?"

"No. But it doesn't change right and wrong. Letting the wrong person be punished for a crime someone else committed isn't a gray or fuzzy area. It's black-and-white, flat-out wrong. Nobody should be above the law or exempt from obeying it, including someone who wanted to be president of the United States. Or my brother. Or you and me."

"You're right, of course," he said. "But it happens. And now that Jamie's dead, it looks like no one else who might know anything about Webb's death is going to talk."

"It's not over," I told him. "Hunter Knight isn't going to give up. And there might be someone else who would be willing to talk."

He gave me an ominous look. "Who?"

"Dori Upshur."

THE IDEA THAT AFTER thirty years Dori Upshur would have anything to say to me—a total stranger—about Webb Landau's murder was about as crazy as you could get. First, I had to find her, presuming I'd been right about seeing her at Jamie's wake last night. Then I had to convince her to talk about a murder that had sabotaged her career and caused her to walk away from her life as a university department chair and a renowned biochemist and vanish into the ether.

Fat chance.

I started looking for her in the most obvious and logical place to go if you want to know what's going on in Atoka and Middleburg: I dropped by the General Store. The OPE sign was lit up and the handmade sign about being temporarily closed was gone.

The rain had stopped a few hours ago and the sun was now poking through the clouds. The sleigh bells on the door jingled as they always did when anyone entered the store, but for once the television in the back room was silent and the empty store seemed eerily quiet. Thelma was quiet, too, still wearing the black dress she had on at the funeral. I found her standing behind the cash register counter with the Metro section of the *Washington Tribune* opened to a full-page appreciation of Jamie Vaughn's life.

She gave me a worn-out smile. "Lucille," she said, folding the newspaper and putting it aside. "What can I do for you?"

"I need a quart of milk," I said, "and some information."

She arched an eyebrow, which disappeared under her lacquered helmet of carrot-colored bangs. I wasn't usually this blunt. "Milk I got," she said. "As for information, not to break my arm patting myself on the back, but I've got quite a photogenic memory, you know. And, of course, people drop by to tell me things all the time because they just plumb like to conjugate here."

"Yes, I know."

"So," she said, blinking behind her thick trifocals, "what is it you want to know?"

"I thought I saw a woman I recognized at Jamie's wake last night, but she disappeared before I got a chance to talk to her. You know how crowded that funeral home was," I said as Thelma nodded. "Anyway, we haven't seen each other for years and I lost touch with her. I wondered if she might have dropped by here, or maybe you heard about her from one of the Romeos."

"What's her name?"

"Dori Upshur."

Thelma tapped her chin with her index finger as if she were pondering the mysteries of the universe. "Sorry, Lucille. Doesn't ring a bell. What does she look like?"

"A bit on the heavy side. Straight gray hair cut in a bob. Glasses. She was wearing a beige trench coat with a red silk scarf when I saw her. And she has a beauty mark above her upper lip."

Thelma's eyes registered recognition when I mentioned the beauty mark. "Her. Why, yes, indeedy, she was in here yesterday morning. Just got into town, in fact. I remember her because of that mole on her face. Reminded me of Marilyn Monroe. She was before your time, but she was a famous actress who was quite the blond bomb shelter."

"I see. Uh . . . Dori didn't happen to mention where she was staying?"

"No, but I asked her. At the Fox & Hound, of course."

The Fox & Hound was a bed-and-breakfast up the street from where I lived. Situated on fifty acres, the sprawling old house was set well back from Atoka Road and had been built just before the Civil War by a wealthy landowner who had added numerous outbuildings and dependencies. The owners of the B&B transformed several of those buildings into luxurious guest cottages, plus there were the rooms in the main house. If you wanted privacy while you were in town, the Fox & Hound was the perfect place to stay.

"How do you two happen to know each other?" Thelma's smile was bland, but this was the quid pro quo. I needed to provide information now that I had received information.

"She was one of my professors in college." I could tell she knew that was a bald-faced lie, but I toughed it out. "Biology."

Thelma gave me a cat-got-the-canary look and my heart plummeted to my feet. "That's kind of funny because she told me she's been working in North Carolina for the last twenty-five years as an environmental conversationalist for one of those nonprofit companies that don't want to make any money. They tell folks to do things like recycling because it helps close the hole in the ozone layer. And you, missy, went to college ten or so years ago right here in Virginia. So how's it you had her for a professor?"

"She was a guest lecturer. For a semester."

Thelma put her hands on her hips. No dice. "What's going on, Lucille? Who is she really?"

If I told her who Dori really was, word would get around from here to Richmond before I even got back to my car. I also knew she wasn't going to let me leave without an answer that sounded a lot more like the truth.

I said, with some reluctance, "She knew Jamie. She was a professor at UVA when he was a student there."

Thelma tilted her head to one side, holding her mouth at a funny angle. "Now that sounds more like it, but still, it seems a bit odd to me."

"What do you mean?"

"Well, a-course I asked her if she was in town for the funeral. She said no, she wasn't. Just here for a day or two to visit a friend." She paused, frowning. "I wonder what she's really doing in Atoka?"

So Dori hadn't gone to the funeral, but she had shown up at the wake.

"Me, too," I said. "And which friend?"

I DECIDED TO DRIVE over to the Fox & Hound. Even though I knew that neither the owners nor anyone who worked there would confirm that Dori Upshur was staying with them since they were scrupulous about protecting their guests' privacy, I figured I could try leaving a note for her and maybe I'd get lucky. As it turned out, I never made it to the bed-and-breakfast because I found Dori where I least expected to see her: at my vineyard.

A lone car was parked by the side of the road and a woman in a beige trench coat and a red scarf stood in front of Jamie's memorial with her back to me. After this morning's downpour, the hundreds of tributes that had been left over the past few days were wilted and bedraggled. The front entrance to my vineyard looked more like a place where people had come to dump trash than to pay their respects. Dori didn't turn around when I slammed the door to the Jeep, even though I knew she must have heard me.

I walked up and stood next to her. She gave me a sideways glance with eyes that looked suspiciously like she'd been crying and said, "Are you following me?"

"Not exactly," I said. "But I was looking for you. This is my vineyard, by the way."

"You're the one who was with Jamie when he died." It sounded like an accusation.

"That's right," I said. "And you're Dori Upshur. I recognized you from pictures in the newspaper. You haven't changed much in thirty years."

I left out mentioning that I'd seen Vanessa's striking photo of her taken at one of her dinners, but I could tell I'd caught her off guard.

After a moment she said in a chilly voice, "You couldn't be more wrong. I walked away from everything I loved thirty years ago. My job, my home, my friends, my life. I changed forever."

"Because of Webb Landau's murder?"

"How do you know about that?" More with that accusative tone. Dori Upshur seemed a lot tougher than the combination mother hen—cum—den mother I had envisioned. Someone who hosted farmhouse dinners with a beloved group of students everyone else jealously referred to as Dori's Darlings where they had far-reaching erudite conversations and sleepovers for those too inebriated to walk or drive home.

I held my ground. "I know about it indirectly from Jamie," I said. There was no point playing games or being coy. "Do you know who killed Webb?"

For a moment she looked taken aback. Then she said, "Taurique Youngblood killed him. There was a trial and he was convicted of murder."

"That's not true—that Taurique Youngblood killed him—and you know it."

Her head snapped up as if I'd struck her, and she gave me a cold stare. "How dare you? You probably weren't even born when it happened. You have no right to pass judgment on something you know nothing about."

"I'm not judging anything," I said. "Just trying to fulfill a dying friend's last request."

"What are you talking about?"

"Jamie didn't think Taurique was guilty. He asked me—no, told me—just before he died to ask Taurique to forgive him."

"Are you implying that Jamie killed Taurique?" she said.

"I'm not implying anything. Besides, I don't think Jamie did it. I think he was full of remorse because maybe he knew who killed Webb. And it wasn't Taurique."

Dori started to pick her way between wilted bouquets of flowers, extinguished candles, and soggy letters and photographs encased in plastic, walking toward the wall and the spot where Jamie's car had crashed. I followed her. This conversation wasn't over.

She stopped and swung around to face me. "And it took Jamie all these years to finally feel bad enough, guilty enough, that he did something about it? Drove his car into your wall because he was so devastated? That's your theory?" Her voice was rich with scorn. "Really?"

I pointed at the pile of stones and the jagged remnants of the wall. "How did you know Jamie crashing into this wall had anything to do with Taurique? All the news stories said he hit it at high speed because he probably lost control of his car. An accident due to reckless driving."

"You're the one talking about remorse." She bent down and picked up a framed campaign picture of Jamie that he'd autographed in his big bold scrawl to someone named Carl and stared at it for a long moment. She hooked a thumb in the direction of the wall. "The easy way out would be to end it all, wouldn't it? Maybe that's just what Jamie did. That's how he dealt with his remorse."

"It doesn't make sense. Why now? Why wait so many years?" I said. "And look at this place. Look at all the people whose lives he touched. Jamie did a lot of good for a lot of people."

Dori shrugged and set the photograph on the ground where she'd found it. "I have no idea why he waited until now. I'm not a mind reader. What do they say? Every saint has a past and every sinner has a future. If he didn't do it, maybe he knew who did and he hated keeping that secret any longer."

"Meaning one of the others who were with Webb at your house for dinner that last night killed him?"

She shot me a curious, uneasy look. "How do you know about that dinner? Who have you been talking to?"

"I read the newspaper articles about the search for Webb and then Taurique's trial. There was plenty of information in there," I said and hoped I was right. "So, who else could it have been if it wasn't Taurique? Or Jamie?"

I waited until she finally said, "It could have been any of them. Including Jamie. That last night before Webb took off, there was such an awful fight between all of them. Everyone was angry—no, furious—at Webb for one reason or another. And they were drinking way too much. I couldn't stand it. Everything and everyone was out of control. So I left."

"That seems like an odd thing to do, instead of trying to put a stop to it. It was your home. A bunch of drunk students fighting and you, a senior university professor, a department chair, just walked out?"

"I had my reasons."

"Because you were angry at Webb, too?"

She gave me a blank stare that meant yes.

"Furious?" I asked.

"Furious enough to kill him?" She laughed without any mirth. "Do you think I would tell you if I did?"

"Probably not. But I do think you'd tell me if you didn't."

"You're clever," she said. "And Lucie—it is Lucie, isn't it?—you really ought to stay out of things that are none of your business."

So she knew my name. I'd been in the news, but it surprised me that she remembered it.

We had reached the rubble of the destroyed stone pillar and the wall. The ground was still scorched and blackened, but after the rain, deep rutted tracks from the tires of the emergency and rescue vehicles were filled with muddy water. Dori and I had to walk carefully to avoid sinking up to our ankles. She leaned forward to touch the remnants of the fire-charred stone wall.

"Jamie made it my business because of his final request," I said to her. "Be careful. The yellow caution tape is there for a reason. You don't want the rest of that pillar to come tumbling down on you. It's not really safe to be here. Come on, let's go."

"Jamie is dead." She pulled her hand away from the wall. "It's nobody's business anymore. It's over."

"Why were you angry with Webb?" I asked her. "I thought he was the star of your department, that he had such a brilliant mind. He was a genius with so much potential that he could do anything he wanted after he graduated."

We picked our way through the flowers and mementos again, heading back to the edge of the ocean of tributes.

She stopped and swung around on me so abruptly that I nearly ran into her. "He was a genius," she said. "But his brilliance was wasted on him."

"What do you mean?"

"Because of his Achilles' heel. Hubris. Do you know what that is?"

"Of course," I said. "Pride. Ego."

"It's more than that," she said. "It's an inflated view of one's accomplishments or capabilities. An unrealistic estimation of just how smart or competent you are. That was Webb. He was brilliant . . . gifted, as you said. An unbelievable intellect. I'd never met anyone like him."

"But?"

"He was lazy, reckless, and a bully when he wanted to be. He relied on his superior intelligence—along with his charm and good looks—to get him out of trouble and invariably it worked. He thought he was so much cleverer than everyone else, and, of course, he was. Nothing was ever his fault. Webb always managed to hang it on someone else."

I was stunned by her passion and still-raw anger. Dori Upshur hadn't left anything behind in thirty years in spite of what she'd told me, any more than I had after my own accident. This was the real wreckage Quinn warned me about. If you can't forgive and move on, the corrosive bitterness eats you from the inside out.

"Did Webb manage to hang some of his problems on you?" I asked, but I already knew the answer.

She shrugged, an affirmation. "What does the Bible say?

'From those to whom much is given, much is expected.' Webb thought he was the exception to the rule. I couldn't abide seeing him waste so much talent. A genius, really. Piss it all away."

"I thought Webb was going to turn in Jamie and Mick Dunne because they falsified data for a project they were working on for him," I said. "Wasn't that why they were angry with him that night? He could have gotten them expelled right before graduation for an honor code violation."

If Dori realized I couldn't have known about that from the newspapers, she didn't say anything. "That's right," she said. "He was. Or at least, he threatened to. But all of them knew hc'd gotten away with worse."

"In other words, everyone at that dinner party had a motive for murder," I said.

"I didn't say that. I said everyone was angry with him. It's not the same thing."

"Don't you think it's odd that the person convicted of killing him really didn't have a motive?"

"The overwhelming evidence against Taurique Youngblood is what convicted him," she said.

We were back where we started, like a vinyl record with a needle stuck in a groove. Let Taurique take the blame because it solved all the problems.

"It didn't take the jury long to decide he was guilty of murder," she went on. "Maybe no one who was at that dinner was sorry Webb was dead. But that's different from actually committing the crime. I'm done talking with you. Stay out of this, Lucie. I'm warning you. You don't know what you're getting into."

"Why did you come here, after staying away for so many years? You looked as if you'd been crying just now."

"That's none of your business," she said. "And just so you know, I've read up on you, too, since you've been in the news. Jamie died in the same spot where a car you were riding in crashed some years ago." She indicated my cane. "Which is why you need to use that."

My hand tightened on the cane. "What of it?"

"That's why you've made this so personal."

"What happened to me has nothing to do with Jamie's accident."

"On the contrary, it has everything to do with why you're so committed to helping Taurique. I've kept up with him," she said. "He has people fighting for him both inside and out-side of prison who want his case reopened. Including someone you know very well."

I felt the blood leave my face. She knew about the St. Leon-ard Project and Greg's role in helping Taurique. "Why would I get involved with the person who was driving the car the night of my accident? I never want to see him again. Unlike Taurique, he belongs in jail for a crime he committed."

"I don't know why you're involved," she said. "I just know that you are. Consider yourself warned: Stay out of this. You'll regret it if you don't."

"Is that a threat?"

"Not at all," she said. "It's a promise."

I shuddered. She sounded like she meant it. I looked down. Directly at our feet was the bouquet of red roses I'd noticed the other morning when I came here by myself to see the trib-utes people had left for Jamie. Unlike some of the other wet, wilted flowers, they still looked fresh and beautiful, as if this morning's rain had revived them. The writing on the attached card had faded, but I could still make out the words.

What's done in darkness always comes to light.

I looked up at Dori. She had stopped here for a reason. "You left those roses," I said. "That note is from you."

"No." She wrapped her arms around her waist as if shielding herself from my accusation. "It's not. I didn't leave anything."

"Of course you did. That note is a warning to anyone who knew about Webb's murder. Who were you warning, Dori?"

"I don't know what you're talking about."

"You've been in Atoka all along," I said, as puzzle pieces fit into place with neat little clicks. "I saw those roses at six o'clock the morning after Jamie's accident. You didn't just get into town for the wake. You were here before Jamie died."

Maybe she'd even seen him the day he died. I still didn't know *why* Webb Landau's murder had resurrected itself after thirty years, but if Jamie had seen Webb's MedicAlert bracelet after all this time, it could have been one of the things that pushed him over the edge. Was Dori Upshur the one who'd given it to him?

Dori's face had gone pale, but she kept shaking her head. "No. No. No."

"You went to see Jamie and you gave him Webb's Medic-Alert bracelet. I thought he'd kept it ever since Webb was killed, but you're the one who had it." I'd just played my trump card. If I was right, it explained a lot of things. If I was wrong, I'd made a stupid miscalculation giving her that information.

But I didn't think I was wrong.

"You have an unbelievable imagination." Her laughter trilled into a half-hysterical cackle. "I had no idea what happened to that bracelet. You're saying Jamie has it? Had it? Where is it now?"

"I don't know where it is," I said, which was God's truth. "But what I don't understand is why you gave it to Jamie after all this time. What changed after thirty years?"

"You're insane," she said, "and you're talking nonsense, making these crazy accusations. Two people are already dead, so consider yourself lucky I've warned you to walk away while you can. Goodbye, Lucie. I hope you're smarter than you seem to be."

I stood rooted to the ground while she left me by the wall and disappeared around the other side of it, presumably heading for her car. A moment later I heard an engine start and then a car pulled out onto the road. My heart was beating so hard I thought it would explode out of my chest.

What was Dori Upshur hiding and who was she covering up for? Herself? Could she have killed Webb? It wasn't out of the realm of possibility: She'd had opportunity and motive. Maybe she showed up after all these years because she learned of the St. Leonard Project's intention to try to reopen the case against Taurique. Had Dori come to town to warn Jamie not to talk about what he knew, just as she had warned me a moment ago?

And now he was dead.

I walked around the edges of Jamie's memorial looking more closely at the things people had left, unsure what I was searching for. Maybe there was another note like the one

Dori—because I was sure she had sent it—had left with the roses. After ten minutes when I hadn't found anything unusual, I gave up and started to walk back to the Jeep.

That's when someone took a shot at me.

Eighteen

For a crazy instant I told myself the two popping sounds were fireworks, even though I knew better. Then another bullet whizzed past me, inches away, and I dove behind the crumbling stone wall. The next bullet hit a chunk of wall above my head and razorlike shards of stone flew in every direction. Something that felt like a stiletto stung my right cheek, and more pieces of stone and mortar ricocheted off my arms and legs. The side of my face felt like it was on fire. The next shot was even closer. I pulled my phone out of my jeans pocket. Whoever was shooting was getting closer. I was unarmed, alone, and if I didn't get out of here soon, I was as good as dead. The only other place that offered any shelter was the Jeep, but it was at least twenty yards away. Even if I could run like I used to when I ran cross-country in school, I still wouldn't make it across that expanse of open space without giving the shooter an opportunity to perfect his target practice.

Quinn's picture was at the top of my favorites list on my

phone. I tapped it and called him as I scrambled to put some distance between the shooter and me. My bad foot twisted as I hit a patch of mud that was as slick as black ice. I grabbed a chunk of wall to keep from landing on my rear, but the effort cost me my phone, which plunked into one of the bigger mud puddles and disappeared. I took a deep breath and fought down panic. Both my parents had died violent deaths on this farm, my father from a bullet wound. I would not be another Montgomery to die the same way. I'd already survived one accident at this wall.

The whine of a truck engine—Quinn's truck—speeding toward me down Sycamore Lane was such a relief I nearly wept for joy. Quinn, thank God, must have heard the shots and maybe my call had gotten through before my phone hit the water. Either way, I flattened myself against the wall as the truck barreled through the sawhorse barricades we'd set up to keep people from using the road, scattering them as if they were made of balsa wood. There was another shot, and this time I knew it was Quinn, firing one of Leland's shotguns out the truck window. He pulled up beside me and flung open the passenger door.

"Get in!"

I flew across the few feet to the truck as swiftly as my bad leg would let me and hurled myself inside. For the second time in a week, I lost my cane as it caught on the seat cushion and bounced out of my hand, landing on the ground.

"Forget the cane. Let's get out of here." He spun the truck in a U-turn as a bullet hit the back of the cab.

"Did you see anyone?" I could hardly get the words out.

"No. Get down." He pushed my head below the windshield

and ducked low himself so he was partially shielded by the steering wheel.

I felt breathless. "He's trying to kill me. Kill us."

"We're not going to let him. Take the gun. Cover us till we get out of here. You're bleeding pretty badly, sweetheart. There's a gash on your face."

"It looks worse than it is." I stuck my father's shotgun out the passenger window and fired into the woods. Quinn floored the gas pedal and we fishtailed down the road toward the winery. No echoing shots answered mine.

I swung my gaze around and looked at Quinn.

"I'm firing blanks," I said. "What were you doing with this gun, anyway?"

He handed me a T-shirt that had been stuffed under his seat. "This isn't the cleanest thing, but you can use it to stop the bleeding until we get that wound on your face taken care of. And what do you mean what am I doing with the gun?" He sounded indignant. "Lucky for you I had it. I told you the other night I might borrow something from your father's gun cabinet to put the fear of God in the next person I catch dumping trash by the vines. Or having outdoor sex."

Before I could utter an astonished protest he added, "And you know perfectly well I'd never use live bullets."

"Right," I said in a faint voice. My blood had soaked through his T-shirt. I found a clean spot and pressed it against my cheek again as Quinn started to turn in to the winery parking lot.

"Let's not go here," I said. "Not the winery. There are too many people—guests, staff—if he follows us. It's too dangerous. And he wasn't firing blanks." I looked out the back window of the cab. "I don't see anyone."

"He'll have to show himself if he leaves those woods and heads to the winery," Quinn said, but he didn't turn in to the winery driveway and kept on going. "Where to?"

"Not the house, either. Persia's there with Hope." My breath had slowed but my heart was still hammering in my chest. "The shots came from the direction of Mick's farm. What if the shooter is on horseback? It wouldn't take him long to catch up with us."

Quinn blinked and turned to me. "Are you saying you think Mick Dunne was shooting at you?"

"No. Jesus. No, of course not. But whoever it was must have crossed onto our property from his land. That way they wouldn't be seen."

Quinn picked up his phone from the console and tossed it in my lap. "Call nine-one-one. We need help. Ask for an ambulance, too." He touched the side of my face near the bloody gash. "You need to get that taken care of."

The wound throbbed, but I shook my head. "No ambulance. I'm sure the blood makes it look worse than it is. Drive to the cemetery. It's on a hill and we'll have a three-hundred-and-sixty-degree view so we can see anyone who decides to follow us." I hit the emergency button on Quinn's phone and identified myself. "There's an active shooter in the woods at Montgomery Estate Vineyard by the front gate. Please hurry . . . and be careful."

A COUPLE OF DEPUTIES from the Loudoun County Sheriff's Department searched the woods near the vineyard entrance after arriving with screaming sirens and flashing lights for the second time in less than a week. Not surprisingly, they didn't find the shooter, though they did find places where the brush had been trampled. But whoever it was had been on foot, not horseback, so I'd been wrong about that.

Bobby Noland—Kit's husband, my childhood friend, and one of the senior detectives with the sheriff's department—called at five thirty to say he was on his way over to talk to me about what happened. By then I had showered and changed out of my blood-spattered clothes after insisting to both Quinn and Persia that the cut on my face would eventually heal just fine. Still, I'd kept Quinn out of the bathroom when I got undressed so he wouldn't see the scraped raw skin and newly blooming bruises on my arms and legs in the places where chunks of the wall had ricocheted off me.

He had turned on the six o'clock news and the two of us were in the parlor watching television when Bobby rang the doorbell. Jamie's funeral had been the lead story, and Pippa O'Hara had covered it with her usual swashbuckling flair. Journalists hadn't been allowed inside during the service, so she'd done her stand-up with the church in the background over her shoulder as funeral-goers were leaving. She'd even gotten a couple of people to comment about what a sad occasion it had been.

"I'll get it," Quinn said, and a moment later he and Bobby walked into the parlor. I picked up the remote and switched off the television. Bobby was holding my cane like a trophy he'd just won in one hand and my waterlogged phone in the other.

Though he was only two years older than me, his job had aged him. His military-short sandy hair was now salt-and-pepper and his blue eyes had the world-weary look of someone who witnessed the worst, most unspeakable things man can do to his fellow man—or woman—on a daily basis.

He took one look at my face and said, "I'd hate to see the other guy. What happened?" He handed me my cane and my phone.

I grinned and the gash felt like it was splitting open. "Ouch. He got away. I wonder if my phone is dead for good?"

"Drink, Bobby?" Quinn asked. "Have a seat."

"Wish I could, but I'm on duty."

"Sweetheart, you want a Scotch?" Quinn asked me.

"Please. On the rocks."

Bobby took the wing chair across from me after pulling a spiral notebook with a pen stuck through it out of his back pocket. "Try putting your phone in a sealed bag of rice and drying it out for twenty-four to thirty-six hours. It might work."

I held the wet phone between my thumb and index finger like it was a lab specimen to examine. "I'll try it. Damn. I just got this phone."

"So tell me what happened," he said as Quinn came back into the room with two Scotches and sat beside me on the sofa.

I told him.

When I was done, he said, "Obviously not a hunter, not at this time of year. Did you call out or anything? Yell, 'Hey knock it off, there's someone here'?"

"He was looking for me," I said. "I didn't want to help him out."

He tapped his pen on his notebook and frowned at his notes. "Who's got it in for you, Lucie? Bad enough to want to kill you?"

"Tell him," Quinn said to me. "Tell him everything."

Bobby leaned back against the chair and crossed one leg over the other. "I thought you just did," he said. "There's more?"

I knew he'd read the same stories about Webb Landau's murder and Taurique Youngblood's trial and conviction that I had, since Kit had made him copies of the ones she'd given me the other day. I also figured Kit had confided in her husband, telling him what she'd learned about Jamie's political campaign using donation money to pay personal and business expenses. What he didn't know was that I'd visited the St. Leonard Project in Washington and discovered that Hunter Knight—with the help of his brother in prison—was pushing to reopen Taurique's case and review the conviction.

So I told Bobby about Jamie's dying request and Vanessa identifying Webb Landau's MedicAlert bracelet. I also told him about my meeting with Hunter Knight yesterday morning.

"Elena and Garrett made up some story about 'Rick'—since that's who I originally thought Jamie was talking about—being a campaign donor who'd had a falling-out with Jamie and told me they'd take care of talking to him," I said. "So they lied. Mick Dunne did, too. I'm also fairly sure Vanessa Pensiero stole Webb Landau's MedicAlert bracelet off my dresser last night when she came to pick up her grandson, so she's upset with me. And then there's Dori Upshur, who told me that if I knew what was good for me, I'd stay out of this. She says Taurique murdered Webb, end of story."

Bobby chewed on the end of his pen and thought for a moment. "Okay, about ten or fifteen minutes after Dori Upshur threatened you and left you at the front entrance to the vineyard, someone started shooting at you from the woods. What makes you so sure it wasn't Dori? You keep saying 'he' and 'him.' But she's the only one who knew where you were. Right?"

Bobby deals in facts and reality. Things you can prove and verify with hard evidence. Hunches—especially an eyewitness's hunch—don't go down well with him because more often than not he says they're wrong. We all recount our stories to fit what we swear we saw. Or what we're sure we knew. The dress was red. The woman was blond. Later you find out from a photo that it was a brunette in a tracksuit.

"I suppose that's true," I said. "I don't know, Bobby. It doesn't feel right to me that she circled back and started shooting at me."

"A feeling, huh?" He gave me a look that left no doubt that feelings ranked a couple of notches below hunches on the facts-and-reality spectrum. "Right. I'll talk to her and see if she has a gun permit."

He thumbed through his notes again. "So based on what you told me, the entire cast and crew who were there the night Webb Landau disappeared have an interest in you staying out of Jamie's business. Who among that merry band knows you talked to Hunter Knight?"

"Nobody."

"Did you tell anybody else?"

"Aside from you and Quinn? Kit gave me the St. Leonard Project's phone number, but I haven't spoken to her since then. And Eli and Sasha know."

"Sasha?" he said. "Jamie's daughter. Jeez Louise, Lucie. Maybe she talked to her mother. Or her stepmother. That would ratchet things up a couple of notches if word got out that you had a meeting with someone who wants Taurique's case reopened."

"I don't get it," I said. "Why go after me? I don't know who killed Webb."

"But you are reassembling the puzzle pieces. And, to mix metaphors, rattling cages."

"And so will Hunter Knight," I said. "Tell me, Bobby, why was Jamie's death ruled an accident?"

"Above my pay grade," he said. "I don't make all the calls."

"Someone was pressuring the sheriff's department to do it, weren't they? Maybe Elena and Garrett, for example?"

"I don't know."

"All right. If it were your call, do you think maybe it was suicide?"

"If it were my call, I wouldn't rule out homicide. But that doesn't leave this room. Understand?"

"Homicide?" Quinn set down his Scotch on the coffee table. "Are you serious?"

"Look at it this way: If Jamie Vaughn was ready to start talking about what really happened to Webb Landau, now he's not going to, is he? And who else is stirring things up?" He gave me a pointed look.

"Me."

"Which is why maybe someone decided you needed to be shut up as well."

"Jesus, Bobby." Quinn's arm went around my shoulder. "You're talking about friends and neighbors here. People we know."

"More often than not, a murder victim has some tie to the killer."

I shuddered. "Now what do I do?"

"Be careful. Watch your back," he said. "Officially, the investigation into Jamie's death is closed, but it doesn't mean I can't do a little looking around on my own time. Go talk to Hunter Knight and maybe set up a meeting with Taurique Youngblood."

"Can you let us know if you find out anything?" Quinn asked.

"It depends. If I can, I will. In the meantime, Lucie, you need to promise me you'll back off this, okay? Drop it."

"She will," Quinn said. "I guarantee it."

"Good," Bobby said, "I was hoping you'd say that."

"I don't understand why you think Jamie's death could have been a homicide," I said.

Bobby held up a hand and started ticking off items on his fingers. "One, no suicide note. Two, he was on his way to a meeting with your cousin, which he'd called to confirm. And three, four, and five, when we checked out his office, we found an empty whiskey bottle, a drink glass, and traces of something else, which we had tested. It turned out to be isopropyl alcohol, plain old rubbing alcohol. That's why Jamie seemed so out of it when you saw him—drink enough of that stuff and it's as if you're blind drunk, your speech is slurred, and your coordination is wonky. Eventually you start throwing up."

I nodded. He was describing Jamie to a T that day.

"Except for one thing," Bobby was saying. "There were no prints on the doorknob to his office. It had been wiped clean. We should have at least found Jamie's prints."

I caught my breath. "Who was with him?"

"I don't know," he said. "Maybe nobody. Or maybe someone

went back after he died and staged the whole thing to make it look like suicide: But whoever was there, I sure as hell plan to find out."

"If you're right," I said, "and it's the same small circle of people who were at Dori's house, then the suspects are all either members of Jamie's family or his closest friends."

Bobby nodded. "Like I told you, there's almost always a connection between a victim and the killer. So it wouldn't surprise me. Except for one thing."

"What's that?" I asked.

"The victim isn't usually someone who nearly got elected president of the United States six months ago."

Nineteen

The Goose Creek Hunt held its annual spring Point-to-Point steeplechase races each year at Glenwood Park, a lush, green course with fences, hurdles, and a fieldstone grandstand commanding sweeping views of the countryside that were bounded in the distance by the hazy blue-violet Blue Ridge Mountains. The course had been built in 1932 on 112 acres of farmland owned by one of Virginia hunt country's most famous sportsmen, and the Goose Creek Hunt had been racing there ever since. Mick Dunne was their master of the hunt, plus he also played polo, so he was a skilled, experienced horseman and hunter. Elena Vaughn rode and hunted as well; so did Jamie's sons.

I didn't want to think about the possibility that one of them took a shot at me yesterday—especially the day of Jamie's funeral—but if Bobby was right, they all belonged on the list of suspects.

Quinn and I had been invited to Mick's race day tailgate

party Saturday afternoon as we always were, partly because we were friends and next-door neighbors, but more important, for the past century my family had allowed the Goose Creek Hunt to ride through Highland Farm as part of their territory.

"Are you seriously thinking about going?" Quinn asked me as we sat drinking coffee at the kitchen table on Saturday morning. I'd made the coffee so it didn't taste like the usual nonpotable rocket fuel he brewed. Just now he was acting as if I'd told him I planned to walk through D.C.'s meanest and most violent streets by myself at two A.M.

"Bobby thought it would be a good idea for you to lie low for a while," he added.

"No one's going to do anything in front of a race day crowd at a posh tailgate," I said. "What's the alternative? Hide under the bed? Until what? Until when? I can't live like that, Quinn."

What I didn't want to tell him was that I hoped showing up at the tailgate—especially with my Technicolor bruises—might surprise and unnerve someone enough that I'd get a clue about the identity of the shooter. A lot of drinking went on at these parties. Maybe someone would get careless.

Heavy footsteps thumped down the back staircase, and a moment later the door to the kitchen flew open. Eli, with his usual wild man morning hair, walked in before Quinn could answer me.

"Morning, all." Eli started to head straight for the coffeepot like he was navigating on radar, but he stopped when he saw me, a pained expression in his eyes as he took in my face. Even though things were strained between his girlfriend and me—over her mother, no less—I was still his sister and blood was blood.

"How are you doing?" he asked. "That's a hell of a shiner, Luce. You were lucky yesterday."

What hung in the air between the two of us was an acute, combustible awareness that maybe this had happened because I was asking too many questions about Webb Landau's death. And a lot of them seemed to involve Sasha's father, Jamie Vaughn. I knew Eli. He hated confrontation and he wanted me to quit poking a hornets' nest.

"I'm okay," I said. "It'll heal."

Eli poured himself a mug of coffee. "Before Hope and I pick up Sasha and Zach for Mick's tailgate this afternoon, I'm meeting a stonemason at the main gate to get a price for rebuilding the wall," he said, heaping teaspoons of sugar and pouring a generous dollop of milk into the mug. He gave me a significant look. "Which needs to be fixed ASAP so no one gets hurt anymore. He's the best guy around. I've used him on a couple of jobs. When he's done, no one will be able to tell what's new from what was already there."

"The crew is there now removing the flowers and candles and other stuff," Quinn said. "It should be cleaned up before your meeting."

I stared at the two of them in amazement. I hadn't known about the stonemason meeting or the crew cleaning up Jamie's memorial. But that wasn't what caught my attention. "The children are going to the tailgate?" I asked.

"Yeah, why? Hope loves horses. Sasha said Mick invited all the Vaughns since they're not doing their own tailgate, under the circumstances. The kids will have a ball. Elena's not going, but Vanessa will be there."

Vanessa. That was for my benefit, a warning.

"There's a chance Mick knew something about the person shooting at your sister yesterday," Quinn said. "Whoever it was probably came through his farm. Unless, of course, he *was* the shooter."

Eli took a loaf of Persia's homemade Sally Lunn bread out of the bread box. He cut two slices and stuck them in the toaster. Then he faced me and said, sounding testy, "Mick? You've got to be kidding me. Sasha and I talked about this last night. I know you think the shooter could have been anyone who was at the dinner the night Webb Landau disappeared, and that includes Mick. Except there's no way he could have done it."

"Why not?" I asked.

My brother gave me another meaningful look. "Because he's a crack shot. If he wanted you dead, Luce, you'd be dead. Mick Dunne wouldn't miss."

IT HAD RAINED AGAIN during the morning, which left the Glenwood Park racecourse damp and soggy and turned the dirt road that ran through the area dividing the tailgate parties between the patrons with spaces along the fence and those who were next to the stacked stone wall into a muddy mess. Mick liked to be close to the finish line, so his spot was always next to the fence by the judge's stand. Eli, Sasha, Vanessa, and the two children were already there when Quinn and I arrived fifteen minutes before the first race was scheduled to start at one o'clock. Someone—probably Sasha—had brought a waterproof blanket that had been placed on the ground next to the fence in front of rows of folding chairs that were mostly occupied by friends and neighbors. Hope and Zach lay on their stomachs on the blanket, playing with a bucket of Lego blocks and ignoring two untouched plates of food, lost in their own world. Vanessa and Sasha stood next to them, passing binoculars back and forth as the horses came up from the paddock for the first race. The sky was still heavy with low, rain-gorged clouds that nearly obscured the mountains, and the day was cold and raw.

People dress up for a hunt country tailgate regardless of the weather because this is a world that still hews closely to time-honored traditions and customs. Women wear pretty silk dresses, elaborate confectionary hats that will fly away in a strong wind, and high heels that are guaranteed to sink into the mud and be ruined by the end of the day. Others dress more sensibly in boots or Wellingtons worn with blazers, a sweater or blouse, and trousers. For men the attire is tweedy sports jackets, jaunty bow ties, silk foulards, and straw boaters or flat caps. Jewelry, ties, scarves, and even belts are always fox or hunt themed. Later there will be a competition for best hat and tie and another for best tailgate. These things happen every year with such familiar regularity that you can almost set your watch by them.

The world of foxhunting and horse racing is rarified, and I know there are many who find it snobbish and elitist, a hobby of the idle rich. But it is a way of life around here that binds our community together, and it's the world I've grown up in. When everything else around me seems to be changing at the speed of light, for a few hours, time will rewind in Middleburg, a hunting horn will blow, amateur riders on Thoroughbreds will hurdle over post-and-rail fences or race on golf course–perfect turf the dazzling color of emeralds, and friends and family will eat, drink, laugh, socialize, cheer loudly, and place one-dollar bets on the outcome of a race as if it is of life-altering importance.

I opted to wear boots and a rain slicker with slacks and a turtleneck instead of a dress for Mick's tailgate, which had an unspoken "no jeans allowed" dress code. The more casual attire seemed to go better with my bruised eye and the gash underneath. My injuries didn't go unnoticed by anyone, especially Mick, who came over as soon as he saw us arrive.

"I heard someone took a shot at you yesterday, Lucie. Thank God you're okay, but that's a hell of a bruise and a cut." His face revealed nothing but worried concern.

"Whoever did it might have been coming from your property. Do you know anything about that?" Quinn asked before I could reply.

Mick flashed a startled look at me before he answered Quinn. "No, I do not. Between the two of us, we've got hundreds of acres. It's bloody impossible to know if someone who doesn't belong there wanders onto a corner of my land. Or yours, which is probably what happened yesterday."

He sounded angry and offended, apparently believing a stranger had been the shooter. I glanced at Quinn. We'd already had the conversation about interlopers having sex or tossing empty beer cans near the vines without our knowledge. Mick was right. We couldn't control everyone who strayed onto our property.

"Jamie's death has brought all kinds of kooks out of the woodwork," Mick was saying, still upset. "The sheriff's department had a car at the bottom of Elena's driveway to keep out curiosity seekers and people looking for souvenirs for the past few days. Some of the same crazy conspiracy theorists who still think JFK's assassination was a plot are saying now that maybe Jamie was assassinated as well. There've been stories on the Internet—haven't you seen them? People will believe anything these days. You've had hundreds of people stop by that memorial at your vineyard. I'm sure there have been a few nutters among them. You've been on the telly, Lucie. People know you were with Jamie that day."

And now one of those kooks took a shot at you. He didn't say it, but there it was.

I felt a small rush of relief that Mick had so easily dismantled any theory of yesterday's incident being related to Webb Landau's murder, but my brain was whirring. Was he right? Some nut—or *nutter*—who was convinced there was something sinister about Jamie's death had decided to bring a gun to the vineyard memorial? *What conspiracy stories* on the Internet?

Quinn cleared his throat.

I said in a faint voice, "I suppose you could be right."

"I think you two need a glass of champagne." Mick clapped his arms around Quinn and me. "And we're wrapping up bets on the first race. A novice rider flat. Elena's got a horse in this one. Get out your dollars and pick a winner. You know where the bar is and there's plenty of food. Eli's in charge of betting, so go find him as well."

The bar had been set up as usual next to Mick's Land Rover, which had been backed into his tailgate spot and the trunk left open to reveal enough alcohol to supply a Kentucky Derby–size crowd. A long table covered with a hunter green tablecloth and an arrangement of yellow and white roses in a silver vase was surrounded by more bottles of top-shelf liquor and mixers. Two open coolers on the ground held beer and water. Bottles of champagne sat in an ice bucket, and there were multiple bottles of red and white wine on the table next to a silver punch bowl filled with ice and a stack of plastic cups. Another large table dominated by a bronze statue of a foxhunter on a horse held platters of roast beef, salads, quiche, chicken wings, smoked salmon, and assorted hors d'oeuvres. Next to it was a dessert table. Mick always put out enough food to feed everyone in Atoka. For a couple of meals.

Quinn poured two glasses of champagne. "Do you think Mick is right, that it was a stranger?" I asked him under my breath as he handed me my glass.

"I don't know. I guess he could be. According to Frankie, we've had some strange people stopping by the tasting room for a drink after they visited Jamie's memorial."

"Maybe we can forget about this for a while," I said. "Let's find Eli and bet on the race."

I turned, nearly colliding with Owen Vaughn and knocking into the drink he was carrying. He raised his arm to avoid spilling it, but not before some of the liquid sloshed over the edge of the glass. His eyes looked slightly unfocused. Whatever he was drinking, it wasn't his first.

"Owen, I'm so sorry." I grabbed a couple of paper napkins from a nearby table and passed them to him. "I didn't realize you were right behind me."

He wiped at the liquid on his hand. "Lucie. Quinn. I wasn't expecting to see you here. I heard someone shot at you yesterday, Lucie, right in front of Dad's memorial. I didn't realize you got hurt." His words were slurred.

Of the twins, Owen was older by an hour, and he was the one who had worked more closely with Jamie in his real estate business. Oliver ran the winery. Though they looked alike—both redheads with their mother's fair skin and green eyes—they were fraternal, not identical, and no one ever mixed them up. Their differences were even more apparent in their personalities, as if God had decided that each of the gifts could be given to only one twin, with no sharing. Owen was the talker, the negotiator, the dazzler, the one with the mercurial temper. Oliver was circumspect, thoughtful, and cautious.

Like both of them, I had grown up in the shadow of a strong father with a forceful personality, but Leland had always been harder on Eli than on either Mia or me. We were girls. Eli was his son. After a while, Eli took a backseat when Leland was around and never tried to compete or outshine him. Owen and Oliver seemed to have adopted the same survival tactic, becoming pale likenesses of Jamie. Now that he was dead, I wondered how they'd cope. Would they unravel as I did when my mother, who was my touchstone, died? I'd been so angry at her violent and unexpected death that I'd gone looking for trouble—and that's how I found Greg. The look in Owen's eyes right now reminded me a lot of me.

"Luckily whoever it was wasn't a good shot," I said. "The sheriff's department is looking into it. I fell and that's how I got the black eye. What about you? How are you doing?"

He gulped his drink and his eyes skittered away. "Dealing with it," he said. "I'm here because Dad would expect me to carry on as usual. He'd expect tonight's dinner to go on as well. His campaign debts didn't vanish just because he died."

He spoke with enough force that I wondered if he knew just

how massive those debts were and also that his father's real estate business was in financial trouble. How much had Jamie shared with his sons?

Dominique said she hadn't been paid for some of her services for the Jefferson Dinner and that she thought the Vaughns had already spent the ticket money they received. They couldn't afford to cancel.

"Hey." Eli came up behind the three of us. "Lucie, Quinn, are you going to bet? The horses are almost at the starting gate. What about you, Owen? You haven't bet, either."

Quinn pulled two dollars out of his wallet. "For Lucie and me," he said. "I'll take Foxy Loxy. I like the name."

"Put me down for Three's a Crowd," I said. "Elena's horse. For luck." I smiled at Owen, who pulled a crumpled bill out of his pocket and gave it to Eli.

"Me, too. Three's a Crowd. Excuse me, I think I'll freshen up my drink," he said.

"You gave me a twenty," Eli said. "Let me give you change."

Owen had already started to move toward the bar. "Keep it," he said over his shoulder.

"He's pretty lit," Eli said. "I'll give him his money later."

Quinn and I followed Eli down to the fence where Vanessa and Sasha were still watching the horses line up on the far side of the course. Eli stood next to Sasha, who leaned over him and said to me, "Eli told me what happened yesterday, Lucie. I'm glad you're all right."

"Thanks," I said. "Me, too."

"Mom's glad, too. Right, Mom?" She nudged Vanessa.

I appreciated Sasha's efforts to patch things up after yesterday's unpleasant conversation at the church hall, but Vanessa's grim smile told me she had neither forgiven nor forgotten.

I smiled and ignored Vanessa's snub. "I heard the three of you went back to Elena's yesterday after the reception and spent the afternoon at Longview."

Sasha nodded. "People dropped off so much food Zach and I ended up staying for dinner."

"What about you?" I asked Vanessa.

She said in a stiff voice, "I didn't go."

"Mom went back to my place for a nap," Sasha said.

A hunting horn interrupted our conversation and a smooth voice said through the loudspeaker, "The flag is up. And away they go."

I caught Vanessa's eye. She knew what I'd just done: established that she had no alibi for her whereabouts yesterday afternoon. I knew from Eli that Vanessa could ride and hunt just like everyone else in the Vaughn family. And even though she wore that orthopedic boot, Vanessa could still get around. If she were really at her daughter's home yesterday when someone shot at me, now she had no one to corroborate her story. She could have been anywhere.

Including my vineyard.

Vanessa gave me an icy smile. "Tell me, did you ever find the MedicAlert bracelet, Lucie?" It was a deliberate dig meant to provoke me because she knew very well I didn't. She'd taken it and, as Quinn said, probably destroyed it.

"No," I said. "It's gone."

Eli elbowed me. "Hey, Luce, that's your horse. Three's a Crowd. Elena's horse is out in front. You're going to win."

A lone rider in lemon-yellow-and-navy silks had moved out in front of all the others, rounding the last turn before the finish line. Around me, everyone was hollering and cheering. Over the noise and jubilation of the crowd, Vanessa moved so that she was standing next to me.

She leaned over and said in my ear, "Looks like you're in luck, Lucie. You made the right choice." She paused and added, "This time."

Twenty

Quinn wanted to go by the winery when we got home from the Point-to-Point to check whether the crew had finished cleaning the oak barrels we planned to use for 750 gallons of Norton once we moved it out of the stainless-steel tank where it was currently aging. I wanted to find the business card Hunter Knight had given me and call him. My cell phone was still drying out in a bag of rice, so I needed the landline, and I didn't want anyone overhearing me, including Quinn.

Especially Quinn.

I hadn't told him about my most recent conversation with Vanessa and the new possibility that had uncoiled itself like a deadly snake in my brain: that she had killed Webb and deliberately misled me all along. And she'd just delivered a not-too-subtle threat to watch myself.

Hunter's phone rang half a dozen times before it went to voice mail. I was tempted not to leave a message, but he'd see who had called him anyway, so I said, "Hunter, it's Lucie Montgomery. Could you please call me as soon as you get this? I'd like to talk to you about the testimony at Taurique's trial, specifically the alibis of everyone who was at Dori Upshur's dinner the night Webb disappeared." I paused. I'd already said more than I wanted to in a phone message. "That's it. Thanks. Goodbye."

The only version I'd heard of what happened the night Webb vanished was Vanessa's, and now I wondered whether it would match what was said under oath at Taurique's murder trial. Bobby had asked me why I was so sure the shooter was male and I couldn't tell him, except that it was a hunch.

Maybe I was wrong and it was a woman. Just not Dori.

Maybe it was Vanessa.

I WAS IN THE kitchen drinking a cup of chamomile tea for my twitchy nerves and waiting for Quinn to finish changing into a suit for the Jefferson Dinner when Eli walked in holding a royal blue velvet jewelry box in his hand. He, too, was wearing a suit.

"You look pretty," he said. "And that purple dress kind of matches your eye."

I set down the tea and punched his shoulder. "If you ever say something nice to me, hell will truly have frozen over."

"I'm joking," he said. "Honest. You do look really pretty."

Appeased, I said, "Thanks. There's something I want to talk to you about. And why are you all dressed up? You look nice, too. Isn't that your lucky tie?"

His cheeks turned red and he opened the jewelry box.

Inside was Granny Montgomery's delicate amethyst-and-diamond dinner ring. "I'm giving this to Sasha tonight. I'm taking her to dinner in D.C. I've had it for years since Granny left it to me for my future wife. It wasn't big enough or showy enough for Brandi—plus she hated anything that was old or antique—so I hung on to it."

"Wow." I looked at my brother. "Is it . . . an engagement ring?"

He snapped the box shut. "No, it would be lousy timing, right after her father died. But it is kind of a pre-engagement ring. We love each other and Hope and Zach get along like brother and sister. I can't imagine my life without her." He gave me an anxious look. "Do you think she'll like it? Am I rushing things?"

"Who wouldn't like it? That ring is gorgeous. And I think she's crazy about you."

He broke into a grateful smile. "I hope you're right. So what was it you wanted to talk about?"

No big deal. I'm just wondering if your future mother-in-law might be a murderer, is all. I'm waiting for a call from Hunter Knight to verify a few things, specifically Vanessa's story about what really happened the night Webb Landau disappeared.

"It can wait," I said. "Is Persia babysitting?"

"Didn't you hear? An old friend of hers is in town from Jamaica so she's having dinner with him in Leesburg."

"Him?"

"She told me not to go getting any ideas, so I think it's just a friend-friend. Not a dinner date."

"Oh. Who's looking after Hope?"

"I'm taking her over to Sasha's."

"Vanessa's taking care of her?"

"Yup. And Zach." He made a face at me. Annoyed. "Come on, Luce. She's not the Wicked Witch of the West. Cut her some slack. Hopefully, she's going to be my mother-in-law someday. I know you two got off to a rough start, but she's a good person. She has to be, to raise someone as wonderful as Sasha."

I nodded. Truce. "Enjoy yourself tonight. And good luck."

"Thanks." He gave me a self-conscious grin. "I'd better get Hopie or we'll be late."

He was whistling as he went up the back staircase to my niece's bedroom. It had been a long time since I'd seen him this happy.

I dumped the rest of my tea down the sink, sick at heart. What if I was right about Vanessa? I didn't know which would be worse: finding out that she murdered Webb Landau and had covered it up for thirty years, or my brother realizing I was the one who put the puzzle pieces together and blew up his world and Sasha's. The first would be bad enough. We'd never, ever survive the second.

"YOU'VE BEEN QUIET," QUINN said as he pulled in to the Goose Creek Inn parking lot half an hour later. "Is something wrong?"

"No, nothing."

"Come on," he said.

I didn't want to tell him the truth. So I said, "Eli's giving Sasha our grandmother's diamond-and-amethyst dinner ring tonight. He called it a pre-engagement ring and he's taking her to dinner in D.C. The kids are at Sasha's place with Vanessa since Persia had a dinner date."

"Wow." He looked amazed. "How'd I miss all that?"

"You've got to be quick. We Montgomerys move fast."

He opened the front door and held it for me, shaking his head. "Still so much to learn about you and your kin."

I grinned and he leaned over for a quick kiss. "We're just full of surprises," I said.

He let out a low whistle as we stepped inside. "Obviously that includes your cousin. Take a look at this place."

Though Dominique had told me about her plans for the dinner menu, she had said nothing about transforming the Inn so it looked as if we'd been transported back to colonial Virginia in the late 1700s. Dozens of candles in hurricane lamps gave the place a dreamy soft-edged look. The strains of a string quartet playing what sounded like Hayden or Mozart came from another room, and waiters in colonial attire took our coats and checked our reservations. I nearly didn't recognize the maître d', who wore a gray wig with a cascade of sausage-like curls, until he winked at me.

"All guests are being asked to put away their phones for the evening," he said to us. "No texting, no selfies, no social media. In the seventeen and eighteen hundreds people *talked* to each other."

Quinn grinned and turned off his phone. I set mine to Mute. "What about the press?" I asked.

"Except for official photos at the beginning and end of the evening, the same rules apply. No live tweeting. They can take their notes the old-fashioned way: Write it down. We see so many guests here preoccupied with their phones all through dinner, no one paying attention to the meal or to each other. So for once Dominique is laying down the law. She wants a return to civility and actual dinner table conversation with the people you're dining with."

"You didn't turn off your phone," Quinn said to me as we walked into the main dining room. "Are you expecting a call?"

He still didn't know I'd phoned Hunter Knight and asked him to get in touch. "Eli and Sasha are in Washington," I said. "If anything comes up with Hope while she's at Vanessa's, we're close by. Besides, I'm just hoping it works again, remember?"

"Oh. Right."

A waiter in a brocade waistcoat, ruffled shirt, breeches, and white stockings offered us glasses of Madeira from a silver tray. "Madeira was one of Thomas Jefferson's favorite drinks," he said. "Very popular in his day. Enjoy."

"That boy," Quinn said after he took a sip, "had good taste."

"I wonder if our Madeira will taste anything like this," I said.

"Don't I wish."

Last year Quinn decided to make Madeira—a first for us—experimenting with a barrel of Vidal Blanc he'd put aside, even though it wasn't one of the traditional Portuguese grapes normally used for the wine. Madeira has the distinction of being the only alcohol in the world that never goes bad. The addition of spirits stops fermentation—we'd added distilled grape spirits from California, or essentially raw brandy, to ours—plus it's also cooked, which further stabilizes it. Some people call it an indestructible wine.

In Jefferson's day, casks of Madeira—finished wine—were

put on ships that traveled the world, allowing the alcohol to mellow at sea. Quinn set ours out in the sun last summer when we had weeks of one-hundred-plus-degree days of withering heat. If he had his way, it would mellow for another fifty years in glass barrels in the attic of Highland House. There's no such thing as Madeira that's too old.

"I'm going to find the sommelier and ask if I can take a look at that bottle," Quinn said. "I'll find you before we're seated for dinner, okay?"

The two of us always split up when we throw a party or host an event at the winery so we can meet as many guests as possible. Socializing, making small talk, ensuring everyone is having a good time and that there are no wallflowers is part of the job. Later after everyone goes home, we pour a nightcap or a glass of wine from a half-full bottle, sit down, put our feet up, and catch each other up on who we talked to and what we learned.

The moment Quinn left, someone came up behind me and touched my arm. I turned around and found myself staring at Oliver Vaughn. "Lucie," he said, "I've been looking for you. Can we chat for a moment?"

I followed him to corner of the dining room where we were by ourselves. In the reddish-gold light of a nearby candelabrum, his face was sharp angles and shadowy planes, his eyes black holes. He looked exhausted.

"We just got here," I said. "Quinn went off to see what he could learn about the Madeira you're serving. It's amazing."

"Dad bought a case of it ten years ago," he said. "It was already fifteen years old. It's aged quite well. Glad you're enjoying it." His smile was strained.

"Are you going to be all right tonight?" I asked. "This evening has got to be tough for you and Owen."

"I'll be fine. Owen's had a few. He was drinking at the Point-to-Point, but Mick and Garrett gave him some coffee and now they're making sure he remains upright until dinner's over. I think they took him outside for some fresh air." He gave me a twisted grin. "Look, I just wanted to ask if you're still okay talking about Daniel Norton and the Lemosy story after dinner. Those bruises . . . I mean, are *you* going to be all right?"

I was touched by his sweet concern, especially with everything else going on in his life.

"Quinn and I are here as your mother's guests and we get to sample the 1876 Norton," I said. "It's the least I can do. Your dad did a lot to put Norton back on the map for Virginia wineries. It's important for someone to tell his story."

"Thanks. Mom didn't really go into detail about asking you to talk. She just told me that you said you would." It sounded as if he left the sentence unfinished on purpose, and an uneasy thought curled into my mind.

The real reason he pulled me aside was to find out what I was doing here, why I'd been given two twenty-thousand-dollar tickets at the last minute. If neither Elena nor Garrett had told him they bought my silence about his father's death, then it wasn't my place to enlighten him, either.

"Your mother thought I seemed like the logical person to ask since I'm related to Daniel Norton," I said, keeping my voice neutral.

"I thought maybe it had something to do with you being with Dad . . ." He stumbled and said, ". . . at the end. When he died."

"What do you mean?"

He knew I was stalling. "You tell me."

"Can I ask you something?" I said. "Actually, two questions."

He gave me a wary look. I hadn't answered his implicit question. "Go ahead."

"Why didn't you move the Norton directly to the Inn from your winery? I heard it also ended up at Longview. And do you know what it was that your dad wanted to talk about with my cousin? He was on his way here that day. Apparently it had something to do with the Norton."

"Dad took care of moving those bottles." His curt reply implied he hadn't been asked or consulted. "And, no, I have no idea what he wanted to talk about with Dominique. The last few days before he died, he seemed really preoccupied and short-tempered. I gave him wide berth, and the last time I spoke to him we argued. Now I have to live with that . . . Look, don't repeat any of this, okay?"

"Of course not." So Oliver hadn't been part of the decision to move the old bottles to Longview before they came to the Inn. "Do you have any idea why or what was upsetting him?"

"No. But I have a feeling you do." He leaned his face into mine. "I want to know what's going on, Lucie."

"Then you should ask your mother," I said again.

"I'm asking you." He paused. *"Please."*

It was that *please* that changed my mind. It didn't seem as if Oliver knew about Webb Landau or Taurique Youngblood any more than Sasha had until I told her about my conversation with Vanessa. I wondered how much Jamie had confided in Oliver, or if he'd kept his financial problems from one or both of his sons as well.

"This isn't the time or place," I said.

"Later tonight, then. After the dinner and the auction."

"Is Owen going to be part of this conversation?"

"Ah . . . no. Just me and you." From another room came polite applause as the string quartet finished playing. He said in a tired voice, "I need to know the truth, Lucie."

He stopped a waiter who was passing by with a half-full tray of glasses of Madeira and swapped my empty glass for a full one. Then he took one for himself. After the waiter moved on and it was just the two of us again, he clinked his glass against mine.

"*In vino veritas.*"

I nodded and we both drank. I knew what he meant. In wine there is truth.

Oliver Vaughn wasn't going to like what I had to say. But somehow, I think he already knew that.

DOMINIQUE'S DINNER WAS AN homage to Jefferson's favorite dishes and his love of French food acquired when he was minister to France from 1785 until shortly before the French Revolution in 1789. Handwritten menus at each place listed the courses: deviled eggs with anchovies, macaroni and cheese, Bibb lettuce with baby peas, spinach timbale, fingerling potatoes with bacon, and broiled salmon with tomatoes, onions, and tarragon. Dessert was apple pie and Jefferson's favorite vanilla ice cream. The wines served with each course— Château d'Yquem, Château Petrus, Domaine de la Romanée-Conti, Château Lafite, all of which Jefferson would have known and loved—had come from Jamie's eight-thousand-bottle private wine cellar and had price tags that I knew were in three digits.

If he had been here, Jamie would have been the master of ceremonies, but Oliver had done his homework and did a good job of explaining why each dish had been chosen, along with the wines that had been paired with the different courses. Just before dessert was served, he introduced me, explaining my relationship to Daniel Norton's second wife. He also explained that I'd been asked to talk about Jamie's efforts to debunk the W. F. Lemosy account that Dr. Daniel W. Norton had not been the first to discover Virginia's only native grape, one that bore his name.

After I finished my talk and took my seat, Oliver stepped up to the podium again. "Before we get to the main event of the evening, I'd like to propose a toast to my father," he said lifting his wineglass. Chairs scraped as everyone got to their feet and a few people said, "To Jamie."

"When Dad learned the story Lucie just told of Daniel Norton not getting credit for the uniquely American grape named for him because W. F. Lemosy falsely claimed his father had discovered it first, my father wanted to right that wrong," he said. "To make sure credit went where it was due. It was part of the reason he bought those three bottles of Norton from the wreck of the *Virginia Belle* and worked hard to set the record straight.

"Dad had a strong moral compass, and he tried to instill his values of right and wrong in my brother and me. He would have made a great president, as I'm sure you all agree."

His next words were drowned out by applause and cheering. When it died down Oliver was saying, ". . . fought for what was right rather than what was easy, for what was good rather than what was popular. My dad remained true to his beliefs until the day he died, and I'm proud to be his son." He hoisted his glass again. "To Jamie Vaughn."

Oliver's eyes found mine. His were challenging and, it seemed, defiant. Had I misjudged him earlier this evening? Was he—along with Elena and Garrett—complicit in the cover-up to keep the details of his father's death from coming to light? And more to the point: Did he see me as a problem to be dealt with now that he realized I knew more than I ought to about Jamie's accident?

I raised my glass, looked him straight in the eye, and drank. Neither of us blinked.

THE NORTON UNICORN WINE was served in balloon glasses to give it as much opportunity to breathe as possible, though the lucky twenty-five who got to taste it were given only a very small amount. Before I even lifted the glass to my nose, the perfume and scent were so intense and focused that I knew it was going to be a powerful, elegant wine. I closed my eyes and drank, hearing the comments that floated around me, including an offer to give up a firstborn child for a single bottle and someone else claiming it was better than sex.

Garrett Bateman stepped up to the podium, a triumphant look on his face. "I believe the verdict is in. Jamie's Norton is simply incredible, an amazing vintage. We'll give everyone a little time before we start the bidding in ten minutes."

Quinn and I had been seated at separate tables across the room from each other. I looked for him in the crowd that had started to mingle again and didn't see him until he showed up at my side.

"I need to talk to you," he said, "in private."

I followed him to a corner where we were on our own. "What is it?"

"The wine," he said. "It's fabulous."

"I know."

"No," he said. "Too fabulous. It shouldn't have held up this well after a century. The color's wrong; it should be more brick red than blood red. When you look at the edge of a wine—at the side of the glass—you should see where the color's not holding up. There should be some oxidation, some madeirization. What we drank is too jammy and there's too much fruit."

It is hard—no, impossible—to detect whether a wine has been doctored strictly from tasting, but Quinn had a point. Wine is a living thing and its natural progression is to eventually end up as vinegar. The odds of catching the moment of brilliance for such an old wine—the unicorn moment—at precisely the right time was a crapshoot. Whatever had preserved the Norton all these years could vanish in a flash, and when that happened the wine would go flat and lose its life. The light would go out of it. But it could also go the other way: It could surprise you by changing and becoming even more remarkable the longer it was open. What Quinn was saying was that the Norton we just drank hadn't changed or evolved as it should have done.

"Do you think it's been doctored?"

"I don't know, but honestly, it wouldn't surprise me. I want to see if I can get a look at that bottle and the cork. I think it's been opened before tonight. At least the one we drank was."

"How are you going to prove it? No one's ever tasted a Norton from the 1870s. Who's to say this isn't exactly what it tastes like?"

"Come on, it wouldn't be that hard to fake. And you know as well as I do that it happens all the time in our world. Add some old brandy, a great bottle of Zinfandel, maybe even some malic acid since Norton's the only grape with a fifty-fifty ratio of malic and tartaric acid . . . voilà, you've got a world-class Norton. I'm from California, remember? I've tasted my share of fabulous old Zins. This wine reminded me of them. A little too much."

I gave him an odd look. "You could make fake Norton with brandy, Zin, and malic acid?"

"Yup," he said. "I could."

My phone, which was inside my evening purse, suddenly vibrated. "Oh, my gosh," I said, pulling it out of my purse. "My phone's working again."

"Who is it?" Quinn asked.

The display read *Knight, H.*

"It's . . . Eli. I'd better take this. I'll slip into Dominique's office since we're not supposed to be caught using phones tonight."

"I'm going to find Oliver. I'll find you later."

The back corridor where my cousin's office was located was dimly lit and her door was closed and locked. The corridor was empty. I hit the green button on my phone and said hello.

"Lucie," Hunter Knight said, "I just got your message. What's up?"

"Thanks for calling. I was wondering whether you had the testimony from Taurique's trial when everyone at Dori's house the night Webb disappeared explained their whereabouts. What they said under oath."

"I do have that information. Where are you?" he said. "It sounds noisy."

"At the Goose Creek Inn at Jamie Vaughn's Jefferson Dinner. His bottles of 1876 Norton are about to be auctioned off. There are a couple hundred people here."

"Can you talk?"

I stuck a finger in my ear so I could hear him better. "Yes."

"May I ask what prompted this call?" he said.

"Someone took a shot at me yesterday when I was by myself at Jamie's memorial. Mick Dunne believes it's probably some nut who thinks there's a conspiracy behind Jamie's death, just like JFK. Another theory—which is less appealing to me—is that somebody close to Jamie believes I might be stirring up new questions about Webb's murder."

He sucked in his breath. "My God. Are you all right?"

"I'm fine. And, just so you know, everyone who was at the dinner the night Webb vanished is in town. Including Dori Upshur. I saw her at Jamie's wake and met her at his memorial at the vineyard yesterday after the funeral. Just before the shooting started."

"Dori Upshur is there? I wish you'd told me." He sounded stunned and a bit irritated. "I finally tracked her down and left a message at her office in Chapel Hill yesterday."

So he was back on the case now that Jamie's funeral was over.

"Well," I said. "I just did."

"Right." I could tell he was still irked. "I've got a whiteboard with a time line and everyone's whereabouts on it right here, plus any witnesses who could corroborate their stories. I'll go over it, but only if you promise to let me know if you hear something that doesn't jibe with what you know, okay? Don't keep me in the dark."

"I promise."

By now I felt I knew what happened that evening as well as if I'd been there myself, and Hunter's version tracked with what Vanessa had told me. The drinking, Dori's departure, Webb crashing off on foot. That left Jamie, Mick, Elena, and Vanessa in the house.

Dori claimed she'd spent the night in her office after driving around for a few hours, and a janitor corroborated that she was there in the morning but couldn't say what time she arrived the night before. Jamie's alibi about leaving later on held up: He'd walked from Dori's to a bar on the Corner and stayed until closing. Someone saw him coming back to his room on the Lawn. He'd seemed fairly inebriated and he was seen there the next morning.

"Vanessa, Mick, and Elena spent the night at the farmhouse," Hunter said. "They're each other's alibis. They were there all night."

Something pinged in my memory.

"Vanessa told me she fell asleep in a bedroom by herself and found Elena in the kitchen the next morning," I said. "Mick was still sleeping upstairs so Elena woke him and the three of them went back to Grounds—the UVA campus—in Mick's car. Elena drove because Mick's hand was still hurting from where Webb had cut him with a kitchen knife."

"According to the court testimony, Vanessa said all three of them were together for the night," Hunter said. "And that

Mick drove the girls back to school the next morning. Elena and Mick said the same thing."

"So either Vanessa lied in her testimony or she forgot a few details when she told me what happened," I said. "It's been thirty years. That's a long time. She also told me that the next morning Mick was wearing a different bandage on his hand. He'd changed so he wasn't using the red bandanna she borrowed from Elena. It was a white bandage and she said you could still see where the cut had bled through."

"If Vanessa lied in her testimony," Hunter said, "she gave the other two alibis for that night."

"There's something else I need to tell you. Jamie had Webb's MedicAlert bracelet when his car crashed into my wall. He dropped it and I picked it up. Vanessa told me who it belonged to. I think she stole it from my bedroom when she came to pick up her grandson the day before yesterday. At first I thought Jamie had it all these years, but after I talked to Dori Upshur yesterday, I have a feeling she's the one who gave it to him. Right before he died."

Hunter let out an expletive. "You're just telling me *this* now? Jesus, Lucie. What else?"

"Hey," I said, indignant. "Back off. I might be the one in someone's crosshairs, not you."

"Okay, okay." He sounded calmer. "Look, how about if I come out there tomorrow and we spend some time going over all this? It could be a breakthrough for Taurique." Optimism had crept into his voice. "Thanks, Lucie. I owe you."

My phone buzzed. "Hunter . . . I've got to go. My brother's calling. I'll see you tomorrow at the vineyard. Ten o'clock?"

"Sure," he said. "Have a good night."

I switched calls and said, "Eli, are you okay?"

"Yeah," he said. "Fine, just fine, but I need a favor. Change of plans. Can you pick up Hope and bring her home? We might spend the night in town."

"Sure," I said. "As soon as we leave the Inn, we'll get her."

"There's something I need to tell you," he said. "Hope's feeling—"

The line went dead.

"Eli?" I hit Redial, but my phone went to a blank screen. "Damn."

"Lucie?" I turned around. Mick Dunne stood in the shadows watching me, his arms folded across his chest. "Is everything all right?"

My heart skipped a couple of beats. How long had he been here and how much had he overheard? My entire conversation with Hunter? Part of it? I tried to replay it in my head. If Mick had heard any of it, he'd know I knew everything there was to know about the night Webb disappeared. Except who really killed Webb.

I forced myself to say, "Everything's fine. That was Eli. He asked me to pick up Hope from Vanessa's and bring her home. He and Sasha are going to be really late."

Mick stepped out into the light where I could see him, a perplexed look on his face. "Vanessa's? That can't be. Hope and Zach are at Elena's. Vanessa drove back to Charlottesville tonight. Something came up."

"Are you sure?" Now I was confused. "Eli told me Vanessa was babysitting."

"No," he said. "In fact, Elena just called. She said Hope's not feeling well and she was wondering if I could find you and ask what she should do."

Was that what Eli started to tell me before his phone went dead? That Hope wasn't feeling well?

"What's wrong with her?"

"I don't know. Elena said she's pretty upset. You want to drive over there and see for yourself? It's only five minutes away. I'll take you."

"I should get Quinn."

"We'll be there and back before he knows you're gone." He came over and put his arm around me. "Come on, love. Let's go. This won't take long."

I tried to wiggle out of his grasp. "Let go of me, Mick. I need to find Quinn."

His arm tightened. "Lucie," he said. "Don't you want to find out if Hope's okay? I know you wouldn't want anything to happen to her."

My dinner suddenly felt as if it were going to come back up on me. "No," I said. "I wouldn't."

"Good. I didn't think so. Let's go." He leaned forward—deliberately—so I could see the shoulder holster and his gun. "Not a word, darling. Not a word. Or you'll regret it."

Twenty-one

No one saw Mick propel me out a side door of the Goose Creek Inn, his arm still wrapped around my shoulder like a steel vise. My phone was dead, Quinn's was turned off, and, with the excitement of the auction and the boisterous crowd milling around inside, it could be awhile before he realized I was gone. Mick helped me into the Land Rover as he had done so often in the past when we were dating. This time it was different, his cold efficiency and a barely concealed simmering anger.

"Why do you have a gun?" I asked. "I'm not going anywhere. I can't. You know that."

"You never know when it might come in handy," he said.

I had spent nights in his bed. Swum naked with him in his magnificent infinity pool where it seemed we could reach out and touch the mountains and the stars. I once thought I was in love with him until I realized he was too restless—maybe too selfish—to fall in love with anyone for longer than a brief interlude.

"Were you the one who shot at me yesterday?" If he said yes, I couldn't bear that much betrayal.

He started the car. "If I'd wanted to kill you, Lucie, I would have. I just wanted to scare you." He spoke in such a matter-of-fact voice that I wanted to slap his face.

I would not give him the satisfaction of knowing he'd gotten his wish. Instead I said, "Did you kill Webb Landau?"

His eyes widened, and I was glad I'd stung him and returned the favor. "You shouldn't ask so many questions."

The Land Rover's high beams lit up the dark, quiet countryside as we sped along Sam Fred Road. No friendly headlights appeared from the other direction and no red taillights appeared in the rearview mirror.

"Did you kill Webb?" I asked again.

He gave me a look and I knew he wasn't going to answer.

We slowed down and he prepared to turn in to the entrance to Longview. No brown-and-gold sheriff's department cruiser blocked the driveway.

"What happened to the deputy who was here for the last few days?" I asked.

"He left after the funeral yesterday."

"Oh."

We pulled in to the circular drive in front of the house and he parked by the door.

"Get out," he said. "And don't try anything. I've got the gun, remember?"

I stumbled on the doorstep in spite of my cane, and he caught my arm. "Don't be so bloody clumsy."

I yanked my arm out of his grasp. "Don't touch me. I want to see Hope."

He opened the door. "Inside, please."

The door was unlocked and he hadn't rung the bell. We were expected. I stepped into the circular foyer. It looked as it had the other day with a spectacular floral arrangement from the garden show sitting on a mahogany table in the middle of the room and other bouquets, clearly sent in sympathy, that were grouped together on a long console table. It seemed like an eternity since I'd come here to offer Elena my condolences.

No maid this time. The house seemed eerily quiet and unsettled. Where were the children?

"Go through to the drawing room," he said.

"First I want to see Hope."

"Do as I say." He patted his holster underneath his jacket. A warning.

Elena was sitting on the white leather sofa, exactly as she had been the other day. She wore jeans and a black turtleneck and held a large glass of red wine. A nearly empty bottle sat on the coffee table in front of her, and she had the determined look of someone who planned to finish it off and move on to something else. With a small shock I realized the wine was a California Zinfandel. When she saw me, she set her glass down. I felt like a truant kid who'd been brought to the principal's office against her will.

"Where's my niece?" I said. "Where are Hope and Zach?"

Elena looked at me in surprise. "How should I know?"

I turned to Mick. "They're not here, are they?"

"No," he said, with the ghost of a smile. "They're not."

Part of me was relieved the children were safe, but part of me knew I'd been stupidly baited. "Well played," I said with sarcasm. "I assume they're with Vanessa after all."

He shrugged and said to Elena, "She was talking to some-body on her phone at the Inn a little while ago. I think it was Hunter Knight. Then her damn phone died."

Elena exchanged a coded look with Mick. Somehow I thought they'd already worked out the details of how the rest of this evening was going to go.

"Lucie," she said, and she sounded genuinely regretful, "I told you to stay out of my family's business, didn't I? Why did you have to get involved?"

Her words were slurred. Maybe it wasn't her first bottle of Zin. The pocket doors to the beautiful mirrored bar had been pushed open as they had been the other day. Tiny interior spotlights illuminated dozens of bottles of alcohol and the facets of rows of crystal glasses so they sparkled like diamonds in the reflection.

Zinfandel and brandy, Quinn said. You could make a good fake Norton by mixing the two of them. If the wine had been altered as Quinn suspected, a smart biochemist like Elena would know how to make a "new" old wine that tasted like what everyone expected a 140-year-old Norton to taste like. It would explain why the bottles had been brought to Longview from Vaughn Vineyards before being moved to the Goose Creek Inn. It would also explain why Oliver wasn't consulted on the details of transporting the wine.

"You already know why I got involved in this," I said to Elena. "Though I still don't know which of you killed Webb Landau. Dori Upshur said it could have been anyone who was at that dinner the night he disappeared."

I had the fleeting satisfaction of watching their stunned

reactions, but it was short-lived because Mick prodded me in the back with the barrel of his gun.

"Dori." Elena practically spat her name. "Don't talk to me about her. She has no business pointing the finger at anyone else. She's in this as deep as we are."

"Elena." Mick shot her a warning glance. "Stop talking."

"What do you mean?" I asked her.

She picked up her wineglass and took a long, deep drink. When she set it down again she said, "As soon as Jamie announced he was running for president, Dori showed up. Said she needed money and she'd keep quiet about Webb if I paid her because we wouldn't want a scandal like that to get out, would we? Help her out, she said."

"Elena." Mick's voice was harsh. "For God's sake, shut up. You're drunk."

"*You* killed Webb?" I asked her. Somehow I hadn't expected it would be Elena.

"No, I didn't," she said. "But I could have done it after what he did to me."

"Dori had Webb's MedicAlert bracelet," I said. "She gave it to Jamie right before he died. What I don't understand is why she would give it away now, give away her only leverage if she was blackmailing you for money."

Elena sat back against the sofa and stared at me, her mouth working as if she were trying to hold back from spitting out something else. But this time she remained mum and so did Mick.

I tried to figure it out. "Unless Dori had something else that's more important. Like the murder weapon. The real murder weapon, not the tire jack that conveniently had Taurique's fingerprints on it because he helped Webb change a flat tire."

Elena's face gave her away. She looked like she was about to explode.

"That's enough, Lucie." Mick gave me a rough shove.

"I didn't kill him," Elena said again.

I was running out of suspects. If Elena didn't do it and Dori didn't do it, that left . . . Jamie and Mick. Possibly Vanessa, though Elena wouldn't have protected her all these years.

"So who were you protecting if you paid blackmail money to Dori?" I asked Elena, and then it dawned on me. "*Jamie?* You were protecting Jamie because he killed Webb?"

"Jamie's dead," Mick said. "It's finished now."

Elena looked like she was caught in the headlights of an oncoming eighteen-wheeler.

I couldn't believe it. Jamie was the guilty one after all.

"It's not over," I said. "There's still Taurique Youngblood. Even if Jamie is dead, Taurique deserves to get his life back. And Hunter Knight plans to help him."

"We need to shut her up for good," Mick said to Elena.

"You're the one who had the dumb idea to bring her here. She's your problem, Mick. All of this is your problem."

Mick stiffened at the insult. "Not as dumb an idea as you think, sweetheart. I'll take her for a ride. Come on, Lucie. Let's go."

"No."

"I wasn't asking."

He reached for my arm, but before he could grab me I swung my cane and it landed on his wrist. The gun flew out of his hand, skidding across the floor and ending up in front of the bar. Mick swore and clutched his wrist. I had only a few seconds until he recovered. I turned and swept the hooked end of my cane across a row of bottles of alcohol in the beautiful mirrored bar, tugging them off the shelves. Bottles and glasses toppled like dominoes, crashing onto the marble floor, where they splintered into lethal shards and jagged pieces. I was ready to make a second pass when Mick wrapped his arm around my waist and wrestled my cane away, throwing it across the room.

"You're coming with me."

By now Elena was on her feet and unsteadily making her way to where the gun lay in a puddle of booze and broken glass. Maybe if she'd been sober she would have noticed the wet spot on the floor and avoided it. It must have been like slipping on black ice—you never see it coming. Her feet flew out from under her and she went down hard on her back, hitting her head. Her right arm landed on a jagged piece of glass and she screamed as it sliced through her skin. Within seconds a sickly brown pool of blood and an amber liquid—brandy, I think—oozed around her.

"Oh, my God, I think I've severed an artery." She sounded panicked. "Mick, help me. Get something to bandage my wrist and stop the bleeding. I've wrenched my back and I can't get up."

"If we don't help her, she could bleed to death," I said to him in a tense voice. "You owe her. She bandaged your hand the night Webb slashed it with a kitchen knife."

"You *do* owe me." Elena's face had turned white. "You know why."

Mick looked from Elena to me and tossed his phone to her. It hit the floor with a thud by her side. "Call nine-one-one. By the time they get here I'll have taken care of Lucie."

I shuddered as a vision of Greg crawling away from me, and another of Mick carrying me from Jamie's car flashed through my mind. "We can't leave her, Mick." I'd said the exact same thing to him only a few days ago when Jamie was trapped in his car before the fire started. "We need something to make a tourniquet to stop the bleeding. A napkin, a scarf, any piece of fabric."

"The coat closet in the foyer," Elena said and moaned. "Look there."

I turned to leave the room.

"Where do you think you're going?" Mick asked.

"To get something to bind her wrist. Where did you think I was going?"

"I'm coming with you."

A green-and-white silk scarf decorated with foxhunters on horseback wearing their pinks and wily-looking foxes evading them was draped over Elena's raincoat. A yellow tie— one of Jamie's good luck campaign ties—hung on a hook. Somewhere in the house a telephone rang and rang. Eventually I heard the answering machine kick in and a male voice leaving a muffled message. We really were alone, just the three of us.

"Let's go." Mick prodded me. Then he added, as if reading my mind, "There's no one here except you, me, and Elena."

I grabbed the scarf and the tie and went back to Elena. Florence Nightingale I'm not, but I know that the tourniquet needed to be on her arm between her heart and the damaged artery. I used Jamie's tie for the tourniquet and the scarf to bind the gash in her wrist.

"I need your finger for the knot," I said to Mick. "Help me out, okay?"

He knelt beside me and did as I asked.

"You need to go to the emergency room," I said to Elena, tucking the ends of the scarf into the makeshift bandage. "Mick, dammit, you have to take her. She could bleed to death."

"No," he said. "We're leaving together, you and me. She'll call nine-one-one."

"I saved you once, Mick," Elena said in a faint voice. Her eyes were closed and her lips had turned purplish-blue. "You know I did."

"What did you do?" I asked. "Tell me."

"Don't say anything, Elena."

"Tell me." I said.

Her voice sounded dreamy and far away. "Put Webb's backpack in Taurique's trash can. Left his credit card for Taurique to find." She paused and mumbled, "Saved you, Mick."

In the silence that followed, I realized I had been holding my breath.

"You killed Webb," I said to Mick. "And Elena covered it up. Last week Dori Upshur showed up in town and finally told Jamie the whole story after all these years."

What I couldn't figure out, though, was why Dori blackmailed Elena rather than Mick. Why would she think Elena had murdered Webb? My mind raced back over Vanessa's story of that night and what I'd just talked about with Hunter. *The next morning Mick's hand was wrapped in a different bandage, a white one, and the knife wound was still bleeding.*

"Mick wrapped whatever he used to kill Webb with in your red bandanna," I said to Elena. "That's why Dori blackmailed you. She recognized your scarf. Somehow she'd also gotten hold of the MedicAlert bracelet, perhaps found it with the murder weapon. So maybe with all your campaign debts mounting up, you stopped paying Dori, who turned up to see if she could put pressure on Jamie. She gave him Webb's MedicAlert bracelet to prove she was telling the truth. Jamie was so devastated he got in his car and drove into my wall. That's why the last thing he said to me was to tell Taurique he was sorry. Ask Taurique to forgive him. Jamie knew the wrong person had gone to jail for Webb's murder."

"Brilliant deduction, girl detective." Mick had picked up the gun while I was binding up Elena's wrist. Now it was pointed at the two of us, and I wondered if a bath in brandy could possibly cause a gun to jam. "Not that it's going to do you any good. I can't leave you two here," he went on. "So now I'm going to have to kill you both. It'll look like a confrontation between you and then a murder-suicide. Elena kills you, Lucie, and then herself."

"Drop the gun, Mick." Oliver Vaughn stood in the doorway to the drawing room, holding a gun of his own trained on Mick. Quinn was behind him. None of us had heard them come into the house. "The police are on their way, so don't try anything," Oliver said as a siren sounded in the distance.

"You're making a mistake, Ollie," Mick said. "I'm your god-father, remember?"

"There's no mistake," Quinn said. "Lucie, are you okay?"

"I'm fine," I said. "But Elena needs to get to the hospital right away. Call an ambulance."

"I said drop the gun," Oliver said. "Otherwise I'll shoot it out of your hand. I'm a better shot than you are and you know it."

"It's over, Mick," Quinn said. "You heard him. Put it down."

Mick's gun was still trained on Elena and me. For a few seconds that seemed to last an eternity I thought he was going to kill one of us, an explosive ending to a thirty-year-old murder—though whether it would be Elena or me, I couldn't tell. Then he looked up at the ceiling as if he were wrestling with some inner demon, and after a sullen glance at Oliver and Quinn he dumped the gun on the coffee table.

I think everyone in the room started breathing again.

"Step away from Lucie and Elena and keep your hands where I can see them," Oliver said. "Lucie, get the gun, will you?"

I got it and Mick gave me a look of pure hatred. "Why did you have to do this?" he said. "Everything was going to be fine. Why did you have to screw it up?"

Screw it up.

Jamie was dead and Mick let an innocent man go to prison for thirty years of his life that he would never get back for a crime he didn't commit. A lot of people I knew would probably go to jail for their role in covering up what really happened the night Webb Landau was murdered. Mick had murdered Webb to avoid being expelled from school for cheating. The crime hardly seemed to justify the punishment. And then if I was right he had taken Webb's research notes and lab results, along with Elena's work, as the foundation for developing a drug years later that had made him a very wealthy man.

I couldn't wrap my head around the audacity of his self-righteous anger. I looked at him still outraged and furious—a man I'd loved and thought I knew so well—and realized I didn't know him at all.

For that matter, there were things I didn't know about myself—unresolved issues of my own—that had boomeranged back into my life these last few days.

Maybe it was time for another talk with my mother.

And some soul-searching.

Twenty-two

A few weeks after Taurique Youngblood had been released from prison, Hunter Knight called and told me
Taurique wanted to thank me in person for what I'd
done. I drove into Washington with Quinn one early May
morning after Hunter set up a meeting in his office at the
St. Leonard Project.

Dasha, the Howard University law student who'd been
there the first time I came by, told us Taurique was already
waiting in Hunter's office when we arrived. Just as she was
about to walk us across the hall, Quinn told me he thought I
should meet Taurique by myself. One look at his face and I realized he'd planned to do this all along.

"You're the one who wouldn't give up on him," he said.
"Taurique wants to see you, not me. I'll wait here and talk to
Dasha for a while."

I reached for his hands and laced my fingers through his.
"I'd really like you to be there."

He shook his head, smiling, and disentangled his hands from mine. "This one's all yours. You did a good thing, sweetheart."

A good thing. I suppose that depended. Or as Kit had said to me that day at the Goose Creek Bridge: "Where you stand depends on where you sit."

Taurique had finally gotten justice, and Mick Dunne was in jail charged with the murder of Webster Landau, along with a second-degree murder charge in the death of Jamie Vaughn. I never saw him again after that night at Elena's when two deputies took him away in handcuffs. Elena had been released on bail—two million dollars—after being charged with a laundry list of crimes: obstruction of justice, perjury, fraud, and money laundering. She claimed to anyone who would listen that Webb had taken credit for her research on the multiple sclerosis drug that was eventually patented and sold by Mick's company. As if that justified murder. She had also doctored the Norton with Mick's help. Oliver Vaughn had suspected something was up with the wine the night he opened it, plus there was the unscheduled stop at Longview, where someone with Elena's background in biochemistry could easily come up with a blend of alcohol that tasted like what you'd expect a century-old bottle of Norton to taste like. After Quinn confronted Oliver the night of the auction and told him the Norton was too good to be true, it wasn't long before they realized both Mick and I were missing. When Elena didn't answer the phone at Longview when Oliver called, Quinn made a lucky guess that the three of us might be together.

Dori Upshur, who had discovered the murder weapon hidden on her farm wrapped in Elena's bloodstained bandanna after Mick killed Webb, pleaded guilty to obstruction of justice and blackmail. In return for cooperating with the Charlottesville police, her lawyer was trying to negotiate a deal so she wouldn't serve time in prison. The last I heard was that she could end up with probation and possibly house arrest or, depending on how good her lawyer was and if she got lucky, a suspended sentence. Plus she'd been Kit's mysterious informant. Working as a volunteer in the D.C. office of the Vaughn for President campaign staff she'd obtained photocopies of the checks she sent to Kit, a little insurance policy in case Elena stopped paying the blackmail money.

Vanessa got off the easiest. She, too, faced obstruction of justice charges for providing Mick and Elena with alibis the night of Webb's murder, but it looked like she'd end up with probation and no jail time. Neither she nor Jamie had known for sure who killed Webb. If either of them had suspected— how could they not?—they had chosen not to ask. It wasn't my place to judge their motives for remaining ignorant, but at least I understood now why Jamie had felt so much remorse just before he died. First Kit had confronted him about the missing campaign money, which Elena had used to pay off Dori. Then Hunter Knight had paid him a visit, letting him know the St. Leonard Project was working to get Taurique a new trial. Finally Dori had shown up with the MedicAlert bracelet and her devastating but erroneous story that Elena was guilty of murder. So Jamie had gone to his best friend, Mick Dunne, who couldn't let the truth come out. Somehow he'd managed to slip rubbing alcohol into Jamie's drink just before he got behind the wheel of his SUV on his way to a meeting with Dominique at the Goose Creek Inn.

If I had thought we had been bombarded by reporters after Jamie's accident, it was nothing like the scrum of news vans that pulled up in front of the vineyard each day to update the unfolding soap opera involving Jamie Vaughn's family and friends and a thirty-year-old murder that had been covered up so that an innocent man had gone to prison for the crime.

When I entered Hunter's office—alone—Taurique was standing next to the two beat-up chairs in front of Hunter's desk, hands folded together, a grave smile on his face. He was tall and thin, and the tweed sport jacket and khaki pants he wore—I wondered if Hunter had found them for him—hung on his lanky frame.

"Hello, Lucie," he said. "I'm very glad to finally meet you."

I put out my hand. "I'm very glad to finally meet you, too," I said. "*Here.*"

His hearty laugh—acknowledging what I meant—revealed a couple of missing teeth. What I had been expecting was bitterness and maybe anger at a life wasted, but Taurique Youngblood was gentle and kind, taking stock of my cane—acknowledging with a nod that he knew exactly how and why I had to use it—before he covered my outstretched hand with both of his.

"I wanted to see you," he said, "and say thank you. If it wasn't for you, I'd still be inside."

I didn't want to take credit for this. "Don't thank me. It was Jamie. I know . . . it was thirty years too late, but you were the last person he spoke of before he died. He so wanted you to forgive him, Taurique."

He smiled. "The quality of mercy is not strain'd," he said in a quiet voice. "It droppeth as the gentle rain from heaven,

Upon the place beneath: it is twice blest; It blesseth him that gives and him that takes."

I stared at him, open-mouthed.

"Portia's speech to Shylock in *The Merchant of Venice.* I know it by heart. It's what kept me a sane man all these years, Lucie. Kept me from turning bitter and all shriveled up. I had to let those bad feelings, the anger at the injustice of what happened, go, and I did. Prayed every day and night to the Lord my God and Savior and He heard me." His grin broadened. "Took us awhile, but the good Lord and me, we got down together and finally worked it all out."

Hunter Knight caught my eye and I instantly read his mind. *That's why Greg wanted me to do everything in my power to get justice for Taurique. You get it now, don't you?*

I smiled at Taurique. "I admire you," I told him. "You have a good heart. Not many people could do what you did."

"You're wrong. Anyone can do exactly what I did with the help of God. You have it in your heart, too—the quality of mercy. Otherwise you wouldn't have fought for me. I heard a lot about you, sweetheart. I 'spect you know that." He nodded his head in Hunter's direction. "I know what you been through."

"If you need a job, Taurique," I said, "and you decide to stay around here, I hope you'll come see me."

"Thank you, ma'am. I'm still figuring it all out. But I just might."

"Good luck. It was an honor to meet you."

This time he took both of my hands in his and gripped them. "The honor is mine."

I started to pull away because I knew I had to get out of Hunter's office before the tears came.

"*Lucie.*" Taurique looked me in the eye and wouldn't release my hands.

"I know," I said, my voice wavering. "I know."

"I'll let go," he said, "if you will. Deal?"

He wasn't talking only about letting go of my hands. He was asking me to make him a promise. "Okay."

"Good. You know what you got to do."

I took a deep breath and said, "Hunter, the next time you see Greg, please tell him that I have . . . that I am trying very hard . . . that I *will* . . . forgive him."

"I'll do that," Hunter said in a husky voice as Taurique squeezed my hands and let go of them. "I'll do that."

Acknowledgments

As usual, I owe thanks to many people who helped me with the research for this book and who graciously let me pester them with my many questions. Also as usual, if it's wrong, don't blame them: that's on me.

Special thanks to Rick Tagg, winemaker at Delaplane Cellars in Delaplane, Virginia and my winemaker/vineyard adviser of many years, for his friendship and for answering questions at all hours of the night or day. Detective Jim Smith of the Fairfax County Police Department, Fairfax, VA, answered questions about law enforcement and the Virginia prison system. Lois Tuohy graciously invited me to her wonderful tailgate for the Middleburg Hunt Point-to-Point; even though none of the horses I bet on won, I had a fabulous time! Jan Schuler and Joni Lawler explained to me all the work, time, and money needed to make Historic Garden Week happen in Virginia every year. Meriah Crawford, assistant professor of English at Virginia Commonwealth University and a private investigator, answered questions about programs that seek to exonerate those who have been wrongly convicted of crimes, and Peggy O'Neil explained the court system and the appeal process. Dr. Kristin de Nesnera, my daughter-in-law, answered questions about university research projects.

The Wild Vine by Todd Kliman (Broadway, 2010) was extremely valuable in explaining the fascinating and convoluted history of the Norton grape in the United States.

Thanks, as usual, to my critique group: Donna Andrews, John Gilstrap, Alan Orloff and Art Taylor for commenting on and helping with numerous drafts of this book. Love and gratitude to André de Nesnera, my husband, who read the manuscript, offered comments and advice, and uncomplainingly gave me the time and space to write—even on vacation. I married well and I am lucky indeed.

At Minotaur, huge thanks to Hannah Braaten, my wonderful editor, and the many people at Minotaur Books who do so much behind the scenes so you can hold this book in your hands.

Last but never least, love and thanks to Dominick Abel, who makes it all possible.

ABOUT THE AUTHOR

ELLEN CROSBY is the author of the Virginia Wine Country Mystery series, which began with *The Merlot Murders*. She has also written a mystery series featuring international photojournalist Sophie Medina. Previously she worked as a freelance reporter for *The Washington Post*, as the Moscow correspondent for ABC News Radio, and as an economist at the United States Senate. Visit Ellen on the Web at www.ellencrosby.com, or on Facebook at EllenCrosbyBooks, and Twitter @ellencrosby, to learn more.